PENGUIN BOOKS
HOUSE OF CARDS

Sudha Murty was born in 1950 in Shiggaon in north Karnataka. She did her MTech in computer science, and is now the chairperson of the Infosys Foundation. A prolific writer in English and Kannada, she has written novels, technical books, travelogues, collections of short stories and non-fiction pieces, and four books for children. Her books have been translated into all the major Indian languages.

Sudha Murty was the recipient of the R.K. Narayan Award for Literature and the Padma Shri in 2006, and the Attimabbe Award from the government of Karnataka for excellence in Kannada literature in 2011.

Also by the same author

SUDHA MURTY

house of cards

PENGUIN BOOKS

PENGUIN BOOKS
Published by the Penguin Group
Penguin Books India Pvt. Ltd, 11 Community Centre, Panchsheel Park,
New Delhi 110 017, India
Penguin Group (USA) Inc., 375 Hudson Street, New York, New York 10014, USA
Penguin Group (Canada), 90 Eglinton Avenue East, Suite 700, Toronto,
Ontario, M4P 2Y3, Canada (a division of Pearson Penguin Canada Inc.)
Penguin Books Ltd, 80 Strand, London WC2R 0RL, England
Penguin Ireland, 25 St Stephen's Green, Dublin 2, Ireland (a division of Penguin
Books Ltd)
Penguin Group (Australia), 707 Collins Street, Melbourne, Victoria 3008,
Australia (a division of Pearson Australia Group Pty Ltd)
Penguin Group (NZ), 67 Apollo Drive, Rosedale, Auckland 0632,
New Zealand (a division of Pearson New Zealand Ltd)
Penguin Books (South Africa) (Pty) Ltd, Block D, Rosebank Office Park,
181 Jan Smuts Avenue, Parktown North, Johannesburg 2193, South Africa

Penguin Books Ltd, Registered Offices: 80 Strand, London WC2R 0RL, England

First published by Penguin Books India 2013

ISBN 9780143420361

Typeset in Sabon by InoSoft Systems, Noida
Printed at Manipal Technologies Ltd, Manipal

To all the Mridulas who suffer silently

Acknowledgements

I want to thank my editor, Shrutkeerti Khurana, for her incredible dedication that has inspired me to write this book.

I also want to thank Udayan Mitra of Penguin Books India for encouraging and persuading me to bring the book out.

I

The Village

There was a small village in north Karnataka with a population of five to eight thousand. It boasted of a beautiful lake with a temple of Lord Hanuman on its shore. The area was dotted with banyan trees. In Kannada, a banyan tree is called 'aladamara' and 'halli' means village, so the village was named Aladahalli.

Aladahalli had only one main road, with houses on either side, and a bus stand right in the middle of the village. Most people who were from here preferred to stay on and commute for work to the cities nearby: Hubli and Dharwad. The advantages of staying in Aladahalli were a laid-back life, less noise and almost no pollution. The greatest attraction though was the school, which was on a par with any city school, and where the medium of instruction was both English and Kannada. Just like in city schools, the students got a rank based on their merit. Bheemanna's daughter, Mridula, was among the top students in her class and was known for her intelligence.

Bheemanna's family was rich and owned a lot of fertile land. His ancestral house was very old and large. The green backyard was filled with varieties of plants and vegetables. There were jasmine creepers in the backyard; Mridula had long, dark hair and would not step out of the house without a string of flowers in it.

Bheemanna's wife, Rukuma Bai or Rukmini, was from a neighbouring village. She was quite different from Bheemanna and talked less than her husband. They had two children, Krishna and Mridula.

When Krishna was born, Bheemanna had wanted to name his son Hanuman but Rukuma Bai had insisted on calling him Krishna. After a while, Bheemanna had lost to his wife's iron will and started calling him Krishna too. But when Mridula came along three years later, he put his foot down. He had once read a novel in which the name of the main character was Mridula. He liked the name since it was uncommon in this part of Karnataka. So, Bheemanna insisted that his daughter be called by that name.

Little Mridula was a bright student. Rukuma Bai frequently told people that Mridula had inherited the smart genes from her side of the family. At such times, talkative Bheemanna usually stayed silent.

Young Mridula was sitting on the swing under the big banyan tree opposite the Hanuman temple. It was Ugadi time—the New Year festival for the Kannada people, celebrated in the month of February or March. Summer had just arrived. The mango trees sported soft reddish-green leaves and the cuckoos were making lovely coo-coo sounds. Everyone in the village was busy preparing for the festival. Yet, there was a pin-drop silence near the temple.

But for Mridula, nothing mattered. She was swinging without any bondage and with a free mind. From the swing, she could see her house. She was happy.

Mridula was not like everybody, she was different. She had enormous enthusiasm for life and unlimited energy for reading, cooking and sketching. She wanted to spend every minute of the day fruitfully. It seemed that the sun rose for her and the rainbow colours were meant only for her. Every day was to be lived to its fullest and every beautiful minute to be enjoyed.

Years passed. The family was content and happy. Bheemanna had added some basic modern amenities to his home.

Meanwhile, little Mridula had grown up and was excelling in school. She scored a rank in the tenth class. Her teachers insisted that she must study either medicine or engineering. But Mridula did not agree. Bheemanna did not take any decision just for the sake of status in society. He left the decision to Mridula and she insisted on becoming a teacher. But Rukuma Bai was hesitant. Her brother Satyabodha was a bank officer in Hubli. His daughter, Sarla, was six months older than Mridula and not as intelligent. But even Sarla preferred to study engineering in Hubli. Bheemanna advised Rukuma, 'Times have changed. We can't tell children that you should become a lawyer or a doctor or marry a person of our choice. Education and marriage should be according to our children's wishes because these are for ever. After all, it is their life and they have the right to follow their heart and make decisions by themselves.'

Bheemanna always bent the rules when it came to Mridula. She was his life. When people asked Mridula whether she was her mother's or father's favourite, she said, 'I am Amma's girl—and Appa's world.'

Mridula remembered a conversation she had had with her father when she was a child. When an animal in the village fell sick, her father immediately took medicine made from the plants in his garden and treated the animal, without waiting for the animal's owner to call him. After the treatment, Bheemanna was given a bowl of rice and jaggery and five one-rupee coins as his fee. He never kept the fee from treating animals for himself. He would offer the coins to Lord Hanuman and say, 'Mridula, grind all the rice, jaggery and coconut together. Then, add some ghee and give it to the cows. It is good for them.'

As she went about her task, her father would ask her, 'Do you know why God has given the power of speech to humans and not to animals?'

Mridula would childishly reply, 'To talk.'

'No, child. Not just to talk. It is also to share. So, whenever you face difficulty or you receive joy, you must share it with others. But think of all the animals—those poor things can't even share their difficulty with anyone. They have to bear it alone. Mridula, remember—you must always be open. Don't hide. Hiding is a sin.'

Mridula listened very carefully to him.

She grew up in such a friendly and honest atmosphere that she became outgoing and helpful—just like her father.

With her parents' support, Mridula travelled every day to teacher-training classes in Hubli and graduated with a top rank. She quickly got a government job in the village high school. Unlike Mridula, Krishna took a long time to finish his degree. Then he decided to look after the family farms instead of getting a job.

Bheemanna was happy about this decision because it gave him more time for social work. As a result, these days he was seen consulting with others in matters like marriage alliances, in mourning houses and even panchayat talks.

Soon, Rukuma started worrying about Mridula's marriage. One day, she said, 'Mridula is twenty-two years old. My brother is already trying to find a boy for Sarla. The good thing is that they live in a big town. Many good grooms come to Hubli in search for suitable brides. But nobody knows that our girl is here in Aladahalli. Please stop being lazy and find someone suitable.'

Bheemanna laughed at her. 'Your niece Sarla has many hurdles to cross. She isn't pretty and only wants to marry a boy who lives abroad. But there aren't any such conditions for Mridula. Our daughter is beautiful. Arjun Sa predicted that the groom will come to our house seeking her hand in marriage.'

Arjun Sa Badni was a famous astrologer in Hubli. On hearing Bheemanna's response, Rukuma took the vessel that was in her hand and smashed it down on the floor in anger. 'What else has your friend predicted?'

Bheemanna tried to console his angry wife: 'Don't bash the vessels. My grandmother had given us that one. Leave your work and listen to me, Rukuma. Badni says that her husband will become a prosperous man after marriage. You needn't worry at all.'

'How can you believe such predictions, and do nothing? It is our duty to search for someone nice for her. Will you marry her off to a beggar just because of his forecasts?'

'Even if he is a beggar, she will fetch him all the riches.' Bheemanna stood up and walked away to their neighbour's house, knowing that that would end the dispute.

As expected, Rukuma forgot the disagreement a few minutes later and went to the garden to work.

Their neighbour, Champa Bai Kamitkar, was a seventy-year-old woman who stayed opposite Bheemanna's house. She had a huge garden in her backyard with lots of flowers. Each plant was as precious as a child to her. Watering the plants and plucking the flowers took her three to four hours every day. Even though she grew so many flowers, she did not use even one for herself. She sent all of them to the other houses on the street.

Champa Bai's husband had died long ago and they never had any children. So, she had adopted one of her nephews—Chandrakant. He studied in Aladahalli and then went to Dharwad to complete his high school. After that, he studied medicine in Bombay and went abroad. He returned after a few years and married a Bombay girl. Eventually, he started his own hospital and settled there.

Every now and then, Chandrakant asked his aunt to come and stay with him in Bombay but she refused consistently. 'Chandru, Aladahalli is heaven to me. People here are easy-going. Our Bheemanna is like a son to me. I can't stand the crowd in Bombay at this age.'

Champa Bai was fond of her sisters who lived in different cities. She travelled often to visit them. During these outings, Mridula took excellent care of her garden for her and, as a gesture of thanks, Champa Bai gave her the lion's share of the flowers.

2

Young Dreams

When Dr Sanjay heard the 6 p.m. bell in KEM Hospital in Bombay, he was rudely brought back to the real world. He remembered that he had to travel by train that evening. An introvert by nature, Sanjay was passionate about his work. It was his salvation; when he worked, he forgot everything else. He had missed lunch and dinner on many occasions as a result. But today, he was about to catch a train and couldn't afford to miss it. He had requested his outpatient department's Sister Indumati to remind him. And she had. Yet, he had forgotten. He immediately started scrubbing his hands so that he could finish up and leave.

Sister Indumati was the person closest to Dr Sanjay in Bombay. She was an elderly lady with grey hair. She smiled at Sanjay and showed her motherly anger: 'Sanjay, at this rate, you won't get to your own wedding at the right time and I will ensure that your bride marries someone else!'

In a lighter tone, she added, 'I know you. So I sent your luggage with Dr Alex to the railway station. He said that the compartment number is A17. And now, you better run.' Sanjay smiled back in gratitude and left quickly.

Dr Alexander was Sanjay's colleague at the same hospital. He was dark, dynamic, popular, a smart dresser and an excellent speaker. Alex was from Goa and was taking the same train till Londa station to meet his aunt, and then he was going to Panaji.

Sanjay rushed to Bombay's VT station. The platform was crowded. The people on the platform who had come to see others off were double the number of the actual passengers. Everybody was busy either waiting to get into the train or saying goodbye to their loved ones. With the train just about to leave, Sanjay ran faster than P.T. Usha to board a coach. He made it into the train just in time.

Breathlessly, he made his way into the right compartment and sat down in front of Alex. Sanjay looked around and was surprised to see only a few people. He realized that the reduced rush was because the schools had reopened after the summer vacation. As he was catching his breath, he thought about how people dealt with anxiety. They lived with it and tried their best to learn how to control it. He got busy with his own thoughts—like a snail encircling itself.

Alex lit a cigarette and asked, 'Sanjay, why are you going to Hubli? You don't usually travel much.'

A lady passenger sitting close to them did not like the cigarette smoke and covered her nose with a handkerchief. But Alex didn't care; he continued smoking and talking to Sanjay.

Shyly, Sanjay replied, 'My friend Santosh is getting married there.'

'I don't think you are going only for the purpose of attending a wedding, especially when you have a lot of work this week. Are you going to be the best man? Or do you have an appointment with a beautiful girl there?' Alex joked.

'Alex, we don't have the concept of best man in our weddings. Santosh is my good friend but I haven't met him in years because he is now settled in the Middle East.'

'For how long will you be in Hubli? Why don't you come to Goa? We'll have fun.'

'No, I can't. I'll only be in Hubli for a few days. Professor Jog has given me a package to deliver to someone who stays around the area.'

Dr Chandrakant Jog was a professor of gynaecology at GS Medical College and Sanjay was his assistant. Sanjay did not usually like to go to weddings but Santosh had helped him in his tough times.

The train picked up speed. The cool breeze hit Sanjay's face. He was tired and leant against the backrest. He asked Alex, 'Is there a special reason for you to go to Goa?'

'Yes, I want to meet my parents and my girlfriend, Anita. I am going to the Middle East next month. I am not a sannyasi like you. Anita visits me even in my dreams.'

Sanjay was quiet. Then he said, 'You have a good job here. Next year, you can get a postgraduate seat. What's the point in going to the Middle East? Goa is a small state and has two medical colleges. After your post-graduation, you can get a job in either of them.'

'Come on, Sanjay, who wants to be a professor? I want to earn a lot of money. If you want to earn money in a government job in India, then you have to be corrupt. But if I work hard for four years in the Middle East, come back and open a hospital here, I can mint money.'

Sanjay asked curiously, 'Do you think that Anita will wait for you till your return?'

Alex smiled and turned his head towards the window.

The train had reached Karjat station. Alex called out to a vendor selling batata vadas. The young boy claimed that the vadas were nice and warm but handed Sanjay a cold and stale vada. Sanjay did not get upset. He merely said, 'Brother, the vadas are like ice cubes. Please give us something hot.'

'In that case, take my employer's head. It's always hot. But for now, give me five rupees.'

Alex laughed and gave the young boy money; but Sanjay became serious. He was thinking about the poor boy's helplessness. The train started moving again and the smell of batata vadas was all over the compartment.

Soon, it was time for dinner. Two railway canteen boys took their order. Alex ordered a non-vegetarian thali for himself and a vegetarian thali for Sanjay. Sanjay felt ignored. Alex had not replied to his question about Anita. Maybe he should not have asked him such a personal question. Suddenly, Alex said, 'Anita will wait for a maximum of one year. I have told her not to wait for me more than that. We should be practical. If we become too emotional, it is difficult to lead a happy life.'

'Where did you meet Anita?'

'I met her at the Mapusa Church. I was the best man in my friend Marx's wedding and Anita was the maid of honour. That was the first time I saw her. Then I met her again at a New Year's ball. Thanks to the Goan Catholic society, there were many occasions for us to meet and we became good friends very quickly.'

'Is she from Goa, too?'

'No, she is from Mangalore, which is in your state, Karnataka.'

'Oh, okay.'

It was getting dark outside the window of the moving train. Alex was thinking about Anita. 'She is unlike the girls in Goa. She is different.'

For the last two years, she had been in Panaji, the capital city of Goa, working with her maternal uncle Freddy Roderick. After she had completed her Bachelor of Arts degree, Anita's uncle had asked her, 'What will you do sitting at home? I am a dealer for Alembic Pharmaceuticals. Why don't you come and help me?'

Her aunt had also insisted. So, Anita had started working in her uncle's office in Goa.

The real reason for bringing her there was that her uncle and aunt wanted to introduce her to the young and suitable grooms in Goa. Anita was a good singer and always sang for the church choir. She was not interested in studies. She had completed her degree but her main interest was interior decoration. Even though she worked hard in her uncle's office, she worked harder at home-decorating her aunt's house. Anita never made the first move when it came to boys. At Marx's wedding, Alex noticed that she was more beautiful than the bride herself and immediately set his eyes on her. She was fair and had lustrous hair. Many young bachelors wanted to date her.

Alex smiled. Though he had just told Sanjay that she was his girlfriend, he knew that Anita was more than that—he would marry her. He remembered how he had gone out of his way to get her phone number and check her travel itinerary. He would go to Uncle Freddy's house without reason and sit there for hours. He had been worried that some young man would move faster than him and make away with Anita, but Uncle Freddy was smart and had suggested, 'Young boy, don't worry. Take her to parties, picnics and get to know her. But don't talk of marriage right now.'

Uncle Freddy was older, wiser and more experienced. He liked Alex. Sometimes, Alex felt uncomfortable when he visited Uncle Freddy's house. Financially, they were much better off than Alex and his family. They had a nice house and a car. If he wanted to marry Anita, he must maintain her lifestyle. Otherwise, people in the church would laugh at him. After going out with Anita, he realized that she was shy and had been raised differently. She did not care about money. But things were not easy when he met her father.

Anita's father, Mr Pinto, was a strict man. He believed that women must work. He was a senior and honest officer with Mangalore Fertilizers. Apart from Anita, he had two sons— one in the merchant navy and the other based in Delhi. Pinto's family was religious and they never missed Sunday Mass. They regularly contributed to the church and were good Christians.

When Mr Pinto came to visit Anita from Mangalore, Alex met him—but Mr Pinto did not even bother to talk to him. He passed a comment: 'Oh, our Anita is so beautiful. She is getting marriage proposals from places like the merchant navy.'

Alex himself felt that he was only an MBBS doctor and could not compete with any of these proposals, unless he owned a nursing home. The only way to get engaged to Anita was to go to the Middle East, make money, come back and marry her.

But how could he share all this with Sanjay?

While Alex was lost in these thoughts, Sanjay started talking about some professor's post that was vacant in a college in Goa. Alex said, 'Tell me, Sanjay, do you want to remain Dr Jog's assistant forever, or do you want to make money at some point?'

Sanjay did not reply. For now, his aim was to get as much experience as he could and then get a postgraduate degree. Money was not a priority, even though he was not from a rich family.

A short while later, dinner arrived. Sanjay asked, 'Alex, what time does this train reach Hubli?'

'You talk as if you don't know your own state. Ask me anything about Goa. I can tell you whatever you want to know.'

'Goa is small and you have lots of relatives there. But I don't have any relatives in Hubli. I have never even been there. I only know that it is near Dharwad which is famous for its pedas.'

'How do you know that?'

'Sometimes, Professor Jog brings pedas from Dharwad and gives them to the staff.'

'Where are your relatives then?'

'Oh, I have a small family—a mother and a sister. I don't have a father. My sister is married to a bank clerk and they live in Belur. My mother stays in T. Narasipura.'

'You know, Sanjay, Dharwad is also famous for Hindustani music, good colleges, great musicians and she-buffaloes!'

'It sounds like you know more about Dharwad than I do.'

'Yes, Panaji is around three hours by car from Belgaum. I have a few cousins who study in Hubli and Dharwad. But Hubli is also notorious for theft. The maximum thefts take place at the Hubli junction. People say that it is as bad as Bombay.'

Another passenger joined the conversation: 'That's really true. Once, I lost all my luggage at that junction.'

The passenger continued, 'My name is Keshav Rao. I work in the government Secretariat in Bangalore. During one of my journeys, I was travelling from Kolhapur via Hubli and all my bags disappeared at night. The next morning, I had to get down at Bangalore in the baniyan and lungi that I was wearing the night before.'

Alex added, 'There will always be thefts in Hubli because of the crowd. Once, I also lost my bags at Londa junction!'

Sanjay was not a seasoned traveller. So he was shocked listening to Keshav Rao. He was scared that if he lost the small bag with his clothes, he would have to attend the wedding in his baniyan and lungi too. He picked his small bag up from the floor and kept it under his head so that it would be safe and he could use it as a pillow for the rest of the trip too. Soon, he nodded off to sleep.

3
The Beautiful Thief

After completing an intricate mehendi design on Surekha's hand, Mridula got up and wiped her hands on her old sari. She was content and happy with her accomplishment. No one in the village could design mehendi as well as her. So she was invited to all her classmates' weddings. She was helpful and even assisted with miscellaneous jobs at the marriage locations. Surekha was Mridula's classmate and a close friend. All the unmarried girls from their class were invited that evening for the mehendi ceremony in Hubli.

On the eve of the wedding, the clouds were dark and looked ready to pour down. It was the end of Shravan—the rainy season. Though it was only 7 p.m., it was as dark as midnight. Surekha, the bride, was in her room in the wedding hall. She was feeling low. She had lived in the secure arms of her loving family till today but now, she had to step into the outside world with an unknown man. Her eyes were moist just like the clouds—ready to burst into tears at any moment.

In the wedding hall, the atmosphere was joyous. The rustle of the silk saris, the sweet smell of the incense sticks, the aroma of fresh jasmine flowers and the mouth-watering sweets made the entire atmosphere very festive.

Surekha's father had worked in many towns and cities and, therefore, he had many acquaintances and friends. Most of them had come for the wedding. However, the groom's family was from Bangalore and only a few could come. Arrangements for their stay had been made in the same building on the first floor.

Mridula was washing her hands in the bathroom to get rid of the sticky mehendi when she heard the sound of raindrops. The rain started slowly and its intensity gradually increased. Water started entering the wedding hall through the open windows.

Rain brings different emotions to different people. For Mridula, the rain was synonymous with joy—it was nature's gift. She thought, 'The earth is full of dust and is dry in the summer. Rain settles the dust, washes away the dirt and makes the world green. It inspires creativity in poets and artists, but during a wedding, it only brings tension.'

Suddenly, the lights went off because of the heavy rain. Surekha's mother, Leela, became jittery. 'Oh my God! The groom's family and friends are here from Bangalore and they have high expectations.'

Then she saw Mridula and told her, 'Hey, hurry up. Take some candles and matchboxes and light them in all the rooms on the first floor. Unfortunately, the generator will take some time. But I will find Surekha's father and get the petro-lamps organized.'

Mridula could not say 'no' to anyone. That was her nature. She smiled and said, 'Aunty, don't worry. I'll ensure that every room gets a candle.'

First, she lit a candle in Surekha's room. Surekha was holding her hands out waiting for the wet mehendi to dry and her friends were flocking around, chatting and teasing her.

Pandit Thippa Bhatta was sitting in front of them. Meghana, Surekha's naughty friend, wanted to trouble him. 'Panditji, please tell us about the marriage rite called *panigrahan*.'

'The first time that a groom takes the bride's right hand in his is known as panigrahan.'

'Can any boy hold a bride's hand at any time?'

'No. Both the boy and the girl must be unmarried and they must hold each other's hand at the auspicious time.'

'What if a boy holds a girl's hand at a bus stop?' someone asked.

Meghana interrupted, 'Panditji, what's the auspicious time?'

Thippa Bhatta was a seasoned man and not scared of any questions. 'Oh, it depends on many factors,' he said. 'For example, some times are always auspicious. Right now, the time is known as *godhuli* and it is very favourable. If you say yes, I will get a boy for you right now and perform your wedding between six-thirty and seven.'

Meghana blushed and kept quiet.

Mridula was still going from room to room lighting candles but she was able to hear the conversation downstairs.

Meanwhile, the groom's mother was unhappy because of the rain and the power failure. Her sister said, 'You should have insisted the wedding take place in a good Bangalore wedding hall. The generator would have been running by this time. Now, look at this mess. If the rainwater seeps in, where will we sleep?'

They heard footsteps. Mridula entered the groom's mother's room and said, 'Aunty apologizes for the inconvenience. Petrolamps will be here at any moment. Aunty has also called the electricity board. May I light a candle for you?'

Both the sisters looked at her and stared. Who was this girl? She was better than the bride! Then, Santosh's mother said, 'Okay, but don't worry. We'll manage.'

Mridula went to the next room. The groom, Santosh, had a Mysore *peta* on his head and was looking excited. There were many men in the room. Mridula did not stay long. She quickly went from room to room and reached the last one.

There was nobody there. The window was open and it was still pouring. She saw a small bag on the window sill. It was getting wet. Mridula thought, 'If I don't close the window, the floor will become wet and it'll be difficult to sleep at night.'

She kept a candle near the door, went to the window and reached out her hand into the pouring rain. As she grabbed the bag, a warm and strong hand gently took hers. Almost immediately, the clock in the hall downstairs started chiming. It was 6.30 p.m. Meghana shouted, 'Oh, the auspicious time has come.'

Everyone cheered along with her.

It was dark and, for a minute, Mridula was scared. The person did not budge or let go of her hand. Then came a harsh male voice: 'I caught you.'

'What do you mean?' Mridula resisted, trying to get her hand free.

'I know that a lot of thefts take place in wedding halls and at railway junctions.'

'I am not responsible for any theft. Go and lodge a complaint with the police.'

'When I have caught the thief red-handed, why should I go to the police? It is dark and there is no electricity. Hmmm. So you thought you could make away with my bag.'

Now, Mridula understood that the man, whom she couldn't see clearly, had mistaken her for a thief. She got angry and said, 'I'm not a thief.'

'All thieves say that. But I learnt about the activities of this town on the train itself.'

'Learnt what?'

'That Hubli is a thief's paradise. I am unwell and had gone downstairs to get some warm water. If I hadn't come back in time, you would have escaped.'

'Let go of my hand. I'm not a thief. I came here to light a candle and saw water coming in through the window. I just wanted to close it, to save the bag from getting wet.'

'I don't believe you,' the man said.

Suddenly, the electricity came back. In the bright light, Sanjay and Mridula saw each other for the first time. Her sari was crumpled, her hair was untied and her face was tired. Her cheeks were red and flushed with anger. And yet, she was beautiful, with thick, long hair, clear skin and large twinkling eyes. Sanjay gazed at her without shame—like a thirsty man drinking water to his content.

He had touched many young women's hands but the relationship between them was strictly defined—that of doctor and patient. As far as he could remember, this was the first time he had caught an unknown girl's hand. He hardly knew any girls and since he was shy, he was not very friendly with his female colleagues.

Mridula also stared at Sanjay. She noticed that he was tall and not as fair as she was, but he was not dark either. He had curly hair and was built like an athlete. His face was beaming with pleasant surprise. He had well-defined and sharp features. Even though he was wearing an ordinary pair of black trousers and a white shirt, he could easily pass for a model.

By now, Meghana was shouting from below, 'Mridula, where are you? The lights are back. Come fast.'

Mridula threw the bag on the floor, removed Sanjay's hand from hers and ran downstairs. Somehow, she was not upset. She wondered who the man was. Though his hand was strong, it was unusually warm and she knew that he was unwell. She felt a strange attraction to this young man. But she also felt awful knowing that she was probably looking wet and miserable in her soggy sari.

Sanjay looked at his bag. It was not open and the rain was still coming in through the window. He felt sorry for the girl. 'Poor girl, she must have come to help in the wedding. She really did come upstairs to light the candles.'

He felt guilty about accusing her of stealing. Poverty could be hard and he knew it. He chastised himself, 'I should've been more cautious with my words. Mridula is such a beautiful name.'

Sanjay looked towards where Mridula had stood and saw a floral hairband lying on the floor. He picked it up and hoped that he could use the excuse of returning it to apologize to her.

Soon, the pre-wedding celebrations began. Sanjay was meeting Santosh after three years. But despite that, what they had to say to each other was over within a few minutes. Santosh's current friends were also there at the function but Sanjay did not know them. He thought that he had unnecessarily wasted two days of his vacation over this wedding. Then he remembered that he still had to deliver Professor Jog's package somewhere near Hubli. He had to find a way to his destination. He decided to ask someone at dinner.

He glanced around and saw Mridula again. She was dressed in a yellow silk sari and had a string of champak flowers in her long plait. She was wearing jewellery and looked like a golden statue. He was enchanted by her beauty, but felt horrible about the way he had treated her.

At dinner, he found himself sitting next to an old man and thought that he would be the best person to talk to because old people usually talk a lot. Before he could say anything, the old man asked, 'Are you from the bride's side or the groom's?'

'The groom's.'

'Well, I'm from the bride's side.'

Sanjay asked, 'Do you know where Aladahalli is?'

'Of course. It is thirty kilometres from here. Whom do you want to meet there?'

'Champa Bai Kamitkar.'

'How do you know her?'

'I don't really know her. She is related to my professor.'

'What's your professor's name?'

Sanjay didn't like the man asking so many questions but he had no choice. He said, 'Dr Jog.'

'Oh, Chandrakant. I know him well. But Champa Bai travels a lot. Well, if you don't find her at home, you can still meet Bheemanna and go.'

'Who's Bheemanna?'

'An important person in Aladahalli.'

'How do I find his house?'

'That's easy. His house is next to the Hanuman temple and Champa Bai's house is opposite his.'

'How do I go to Aladahalli?'

'That's not a problem. There is a non-stop bus tomorrow at 2 p.m. Otherwise, there is a regular bus every hour.'

Sanjay ate his dinner quickly. When he reached for the water, he found it was warm. Sanjay asked the serving boy, 'Who told you to give me warm water?'

The boy pointed his finger towards Mridula and said, 'She did.' Mridula was smiling at him, but Sanjay felt ashamed. So he just nodded at her.

The wedding took place the next day—and without any rains. The atmosphere was full of glee. Sanjay gave his gift to the couple and decided to catch the two o'clock bus and leave for Aladahalli. At the bus stand, he saw Mridula standing there. He was astonished to see her in simple clothes—like an ordinary girl. This was the best time to apologize to her. He went near her and said softly, 'Miss Mridula, I'm sorry.'

She turned back to look at him. Surprised, she said, 'Why are you here?'

'I'm sorry for my harsh words.'

'Yes, you mistook me for a thief. Maybe because of my wet clothes. You were so impatient that you wouldn't even listen to me, Mr—'

'I am Sanjay, a doctor from Bombay.'

'I didn't ask you for details,' Mridula answered.

'I apologize once again.'

'No, it isn't your fault. The way a person dresses is important.'

The bus arrived and both of them climbed aboard. This worried Mridula. Sanjay looked handsome and said he was a doctor, but why was he following her? As far as she knew, nobody knew him in Aladahalli. If he followed her to the house, then old-fashioned Rukuma would not keep quiet. She would kill her with her questions and his arrival would be immediately broadcast in the small village. The best way out of this was to send him back right now. Mridula asked Sanjay, 'Whose house are you visiting in Aladahalli?'

Sanjay looked at her. Her face had given her away. He knew that this innocent girl couldn't hide her feelings and so he wanted to tease her.

'Yours.'

'Why?'

'I want to meet your parents, explain everything and apologize to them.'

'I have already forgiven you. You needn't come for that purpose.'

'It is my duty to apologize to your parents.'

Mridula got even more worried. When the conductor came, Sanjay bought two tickets to Aladahalli. Mridula felt uncomfortable through the entire journey. She cursed herself, 'Why did I go upstairs with the candles?'

When the bus reached Aladahalli, she got down quickly.

A young boy, Budansabi, was waiting for her. There was a wound on his leg. He said, 'Sister, yesterday the bicycle chain hurt me badly and I thought of you so much. Will you look at it and tell me what to do?'

Sanjay wanted to tell the boy to get a tetvac injection immediately. But Mridula recommended, 'Clean your wound with Dettol and come to my house. I will give you medicine.'

Budansabi said, 'Okay,' and went away.

Sanjay was upset. Mridula was beautiful and her family may be rich but she was not a doctor. She should not advise people without knowing the consequences. He could not control himself. 'Mridula,' he said, 'you must not misguide the villagers. Dettol is not the solution. You have to give him a tetvac. It is a necessity. Otherwise, the consequences can be heavy for the boy.'

Mridula smiled and did not mind his words. She said, 'Oh, is that right?'

'I don't know what you have studied, but you don't have the right to play with somebody's life. You should have told him to go to a doctor.'

'Well, I am a teacher but that doesn't mean that I shouldn't try to help them. Let's do this. From this moment on, whenever we get patients, we will send them to Bombay. However, you should pay for their fare.'

Not waiting for an answer, she walked away. Sanjay was offended because Mridula had made fun of his profession.

He thought, 'She is a careless young girl who is exercising her power because she is from a well-to-do family. I don't want to get into it. I have come here for a specific purpose—to deliver a package, inquire about Champa Bai and report back to my professor. That's what I'll do and then leave quickly.'

A few minutes later, they were passing the Hanuman temple. Mridula was walking ahead of Sanjay. She was worried about what Sanjay would say to her father while Sanjay was wondering why this girl was going in the same direction as him.

At last, they reached Bheemanna's house. Bheemanna was sitting in the veranda. Sanjay asked, 'Who is Mr Bheemanna?'

Bheemanna got up and said, 'I am.'

'I want to meet Champa Bai Kamitkar.'

'Oh, she has gone to Naragund.'

'I am Sanjay Rao, a doctor from Bombay. My professor Dr Jog sent me here to deliver a package.'

Bheemanna was interested in the new visitor. He said enthusiastically, 'Why are you standing outside? Come here and sit down. Don't feel shy. Champa Bai will be back in an hour. You can wait here.'

Then Bheemanna looked at his daughter. 'Why are you standing there like a stranger? See, a doctor has come home. How was the wedding?'

Before Mridula could answer, Bheemanna continued, 'Sanjay Rao, Mridula is my daughter. She had gone to her friend's wedding in Hubli. Surekha and she were classmates and I have known Surekha's father for a long time. Mridula, please make two cups of strong tea for us.'

Mridula went inside and, within a few minutes, brought out two cups of tea. She was smiling. Sanjay took the tea and gave the package to Bheemanna. He said, 'I think I will go back now. My train is tonight. Kindly give this to Champa Bai.'

'No, you can't go like this. You must eat dinner with us. I'll make sure that you reach the railway station on time. You are Chandrakant's student and he's my good friend. How can I send his assistant back without a meal? What will he think? What will our Champa Bai think?'

Sanjay felt uncomfortable. He said, 'No, I will go back. I can't spend so much time here.'

'You won't get bored in our village. You must see the Hanuman temple, the big lake and our medicinal garden. Time will fly. Mridula, please get dinner ready. Sanjay and I are going for a stroll in the village and we'll come back soon.'

Bheemanna made his way out, knowing that Sanjay had no choice but to follow him. Sanjay had never met such an open, straightforward and friendly man and didn't know how to react. Luckily for Sanjay, Bheemanna started chatting about Mridula. 'Our Mridula is intelligent. We stay in this remote village and are finding it difficult to find an educated groom for her. My immediate circle consists only of farmers.'

'You can take Dr Jog's help.'

'Yes, you're right, but it has been more than ten years since Chandrakant came here and Mridula prefers a boy from Karnataka. We have searched for boys, but some of them felt that Mridula is neither a doctor nor an engineer. Some she herself did not like. Our Mridula says, "I don't mind marrying a man with less money. I can also work. But the boy should be good-natured." She thinks differently from us.'

Suddenly, Sanjay remembered Budansabi and asked, 'Does Mridula know anything about medicine?'

'Yes, she has had medical training. We don't have a hospital here. So she gives tetvac injections, helps in vaccination camps and takes care of people. She gives excellent first aid too and is of great help to the village women.'

By this time, they were back in front of Bheemanna's house and found that Champa Bai had returned. Sanjay talked to her and gave her the package. He looked for Mridula but did not see her anywhere. He couldn't believe that less than twenty-four hours ago, he had met a beautiful girl who had enchanted him thus.

After Sanjay returned from Hubli, he daydreamed about Mridula almost every day. While unpacking his bag, he found her hairband. He had forgotten to give it to her! He said to himself, 'I can mail it to her. But I don't feel like doing that. I may not even meet her again. It is better to throw the hairband in the dustbin.'

But he didn't do that.

Over the next few days, his work kept him busy and, gradually, he forgot about the hairband.

4

Destiny

The Hubli Teachers' Association went for a three-week annual trip during the Dussehra holidays. They welcomed teachers from neighbouring villages as well and this year, two teachers from Aladahalli were joining them—Principal Siddarod Hiremath and Mridula.

In the last four years, the Teachers' Association had visited Delhi, Kerala and Tamil Nadu. This year, they planned to go to Maharashtra. All the teachers were enthusiastic and had saved money to spend on the trip. They had reserved an entire railway coach and planned to take a cook with them: that would save them money and the food would be hygienic too. The teachers decided to stay in the local Karnataka Sanghas in the big metros. The tour itinerary included Bombay, Pune, Ajanta, Ellora, Aurangabad, Nasik, Nagpur and a few other towns.

Though Rukuma was not happy, Bheemanna encouraged Mridula's trip. Mridula had never gone outside north Karnataka and was excited at the prospect of seeing more of India. She was packing her bags when Champa Bai came in the evening to wish her a happy journey. Champa Bai was a seasoned traveller and liked to give travel tips to others. She advised, 'Mridula, don't take too many saris. If your first stop is Pune, you can buy a lot of good saris there. Here is Chandrakant's address and telephone number. It is better to have a doctor's address in an unknown city. You can stay with him in Bombay if you want to.'

'Aunty, I saw him twelve years ago and I don't even remember his face. I can't speak Marathi either.'

'Mridula, don't give me excuses. Call him and tell him that you are Bheemanna's daughter. Then he will talk to you in Kannada. It is his native language.'

Bheemanna changed the topic: 'Champa Bai, your nieces are married and are in Karnataka, aren't they?'

Now, Mridula knew that the conversation would never end and that Champa Bai would eat dinner in their house. So she went to the kitchen to help her mother.

The next morning, Mridula left for her trip.

The first stop was Pune. Mridula was the youngest in the group. They visited Parvati Hill, Chaturshringi Temple, Sambhaji Park, Ganapati Temple and Dagdu Halwai. As per Champa Bai's instructions, all the lady teachers visited Lakshmi Road for sari shopping. Mridula had thought that Hubli was a big shopping centre, but now she saw how small the Hubli market was compared to Pune.

There were lots of Rasvanti Grahas and these juice shops sold sugar cane juice in style. Sugar cane was not grown in Aladahalli because the land was unsuitable and sugar cane needs a lot of water to grow. The sugar cane juice they got in Hubli tasted different. Here, they added lemon, cardamom and ginger to the sugar cane juice and kept it on ice. Mridula enjoyed the juice in Pune and drank a lot of it till the day they left.

When they reached Bombay, Mridula got nervous on seeing the huge crowds. The big city, the people and the speed of the trains scared her and she wanted to go back to Aladahalli and its calm. The group stayed at the Karnataka Sangha at Matunga, a locality in central Bombay.

The next day, the group planned to see Elephanta Caves, the Gateway of India and Nariman Point. They hired a bus to take them around the city. But after breakfast, Mridula felt giddy and nauseated. She told the others, 'I am feeling unwell. But please go ahead. There is a housekeeper and a cook here. They will help me if I need anything. I'll take some medicine and I should be all right by the time you come back in the evening.'

The group was concerned but Mridula convinced them that she would be fine after a few hours of rest. So they left for the trip after Mridula promised to call them if she felt worse.

Actually, Mridula was scared. She thought that she must have had too much sugar cane juice. Soon, she got fever and it did not subside even after taking the medicine. A little later, she started vomiting and dehydrating. Her stomach was hurting too. She knew that it was better to be on drip and to drink lots of coconut water in such a situation. She felt helpless. 'If this continues, I will spoil the trip for the rest of the group. People have looked forward to this trip for months. I can stay back in Bombay till I get better—but where will I stay? Had this happened in Aladahalli, things would have been easy. My father would have sent word to a doctor in Shiggaon or Hubli.'

Suddenly, Mridula remembered that Champa Bai had given her Dr Jog's contact details. Though she was hesitant to contact him, she didn't know what else to do. With great reluctance, she dialled the number. When the person on the other end spoke in Marathi, she was puzzled. She said in English, 'I am Mridula, Bheemanna's daughter from Aladahalli.'

In Kannada, the person said, 'I am Chandrakant here. Where are you calling from? Are you in Bombay?'

Mridula told him what had happened to her. Dr Jog gently said, 'Please don't worry. You may need saline. I am already in the hospital on my rounds. I'll send my car and you can come here directly.'

After hanging up, Dr Jog looked at all his assistants and spotted Sanjay. He said to him, 'Sanjay, you are my only assistant who can speak Kannada. You may have met Mridula when you went to Aladahalli. Please go in my car and bring her to the hospital. She may be more comfortable coming here with somebody she knows. Admit her in the women's ward. Meanwhile, I'll arrange a special and comfortable room for her. Poor girl, it must be a big culture shock for her to see Bombay and then, to make matters worse, she's sick too.'

Chandrakant loved his aunt Champa Bai and knew that Bheemanna took care of her. Now, Bheemanna's daughter was unwell and it was his duty to help her. His wife was out of the country so he decided to keep Mridula in the hospital till she was better and then move her to the women's hostel till her group came back to Bombay. He thought, 'Sanjay is a sincere boy—he is from Karnataka and may know her too. I'll tell him to help her for the next ten days.'

Though Sanjay did not show it, he was happy with this new assignment and unexpected opportunity. He had resigned himself to the fact that he would never meet Mridula again. When he reached Karnataka Sangha, he found that Mridula was very sick—she looked like a faded white lotus of the Aladahalli lake. Sanjay asked her, 'What's this, Mridula? Have you come to Bombay to fall sick?'

Mridula replied in pain, 'Sickness is independent of where you are. Food is the actual cause.'

All her colleagues had come back from their day trip and were concerned. They wanted Mridula to go with Sanjay, so that she could get good care and treatment. Principal Hiremath consoled her, 'Mridula, don't worry. We'll be back in Bombay after ten days. By then, you'll be all right and you can join us. If you are in a doctor's care, then we won't worry. I can talk to your father if you like.'

So Mridula had no other choice. Sanjay brought her to the hospital. The ground floor was the maternity ward and the first floor was the women's ward. Mridula was given one of the special rooms reserved only for doctors and their recommended patients.

Sanjay was busy looking at Mridula's medical papers when Alex ran into him. 'Sanjay, why aren't you in OPD on this busy day?'

'There's a special case.'

'Why are you standing outside the women's ward? Is the patient in the special case a girl?' Alex smelt a rat.

Sanjay blushed, 'Yes, the patient is a girl. I met her at the wedding in Hubli.'

'Not bad. At least, you lost something in Hubli.'

'What's that?'

'The most precious thing for a young bachelor like you— your heart. I wish you all the best.'

Alex smiled, put a hand to his heart and walked away.

Mridula was on saline for the next few days; after that, she was back to her usual self. She did not call her parents because she knew that they would worry about her. Now, she had to wait for her group to come back. So she moved to the women's hostel and Sanjay became her only visitor.

'You missed seeing the Elephanta Caves in Bombay with your group because of your illness. I have a holiday tomorrow. May I take you there?' Sanjay surprised himself by making the first move. He hid the fact that he was taking leave just to take her out.

Mridula felt shy and yet, she wanted to go with him. She asked, 'Do you think Doctor Uncle will mind if I go with you?'

'No, you don't have to take his permission.'

It was the first time that Mridula was going out with a man. They went to the Gateway of India since the motor boat started from there. While they were waiting to get into the boat, Mridula looked around. She found this city very different. Everyone was doing something or the other. Not an inch of land was wasted here. When their turn came to get into the boat, Sanjay stretched out both his hands to help her step on board. At that moment, Mridula realized that one of his arms was shorter than the other. Sanjay saw that Mridula had noticed his deformity and felt awkward. But Mridula did not say or ask anything.

The boat started moving towards Elephanta Island. It was full of young lovers, families and college students. One of the bench seats on the boat was not fitted properly. The equipment to fix the seat was available but the boat assistant was unable to do so. The passengers who had paid for the seat were upset and were arguing with the helpless assistant. When Sanjay saw what was happening, he asked for the toolkit and repaired the seat in ten minutes. The assistant was grateful and started talking to Sanjay. 'Sir, our owner doesn't hire any carpenters because of their high labour cost and I don't have any training at all. So customers get upset with me. You are a good mechanic, sir. I'm fortunate that you came today. Thank you so much.'

Sanjay did not reply.

After an hour, the boat reached Elephanta Island. All the visitors were excited. Very few people went to actually see the caves. While walking from the seashore to the caves, Sanjay was unusually quiet. Mridula said, 'Did you notice that the helper thought that you were a mechanic? I wanted to tell him that you are a doctor.'

'Yes. Well, a doctor is also a mechanic—of the human body.'

'That's true.'

'In our hospital, if any medical equipment doesn't work, they call me. I like to repair things.'

'Then why didn't you pursue engineering?'

'There was a reason.' Sanjay became silent and did not say any more.

A short walk later, they reached the caves. There were huge statues carved in the temple wall. It was beautiful. But Mridula was thinking about Sanjay. 'Let Sanjay answer my question in his own time. I don't want to get details about his personal life by forcing him to answer.'

Outside, there were some restaurants, and hawkers selling picture postcards, film rolls, instant photos and T-shirts. It seemed to be a popular picnic spot and not just a place of archaeological interest. Sanjay and Mridula decided to have tea in one of the restaurants. While sipping tea, Sanjay started talking: 'When I was a child, I was normal just like anybody else. At the age of four or five, I climbed a tree. I don't remember this incident at all. My parents told me that I fell down from the tree and became unconscious. My father was the village medical practitioner and he never took money from his patients. But he didn't have any formal education. He prepared medicines at home. So he gave me a home-made remedy, but my arm wasn't set properly. Later, my mother took me to a big hospital and showed it to an orthopaedic surgeon. But it was too late. I had to have surgery. In that process, my arm became a little shorter.'

Hesitantly, Mridula asked, 'Do you have any problem with that hand?'

'No, I don't. It hurts only if I use it too much or lift heavy things. But I feel like the odd man out in any crowd.'

Mridula felt his pain and did not know what to say. Sanjay continued, 'When I had this problem, my mother gave me the courage to face it. She believed that I could be a good doctor despite my defect. She was my strength. My mother is responsible for what I am today.'

Sanjay became nostalgic. His mother, Ratnamma, was a petty moneylender. She loved money and finance. He had told her many times that he did not like her line of work but she said that she enjoyed it. She was right. Everybody should do what he or she enjoyed!

As Sanjay went down memory lane, he recalled that during the PT period in his school, the teacher would ask the students to stretch out their hands. All his classmates would make fun of him then. Sanjay would get upset and chase after them. When he could not catch them, he would go home and cry. Ratnamma would pacify him and say encouragingly, 'Child, this was God's decision. Who knows? One day, you may rule the world with this crippled hand!'

'But you didn't answer my question,' Mridula reminded him.

'Yes. I went to the hospital many times because of my hand. The doctors there helped me. So I also wanted to become a doctor. My father had three sisters and my mother had two. Since most of them died in childbirth, I thought about becoming a gynaecologist, even though I know that most women prefer female doctors.'

They finished drinking their tea and took the next boat back to the mainland.

For the next few days, Sanjay worked for half a day, and then he took Mridula out in the evenings. The days passed quickly and Mridula's last day in Bombay came along. Her group arrived from Nagpur and Mridula planned to join them at the railway station. From there, the group was going to Kolhapur and then to Hubli.

Mridula started packing her bags and decided to wait for Sanjay at the women's hostel. She liked to wait for him. She recalled that when she was admitted in the hospital and was given saline, Sanjay had stayed the whole night with her so that she would not feel alone in a strange city. She had felt shy at the time because she barely knew this young man. Still, she felt an attraction towards him and wondered whether she would see him again after today.

Sanjay was unable to concentrate on his work that day. He could not stop thinking about Mridula. He felt like he had known her forever. He had met her for the first time when it was raining in the dark and had caught her hand in Hubli. But the attraction was the same even in Bombay. It had not faded. He had seen beautiful and innocent girls in the movies and read about them in books, but it was difficult to meet such girls in real life. Sanjay felt lucky to know Mridula.

He thought to himself, 'After she leaves today, when will I see her again? I know that whoever marries Mridula will be fortunate. Usually, people comment on my short arm and question me. Shamelessly, they ask me whether it is hereditary or a birth defect. It makes me feel inferior. But Mridula didn't ask me about it and didn't treat me differently after she learnt about my accident. I've met her parents and seen her home. I know that her family is content, not pretentious or money-hungry. In a marriage, if the wife is ambitious, then a simple person like me will suffer. Why can't I be that fortunate person who marries her? We both belong to the same community and speak the same language. She is intelligent and both of us can adjust quickly if we get married. But no, I may not be good enough for her. She belongs to a well-to-do family and she might think of me only as a good friend. She may not have even thought of marriage. Maybe she likes someone else. Or her parents might want her to get married somewhere else. What if she herself says "no"? Do I have the capacity to bear rejection?'

For a minute, he was scared. Then he remembered Alex's words: 'No Indian girl will make the first move. That has to come from the boy. He has to ask the girl and the worst case is that she will say "no".'

'How do you know whether a girl will say "yes" or "no"?'

'If the girl wants to say "yes", she won't agree immediately. She may say that I'll let you know or I'll talk to my father. If you get that answer, you know that she will say "yes". The girl who wants to say "no" will tie a rakhi on your hand before you can even propose to her. She will publicly declare that you are like her brother. Some bold girl may even slap you. It is rare but you should be ready. Haven't you heard the famous song *Pyaar kiya to darna kya* from the movie *Mughal-e-Azam*? It means that you should love a girl only if you have the courage to do so. Otherwise, you should have an arranged marriage—your parents and you should see the girl together and make the decision in five minutes.'

Sanjay was hesitant to express his love to Mridula but he did not have a choice. He remembered Mridula's floral hairband. It was difficult for him to express his love through words. The hairband gave him a reason to write a letter to her. But now, he had an even bigger problem: he did not know how to write a love letter. He had no experience in this area. The twenty-five-year-old Sanjay struggled like a teenager writing his first love letter.

Dear Mridula,

You may be surprised to see my letter. I am not a great writer and this is my first letter to any girl. I like you a lot. What you see is what I am. I don't want to lie to you. I come from a poor family. We have some land but I don't have any other assets. I don't have a father. My sister is already married. I am not equal to you in terms of looks or money. You already know about my hand. But I am hard-working and honest. I want to spend the rest of my life with you. If you feel the same way about me, then write back. Otherwise, destroy this letter and forget about it.

Sanjay

He read the letter again and again but did not know what else to write. So he put her hairband and the letter inside an envelope and sealed it.

Sanjay picked Mridula up from the women's hostel and took her to VT station. The group was waiting for her there. Mridula joined them and sat at the train window to say goodbye to Sanjay. The engine whistled and signalled that the train was about to leave. Sanjay gave the envelope to Mridula with hesitation. In a low voice, he said, 'This is important, Mridula.'

'What's this?'

But by then, the train had left the station and Sanjay was left standing on the platform, waving nervously.

5

Reflections

Sanjay came back to his room and wondered whether he had done the right thing. Maybe he should have faced her in person, expressed his feelings and said, 'Mridula, I love you.' That may have been far more effective than a letter. But he knew that that would have been much harder for him.

He wondered, 'Would she have read my letter by now? What will she think? She can definitely find someone better than me. She is good-looking and an idealist. She has never seen poverty in her life. In fact, she has not seen the competitive world outside Aladahalli. Why should she marry me? After all, I am handicapped. My mother has a small moneylending business. How can I expect Mridula's family to give their daughter to me?'

Still, he was hopeful. Bheemanna was talkative but not worldly-wise. Mridula was academically brilliant but not street-smart like his sister, Lakshmi. So they might agree. Sanjay was unable to eat his dinner. He lay down but sleep was a thousand miles away.

He could see the overpopulated Parel from his bed. He called Sister Indumati at the hospital and told her to call him only if there was an emergency. His mind jumped back to his childhood.

T. Narasipura, on the banks of River Kaveri, was his home town. He had studied there till his school-leaving examinations. At the time, his father was alive and his sister was unmarried. Their financial condition was bad. His mother, Ratnamma, had not had her moneylending business then. She used to only look after the land. Though she was uneducated, she was smart. She had a lot of knowledge about famines and how to handle them. His father was timid and he consistently worried about what people would say. But his mother was bold enough for both of them.

His father used to tell him, 'We should care about society and what people say.' But his mother would say, 'People will always give you advice, my child, but you must remember to do what *you* think is right.'

Their statements were as contradictory as day and night. Though Amma talked less, her decision was the final one in the family. People said that you should pick your battles. But Appa used to accept defeat easily. He said that there was no defeat or victory in life. Appa was detached.

The clock in the corridor struck midnight. It made Sanjay realize that he hadn't got any emergency calls. Indumati must have diverted his duty to someone else. That was so nice of her. Still, he couldn't sleep. His mind wandered again.

He got good marks in the school-leaving examinations. By then, his father had passed away and his sister, Lakshmi, was married and lived in a joint family. Her husband's family lived in a huge house and all the four brothers worked and stayed together in Mysore. No one was ready to leave the family house and go because they knew that the brother who stayed in the house till the end would inherit it—it was the only family property. Movies like *Hum Saath-Saath Hain* and *Hum Aapke Hain Koun* advocated the importance and advantage of a joint family. But Sanjay had seen the selfishness, jealousy and negative undercurrents in large families and the false portrayal of a well-bonded family to society. It was better that people lived separately and kept cordial relationships with their siblings and parents, rather than staying in a joint family and fighting every day, he thought.

When he wanted to join a college in Mysore, his sister and mother had insisted that he stay in Lakshmi's in-laws' house. He did not want to stay there but he had neither the power nor the economic freedom to disobey his mother's command. He was aware that his mother could not afford to keep him in a hostel and she believed that if he stayed in a joint family, he would be looked after. But that was a wrong assumption. Only a person who stayed with such a family knew what went on. There was fierce competition between the family members. The men had small differences about economic status but the women competed with each other over everything. If one of them bought a sari, the others would also buy one, even if it meant that their husbands had to borrow money. If someone bought gold jewellery, the others wanted to buy something even more expensive. Lakshmi had got used to staying in such an atmosphere and had adapted to the family. She had become one of them. But Sanjay felt suffocated there.

Amma sent two bags of rice for his initial stay, but Lakshmi's sisters-in-law sarcastically said, 'Only rice is not enough. You also need other things like dal and everyday items such as soap, toothpaste, hair oil, etc.'

Then they laughed at him. The children in the house asked him about his short arm repeatedly and made fun of his handicap. Sometimes, he got so upset with Amma and Lakshmi that he felt like staying in an orphanage. At least, he would have had some peace and quiet there.

Somehow, he survived the two years in that house. He was a good student and obtained excellent marks in his pre-university exams. When he decided to study medicine, he knew that he was good enough to get admission in any government college. He deliberately did not apply to Mysore Medical College and he got admission in Bangalore. Amma asked him, 'Sanjay, why didn't you get admission in Mysore?'

He lied to her, 'Amma, I didn't get admission in Mysore Medical College because I have less marks.'

The truth was that he did not want to stay in Mysore or in his sister's house. He knew that it was not a good thing to lie, especially to your mother, but sometimes, white lies are essential to make our lives smoother. He himself had seen his mother lie sometimes, and he did not consider it a great offence. In the last two years, he had matured and heard a lot of lies in the joint family. He told his mother that he was going to study in Bangalore.

When he came to Bangalore, life seemed beautiful. But living in Bangalore was expensive. His eyes swelled with tears when he thought of how much his mother had to struggle to support him. He rented a small room on Santosh's terrace. He cooked for himself and attended college. Santosh's mother was a nice lady; she often said, 'Sanjay, why do you struggle to cook every day? You are wasting your precious time. Eat in our house. I can easily add some extra rice in the cooker every day.'

But he never accepted her offer. During festivals, however, he ate lunch with them. His father had taught him an unforgettable lesson: 'Child, too much is too bad. Even nectar in large quantities will turn to poison.'

It was Sanjay's nature not to get too attached to anyone. He never liked sitting and chatting, getting into personal matters or advising people. That was why he did not have any bitter enemies or good friends. Even with Lakshmi and Amma, he only spoke when needed. He preferred to be by himself—just like a tortoise in its shell.

When Sanjay saw Mridula for the first time, he was surprised. She was a beautiful and blooming flower that swayed freely with the wind. She was genuine and full of affection. Her family's hospitality came from the heart—unlike the house in Mysore where respect depended on how much money a person had. Mridula and her family's lives were filled with positive energy. Each day was celebrated like a festival. Mridula smiled and laughed without reason. Was that why he was attracted to her? Somewhere, he had read that opposites attract. He knew that he was not attracted to her because of her financial status or the fields or farms her family owned. He believed in himself.

His mind came back to the present. Both of them had known each other for only a short time. They had never been friends before. The idea that Mridula might say 'no' to his proposal made him sweat in the cool night. The word 'no' was not new to Sanjay. He had experienced bitterness many times. But he would not be able to take it this time.

When he was studying in Bangalore, his extrovert classmate Vasudha was fairly close to him. They had studied together for five years and were good friends. She was also Santosh's cousin and visited his house often. Santosh used to make fun of Vasudha's friendship with Sanjay. Even though Vasudha was not very attractive, Sanjay used to see her every day and started liking her. At the time, he was in his early twenties. But one day, Sanjay overheard a conversation between Vasudha and Santosh as he was passing by.

Vasudha was saying, 'Santosh, stop teasing Sanjay and me. He is my classmate and a brilliant student. I respect him. But I also pity him because of his hand. Why will a normal girl like me marry him? Pity is different from love.'

Her comments shocked him. He remembered what Amma had said: 'Child, don't express your deepest feelings to anyone unless you are sure about the consequences. You should never share your weakness without thinking it through. Otherwise, people will take advantage of it.'

But Appa had said just the opposite: 'Every person is an island. You need a bridge to connect two islands. That bridge is called a relationship. In life, real affection comes not through hiding but through expressing your true feelings.'

Fortunately, he had followed Amma's advice instead of Appa's. Otherwise, everyone would have laughed at him then.

After this incident, he never talked to any girl until he was in Bombay. His heart was like stone. But it melted like butter next to fire when he met Mridula for the first time. It was not just the attraction—a sense of protection and belonging pulled him towards her. But he didn't know what Mridula felt for him.

When he was thinking about the future after his internship, there was nobody to guide him. Ratnamma gave full freedom to her son to decide his future. She had said, 'Sanjay, you are more educated than all of us. You can understand things much better than I can. I can only advise you that you should not fall prey to wrong things. Think practically and decide.'

Sanjay respected his mother for her frank opinions. But in Santosh's house, both his parents interfered in everything he did. He had too many restrictions, while Sanjay was a free bird. Amma also expected the same freedom from her son. When she started a small shop, he had not liked it but she had still gone ahead.

Alex was one year senior to him in college and they were good friends. During Sanjay's internship, Alex had come from Bombay to meet him and asked him about his plans. Sanjay had said, 'I want to do my post-graduation in gynaecology.'

'That's really good. But getting a seat in government quota in Karnataka is not easy. You have to be a topper. Otherwise, you'll get anatomy or pathology.'

'Yes, I know. I think that I should get some work experience too.'

'Well, if you want to work, then come to Bombay. Do your residency and become a duty doctor in any government hospital. It has its advantages. You get excellent clinical practice and you learn how things work. At the same time, you can also prepare for your post-graduation entrance test. I am working in KEM Hospital. I can get you a job there but it won't be permanent. The salary won't be high either. But if you want to get some experience, Bombay is where you want to be. Work for a few years there and then you can decide what you want to do.'

Alex had given his contact details and left.

Sanjay never did anything in a hurry. So he thought about it. He had never been out of Karnataka and thought that this would be an opportunity for change. He did not want to take the entrance test without preparing for it. He had just heard that one of his brilliant classmates had not got through gynaecology. Maybe he had not done well in his entrance test. But it was a shock to Sanjay. So he thought that the best thing to do was to go to Bombay, get some experience, come back and then take the test.

He was still unable to sleep. Was he scared that Mridula would say 'no'?

When he came to Bombay, he was terrified seeing the pace of the city. The city was overcrowded and he felt like going back to Bangalore. But Alex made his stay comfortable. He turned out to be a true friend. Alex was not academically brilliant, but his strengths were leadership qualities and networking skills. Within a week, Sanjay got a residency with the assurance that later, he would be a duty doctor as well. Usually, intelligent and trained young doctors didn't work in government hospitals. They either joined private practices that catered to everyone or they went abroad to earn more money.

Alex had explained the politics at work, 'Sanjay, there are three units in the gynaecology department. They are headed by Dr Jog, Dr Parekh and Dr Bhosale. Dr Parekh is good but he owns his own nursing home. So he is more concerned about that. Dr Bhosale is a local person related to a minister. So he is constantly busy. The best is Dr Jog. He is impartial, knowledgeable and a great teacher. Also, he is from your state. You will feel more comfortable with him. Though we talk about equal opportunity for everyone, practically, in our country, it is community, language and connections that are important. I recommend Dr Jog. But the decision is yours.'

So Sanjay had joined Dr Jog. But Dr Jog never talked to Sanjay in Kannada and treated him impartially. However, Sanjay spoke in Kannada to patients who knew the language to make them feel at home. That was how Dr Jog found out that Sanjay was also from Karnataka. But it made no difference to him. He was more impressed with Sanjay's sincerity at work.

Sanjay's thoughts wandered back to Mridula and he thought about her reaction, 'Maybe she's making fun of my letter in front of her friends. I have spent almost three years in Bombay now. It is time—I must either do my post-graduation in Bombay or return to Bangalore.'

Finally, he slept.

6

A Second Chance

November and December were the best months of the year in Aladahalli. There were no lashing rains and no windy, hot days. The sky was clear and the weather pleasant. The full-moon day was celebrated with great joy and all relatives and friends came together for a moonlit dinner at the side of the lake or in the mango grove. The entire dinner consisted of special items that were white in colour, such as curd rice, sugary desserts, white chiroti, kheer and jowar roti.

Bheemanna celebrated this festival annually and this year was no different. All his friends had come from different villages. Rukuma's relatives were also joining in. Champa Bai was like family to Bheemanna and her relatives were also invited. Bheemanna had hired a cook from Hubli and told him, 'We're not maharajas or gods. We're mere mortals and can't give expensive gifts to everyone. But we can give them excellent food, cooked with love. Please use a lot of home-made ghee, jaggery and fruits. Whoever joins us for this dinner must remember the food and the company until the Purnima festival comes around again next year.'

After the Maharashtra trip, Mridula had become unusually quiet at home. For the first time in her life, someone had written a love letter to her. Initially, she was shocked. But once she had finished reading the letter, she began to like Sanjay even more. A wedding was an important milestone and she couldn't take the decision on her own. Her parents would have a major say in this. She decided to tell her parents. Bheemanna had not noticed that Mridula was quiet and preoccupied. He was too busy preparing for the festival. Rukuma attributed Mridula's quietness to her brief sickness and tiredness from the trip. She wanted to talk to her but there were too many guests at home and they were keeping her busy. Rukuma's brother Satyabodha had also come with his wife and children, Sarla and Satish. Satish was not Satyabodha's biological son but his wife's distant cousin who had lost both his parents; Satyabodha and his wife had adopted him as their own.

On the day of the festival, all the guests left for the lake with the cooked food. Bheemanna told them that he and his family would join them shortly. Rukuma had almost finished cleaning the kitchen. Now, only the four of them remained in the house. Mridula thought, 'This is the best time to tell my parents about the letter.'

Bheemanna was sitting on the swing and urging his wife to hurry up. Mridula quietly brought the letter and gave it to Bheemanna. Then she went and stood behind a wooden pillar. Bheemanna read the letter and was surprised. He immediately called out to his wife, 'What's your opinion about that doctor from Bombay?'

Hearing Bheemanna's urgent tone and unexpected question, Rukuma stopped what she was doing and came outside. 'Why do you want to know? And why now?'

Bheemanna said softly, 'Because he has written a letter to our Mridula telling her that he wants to marry her.'

By now, Krishna had also come outside. Rukuma replied, 'We have met him just once and we don't know anything about him or his background.'

'Don't worry. He belongs to our community. You already know that he's a doctor. Now, tell me what you think.'

'How can I give my opinion in such a short time?'

'Well, take your time. Ah, I forgot to tell you one thing.' Bheemanna told Rukuma about Sanjay's handicap.

Rukuma looked disturbed. 'I think we shouldn't pursue this matter. Our Mridula can get a better boy.'

Mridula went inside the house. She wanted her parents to discuss this freely. Krishna followed her; he wanted to know more about Sanjay. 'Mridula, you didn't tell me about Sanjay!'

'Brother, I never thought of him in that way.' She told him what had happened between Sanjay and her.

Meanwhile, Bheemanna said to his wife, 'If everything else is favourable, then his arm shouldn't be the reason to stop the marriage. The boy is handsome and intelligent. We can find out more details from Chandrakant. But let's do that only if Mridula agrees.'

Rukuma was still hesitant. 'What's the hurry? If I tell my brother, he'll get her a better alliance.'

'Your brother is unable to find a match for his own daughter. So forget about it. The boy is decent and that's why he has written a letter. But if Mridula says "no", then there is nothing more to be done.'

Bheemanna called out to Mridula. She entered the veranda like a shy bride. She knew why they were calling her. Bheemanna said, 'Mridula, don't think that we don't have the capacity to find you another boy. We aren't insisting that you marry this boy because it reduces our tension. I believe that we should give our daughter to a boy only if he is good and we shouldn't worry about how rich he is. This is your decision. Please feel free and tell us what you think.'

Without even lifting her head, Mridula replied slowly, 'If Sanjay met with an accident that left him handicapped after we got married, then you wouldn't hold that against him. So I don't have any objection to the alliance if both of you are okay with it.'

Surprised at Mridula's quick and decisive response, Bheemanna and Rukuma looked at each other.

7

Generation Gap

Tirumakudalu Narasipura was a famous pilgrimage town near Mysore and was popularly known as T. Narasipura. There were small shops in front of the Narasimha temple in the town. One of them was Ratnamma's. She was a fifty-eight-year-old widow whose house was right behind her small shop. She sold flowers, incense, camphor, bananas, coconuts and other puja items. Some pilgrims wanted to take a dip in the river Kaveri since they considered it very auspicious. So Ratnamma also kept plastic mugs, soaps and low-quality towels for them. There were many such shops on the same street. Still, all of them managed to make a small profit.

Business was at its peak in May because of the cart festival, a day before Buddha Purnima. This day was also known as Narasimha Chaturthi. Devotees came from different parts of the country to T. Narasipura on this day and there were extra buses from Mysore too. On other days, the crowd was minimal. Usually, only devotees from Mysore visited the place. But they didn't buy anything from the shops. They got their fruits and coconuts from home and went directly to the temple. So most shop owners had an added income during this time.

Ratnamma had a lucrative moneylending business. She was shrewd and, at times, ruthless. When she lent money, she charged an extremely high interest rate. People frequently commented, 'Ratnamma is a hard-hearted lady.'

But she did not get upset. She calmly justified her stand: 'Am I not giving them money when they need it? They know the terms. Why should they get upset when I ask them to return it? Why was Karna of the Mahabharata called great? Because he gave away money and things to everybody. If I start lending money with a low interest rate, there will be a big queue in front of my house. And if I stop asking people to return the money, then they will either take very long or they may not even return it. My business will go down the drain. People will always talk. If they want free money, then I am not the right person to approach.'

Nobody ever knew what Ratnamma was thinking, but she could find out someone else's secret very quickly. She never got upset or raised her voice. Her entire world was money and she kept an account of everything. She never offered tea to her customers either. Recently, the people at T. Narasipura had seen a spike in bad moneylenders. Ratnamma seemed better than most these days.

Even though Ratnamma did not leave her shop and go anywhere, she knew the ins and outs of the entire village. Her argument was that people could talk of philosophy only after they had achieved considerable success in life. She said that people who came to listen to discourses on philosophy never practised it.

One day, Lakshmi called her mother and said, 'Shankar has been transferred to Belur. I want to come and see you.'

Ratnamma did not close the shop even for a day, so it was Lakshmi who always came to meet her mother. This time, there was a special reason for her visit. Sanjay had sent Lakshmi Mridula's photo and had informed her about his upcoming wedding. Lakshmi wanted to discuss this with her mother.

A few days later, Lakshmi arrived with her son, Anil. When the topic of Sanjay's marriage came up, Lakshmi got upset—but her mother was cool. Lakshmi said harshly, 'Amma, whatever you may say, Sanjay has brought disgrace on us.'

Lakshmi had taken after her father and was much more talkative than Sanjay. Ratnamma was silent at her comment. Lakshmi continued, 'I told everyone in my in-laws' house that Sanjay will marry a doctor and open a nursing home. This girl Mridula is just a teacher in a government high school. Now, I look like a fool.'

'Why did you say that? He never said anything like that to me. Did he tell you that?'

'No, he didn't. There's a reason why I said that. My husband's sister Vimla told me that she wanted Sanjay to marry her daughter Usha. I don't like Vimla. But I didn't want to hurt her feelings and said that Sanjay will only marry a doctor. They will laugh at me now. We don't know anything about this girl or where she's from. We have never even visited Aladahalli. Why is Sanjay getting married to a girl from there?'

Ratnamma was not perturbed. 'Why are you upset? The girl is nice looking and Sanjay is educated. He must have met her and thought about it before making this decision. You are increasing your blood pressure by getting upset.'

Sanjay had never talked about marriage to his mother. In fact, there were many parents whose daughters were of marriageable age and they kept dropping hints to Ratnamma. Sethurao in T. Narasipura owned a lot of land and had a good moneylending business too. He had indirectly asked Ratnamma once or twice about her son. Another time, there was a female doctor from Mysore who had asked her about Sanjay and suggested that they could open a nursing home together if they got married. But Ratnamma had not replied. Ratnamma thought, 'When daughters grow up, they become good friends to mothers but when young boys grow up, they become strangers. Lakshmi doesn't understand that. Maybe she will when her son, Anil, comes of age.'

In fact, Ratnamma had not seen Sanjay for almost a year. Once, he had said to her, 'Amma, I'll send you more money. You work too much. You can close the shop.'

At the time, Ratnamma had thought to herself, 'It really isn't too much work for me, but the truth is that he doesn't want me to run a small shop. He must think that it is below his dignity. But I don't worry about such false status symbols.'

A customer walked in and interrupted her thoughts. He asked the price of a towel and a mug. Then he started negotiating with her: 'Oh! That is very expensive. It is much cheaper in Mysore Devaraja Market.'

Lakshmi channelized the anger at her brother towards the customer and said, 'Then you should have bought it from there. Why did you come here?'

Fortunately, the customer was a little deaf. Ratnamma became alert. She knew the fundamental rule: the customer is

God. Wisely, she told Lakshmi, 'Take the child inside and cook for the afternoon.'

Lakshmi gave her mother a dirty look and went away.

Ratnamma started convincing the customer: 'Yes, things are much cheaper in Mysore. We buy goods from there, load them in a bus and pay for the bus and a coolie. We also take money from a moneylender to invest in our shop. We don't have much choice. They may look similar to Devaraja Market in colour but you may not have checked the quality. One has to pay a price for good quality. Please see the quality of the towels and the mugs and buy them only if you are convinced that they are good.'

The customer changed his mind after listening to her. Ratnamma completed the transaction and thought, 'It is difficult to understand customers. Everyone has a different personality. I have to understand them as I talk to them. How will Lakshmi realize that? Her husband, Shankar, is a bank clerk and gets his salary regularly whether he works or not. But my life is full of ups and downs. How can Lakshmi appreciate the importance of money, customers and business when she sits at home all day?'

Ratnamma heard Anil crying and was immediately annoyed. With all the comforts, Lakshmi couldn't look after even one child.

She remembered her past.

With a husband like Narasinga Rao and two small children, life had not been easy. Her husband did not have common sense. Though he was good at prescribing medicines to his patients, he was extremely bad when it came to charging them for it. When she insisted that he ask his patients to pay so that she could get some money to run the household, he would say, 'How can I ask my patients for money? It is Lord Dhanvantari's gift to me. When patients are cured, they give me money themselves. But if I insist that they pay, this gift will disappear.'

Though the people in the village were uneducated, they were street-smart. When they were ill, the patients and his relatives came and touched Narasinga Rao's feet and cried, 'You are God to us. Please save the patient.'

But once the patients were cured, they avoided him. Ratnamma wondered how she would run the house in this town with two small children. That was the time when she decided to look after the fields and open her own business. She remembered how they had struggled for Lakshmi's marriage. Her eyes automatically went to Lakshmi and Shankar's wedding picture on the wall.

Lakshmi was a very beautiful girl. Even today, after having a child, she looked the same. But beauty alone cannot fetch a good groom for a poor man's daughter. Many people took help from Narasinga Rao. But when her husband went with Lakshmi's horoscope and picture to their houses in hope for an alliance, they gave him a glass of water and sweet-talked him. Later, they told him that the horoscopes did not match. Ratnamma's impractical husband believed them but she knew that the real reason was not horoscopes but their lack of money.

After a lot of disappointments, Ratnamma herself had set out to search for a groom for her daughter. Shankar was a distant relative. But there was an age difference of ten years between Lakshmi and him. Fortunately, he did not have parents who would demand a lot of dowry. So, Ratnamma had begged Shankar and he had agreed to get married to Lakshmi. But Narasinga Rao was unhappy. He argued, 'This is not a good match, Ratna. Shankar is greedy and aggressive. He is quarrelsome and cunning too. I don't like his family either.'

But Ratnamma had not cared and Lakshmi had got married to Shankar.

Ratnamma was sweating in the hot summer. She wiped her face with her sari's pallu. There were no customers in her shop and she knew from experience that nobody would come for a few hours. She was about to close the shop for lunch when she saw Mada coming from a distance.

Her thoughts went back to her husband again. 'If all men are like Narasinga Rao, the wife's life is difficult,' she said to herself. 'Men should be aggressive and that is essential for success. Lakshmi talks but she is not courageous. It is good that she has an aggressive husband. However, Sanjay is like me. He talks less but is more courageous.'

By this time, Mada had reached her shop. He had been working with her in the fields for a long time. He said, 'Lakshmi Amma has asked me to plant a tree in the backyard. Which one should I plant? When Panditji was alive, he liked neem trees. Should I plant one in your backyard?'

Ratnamma smiled and replied, 'No, Mada. Plant a champak tree.'

'How much should I dig, Amma?'

'The soil is quite rocky at the bottom. Keep digging until you reach the rocks.'

Mada went off to start digging. Almost immediately, the bells in the main temple started ringing, indicating that it was lunchtime. Ratnamma folded her hands in respect to Narasimha. She did this from habit and not because of devotion. Then she went inside her house for lunch.

Lakshmi was laying places for two people and Anil was sleeping on a mat on the floor. The house was small. It had a room to keep a safe locker, a hall big enough for thirty people, a small bedroom and a kitchen and a dining room. There was no puja room. Ratnamma's logic was that God was everywhere and there was no need for a separate room to worship in. She kept some idols in the kitchen cupboard.

After Sanjay son had started earning, he sent money home regularly. Lakshmi insisted on modifying the mud floors in the house to cement floors. Ratnamma did not like making the expense. She said, 'Why did you waste hard-earned money on this? Had we used the same money in the moneylending business, we would have earned something.'

Ratnamma sat on the ground for lunch. Lakshmi had made ragi balls and vegetable sambar. There was majjige huli in another bowl. Ratnamma got irritated. She thought, 'It is such a waste if Lakshmi makes food like this every day. It is expensive and this kind of food puts a person to sleep. Usually, the women customers come in the afternoons to take loans because the men are away and won't know about it. If I sleep, it affects my business.'

She was about to scold Lakshmi, but saw her grandson, Anil, sleeping on the floor. So she changed her mind. Cleverly, she asked her daughter, 'What do you make for lunch every day in your house?'

Lakshmi was a chip off the old block. She understood what was going through her mother's head. She said, 'My husband always says—what's the purpose of earning money if we don't eat properly and take care of our health? So, I cook two vegetables, sambar, rasam and a dessert every day.'

Ratnamma started eating and did not answer her. 'If Lakshmi spends all her husband's salary in cooking, then she can never save money for a rainy day,' she thought. 'Shankar is greedy and may have his eye on my property. Maybe that's why they spend all their money. I also want to enjoy life and eat good food but I control myself and save every penny.'

She was worried that after she was gone, Lakshmi would inherit a part of her hard-earned money and Shankar would enjoy it and spend it all. The idea of someone else enjoying her money made her uncomfortable. Then she saw Lakshmi's sari. Though it was not silk, it was not cheap either. She couldn't help thinking, 'Why does Lakshmi wear such good saris at home? After all, she is only a homemaker. An ordinary sari is enough. She could have used the same money for something else. But Lakshmi behaves as if she is very rich. I have not bought a new sari for ages.'

A few years ago, Lakshmi had celebrated Anil's first birthday and insisted that her mother come for it. Under a lot of pressure, Ratnamma had closed the shop for a day and gone to Mysore. But she was unable to eat lunch looking at the grandeur of the party. She was shocked at how much money they had wasted on a baby's birthday. The food was expensive and they had bought boutique clothes for the boy. Ratnamma had repeatedly told her daughter not to gift her a sari. Money would have been better. But Lakshmi had not listened and had given her mother a sari. Ratnamma had told Lakshmi to buy the boy a gold chain instead of having such a grand party but her advice had fallen on deaf ears. So, she had wished the child a long life and had not given him any gifts. According to her, wishes and blessings from elders were more precious than any gifts.

Lord Narasimha's wife, Goddess Lakshmi, was very popular. In the Narasimha temple, many people gifted her a sari. The goddess usually wore the sari only for a day. Sometimes, the goddess's sari got stained with turmeric or vermilion. Such saris were given away as *prasad* to people. Once that sari was washed, it was as good as new. If it was a silk sari, then the head priest's wife kept it for herself. Otherwise, Ratnamma usually got one or two non-silk saris every year. She felt fortunate that the sari was the goddess's prasad and she could enjoy it without spending any money. Her wardrobe was full of such saris.

Ratnamma finished her lunch. Just then, she heard the sound of digging in the backyard and went to check what was happening. The backyard was huge. In one corner, there was a honge tree planted by her late husband. As an Ayurvedic practitioner, he had told Ratnamma about its many uses. When he was alive, he had grown herbal plants. Now, Ratnamma preferred to grow pumpkin creepers. She thought that growing herbs like coriander was a waste of money because coriander seeds were expensive to grow, and their only use was that they gave out an aroma during cooking. But growing a pumpkin had more advantages. She could throw pumpkin seeds anywhere and not worry about them. A creeper usually started growing without much care. Pumpkins didn't decay either. So she could keep them for many months in the house. When there were no vegetables in the summer, the pumpkins became expensive. That was a great way for her to make some money.

Ratnamma came back to the house, washed her hands and lay down on a charpoy. She thought, 'What's the use of the honge tree? All the unemployed and young boys sit below the tree and chat to kill time. Sometimes, they even steal pumpkins. Then I have to spend more money on fencing.'

For a minute, she was upset with her dead husband. 'Had he planted half a dozen champak trees instead of the honge tree, we would have earned money by selling flowers to the women who worship Gowri. I wish I could cut down the honge tree. I can get wood from it. But I'm sure that Lakshmi will oppose my decision. She calls the tree "Appa's tree" and is sentimental about it. She doesn't understand my difficulties. The best time to cut the tree is when she is not around.'

Then she thought of her son. Would he also oppose her decision? For a minute, she was worried. It was more difficult to face a son than a married daughter. Then she remembered that her son had fallen in love with a lovely girl. He may not remember T. Narasipura, much less the honge tree.

A little later, there was a dull noise from the site being dug. Mada had hit the rocks. Ratnamma noticed that Lakshmi had come to lie down next to her.

When she was in Mysore for a visit, Ratnamma had seen Shankar bring five rupees worth of champak flowers for his wife every day. She had calculated how much it must cost him per year—more than eighteen hundred rupees! What a waste of money on flowers that wouldn't last for more than twenty-four hours. It was too much for her to take. She knew that Shankar was a loudmouth and his relatives avoided him for this reason. But still, for the welfare of her daughter, she had said, 'Shankar, you should save that money and invest it somewhere, maybe in a fixed deposit.'

Shankar had replied harshly, 'Mother-in-law, we will be able to save even more if we just stop breathing!'

Ratnamma had thought sadly, 'He does not respect my age or my position.'

That was the last time Ratnamma ever spoke to Shankar about money matters. She had also made up her mind never to help this couple financially. She knew that their life was a bottomless bucket. If she ever gave them money, it would be spent very quickly.

She was brought back to the present when Lakshmi broke the silence: 'Amma, you aren't saying anything about Sanjay's marriage. Are you hurt?'

'No, he has to get married some day.' Then she thought, 'Lakshmi has changed a lot under Shankar's influence. She is not really worried about Sanjay's wedding. It doesn't matter to her whether he marries a rich or a poor girl. But she wants the status that will come if her brother marries a girl from a rich family.'

Ratnamma didn't care about status. Though she had some gold jewellery, she kept it in a bank locker and never wore it. She didn't plan to give it to her daughter or daughter-in-law. Gold wasn't just jewellery to her. It was an asset and an investment. If things went badly, she could mortgage or sell it. What was the use of spending money on silk saris? Once they were washed, they were worthless and couldn't be sold.

Her mind jumped to Mridula. 'The girl is from Dharwad district and people there always buy pure gold. It is good that they don't add copper and make intricate designs. If the gold is pure, it melts easily and there is no wastage. Usually, the girl and her parents take care of the wedding expenses. The boy's side hardly spends any money. Mridula's father is a landlord. He can give whatever he wants to his daughter. I don't want to be a part of it. Anyway, the girl is not going to give me gold for the moneylending business. If her family wants to give me a sari, then I will tell them that I want cash and not a sari. I will also let Sanjay know. But whatever he wants to give Lakshmi will be between the brother and the sister. I don't want to interfere. I want to make it very clear that I will give Mridula only a mangalsutra, my old earrings and toe rings. I don't want to spend much. It is also a good omen for a daughter-in-law to get her mother-in-law's ornaments. The greatest gift that I can give the married couple is my blessings. I'm not going to talk about any wedding preparation or have marriage-related discussions. All the negotiations will be left to Lakshmi, Shankar and Sanjay.'

Meanwhile, Lakshmi turned on her side and thought, 'If I had stayed with my mother, then her influence on me would have been more. But I got married at a young age and stayed with my husband in a bigger city. My husband has been transferred to many places because of his job and I have seen a lot because of that. I can't understand why my mother keeps thinking about money. I have one brother and I want him to have a big wedding. Had this been an arranged marriage, I would have negotiated well but now my words will probably fall on deaf ears. If the girl was from Bangalore or Mysore, we would have rented a huge wedding hall. I would have been able to make my sisters-in-law jealous. But Sanjay has really disappointed me. He himself has proposed marriage to Mridula, so naturally the girl's parents and relatives will not respect our words.'

Lakshmi was upset with Mridula even though she had never met her. She knew that Amma wouldn't spend any money on Sanjay's wedding. Amma never gave Lakshmi any gifts when she came to visit her either. On the contrary, she would say, 'Giving saris is such a waste. I'll get you a necklace instead.'

Lakshmi had heard this for years but she was yet to see a necklace. All her sisters-in-law made fun of her. They purposely told her, 'Oh, see the new sari my mother has given me this time.'

Both parties knew that the sari had been bought from the husband's money without his knowledge; Lakshmi was no exception. She took money from Shankar without telling him and bought saris in Mysore. She later told her sisters-in-law that her mother had given her the sari. Sometimes, Sanjay would send Lakshmi money for the Gowri festival and even send her a sari. But Shankar always suspected that that sari too was bought with his money.

Lakshmi was angry with Sanjay for putting her in such a situation. 'Amma may keep quiet about Sanjay's wedding but I will talk. I'll demand a sari from Sanjay and his in-laws. Whom should we invite to the wedding? Amma has many acquaintances because of her business. But none of them are true friends who will genuinely enjoy Sanjay's wedding. Amma has a different principle in life. She says, "If you are running a business, then don't become too friendly with anyone because, inevitably, they'll ask you for a loan. Once people become friends, it is difficult to ask them to return the money. You'll lose the money and the friendship."'

So, her mother did not have many friends.

Lakshmi turned back and saw her mother sleeping soundly. Maybe the majjige huli had put her to sleep.

8

The Strings of Love

Shankar and Lakshmi decided to go and talk to Bheemanna about the marriage arrangements. It was Lakshmi's idea. Sanjay felt that it was appropriate since Lakshmi was older than him and was his only sister. So he told Bheemanna about his sister's forthcoming visit.

After a few days, Shankar and Lakshmi went to Arsikere and boarded the Kittur Express at night. The next day, they reached Hubli at dawn. They planned to return by bus the same night. Krishna was waiting for them at the Hubli railway station. He would drive them to Aladahalli as planned—it was only an hour away.

But when Lakshmi and Shankar got off the train, Shankar changed the plan. He did not like the idea of going directly to Aladahalli. He said, 'First, we'll go to Ajanta Hotel and have a bath and eat breakfast. Then we'll leave for Aladahalli.'

Krishna found this impromptu change of plans a little strange but kept quiet and nodded his head. At the hotel, Shankar pretended to offer to pay the bill but did not refuse when Krishna insisted on paying.

Due to this delay, Krishna, Shankar and Lakshmi reached Aladahalli only at 11 a.m. Rukuma and Bheemanna welcomed them wholeheartedly. They were genuinely happy. Soon, Mridula also joined them. She was wearing a simple white sari with a green blouse and looked absolutely radiant and beautiful even without lipstick or make-up. She reminded Lakshmi of a fragrant white-jasmine creeper. Lakshmi was immediately envious of her natural beauty. She started measuring Mridula's family's financial status by the gold that they were wearing; she was disappointed. Mridula was wearing minimal jewellery—a gold chain, gold earrings and four gold bangles. Her mother was also wearing similar jewellery in addition to her mangalsutra. Lakshmi did not understand why these women were not showing off their jewellery.

She recalled her engagement day. She had gone to her neighbour Subbaiah Shetty's house to get some gold-plated ornaments even though Ratnamma was dead against it. Lakshmi had adorned herself with the ornaments from top to bottom to

impress her in-laws. She had been wrong. Shankar's sister Vimla
was clever enough to realize that the ornaments were fake. She
had sarcastically remarked, 'Oh, these ornaments are available
in Chickpet for a hundred and fifty rupees. My daughter Usha
bought them for her college dance programme.'

Lakshmi heard Bheemanna's voice asking them to follow
him outside the house. Bheemanna took Shankar and Lakshmi
for a walk around the village. They were uncomfortable with
his local Kannada. They had never heard such a version of
Kannada before. Bheemanna, however, talked to them easily
and kept the conversation going. Whenever Bheemanna met
someone during their walk, he would say, 'This is Mr Shankar
Rao. His brother-in-law is a doctor in Bombay. They have come
here for marriage negotiations.'

Shankar found his openness very insensitive. He gathered
that Bheemanna was an important man in the village. He
had enough money in the bank and owned a lot of land. But
Shankar did not understand why Bheemanna was giving away
his beautiful daughter to a handicapped man. He became
jealous. In his marriage, Shankar had only got a beautiful wife,
but Sanjay was lucky enough to have found a good girl and a
rich father-in-law. However, Shankar was disappointed when he
saw Bheemanna's ill-equipped house. He thought of his house
in Belur that had all the modern appliances—though most
of them were bought on instalments. Almost 70 per cent of
Shankar's salary was spent in repaying these loans. By the time
one was paid off, Lakshmi thought of something else to buy. Her
demands were never-ending. She was always competing with
the members of her ladies' club. These days, she was insisting
that he take a new loan and buy a second-hand car. Shankar
thought, 'If I had money like Bheemanna, I would have bought
a Mercedes-Benz and a three-storey building in Hubli.'

He pitied Bheemanna for not enjoying life's luxuries. But
one thing was apparent—Sanjay had made quite a catch.

Rukuma went inside the kitchen to finish the preparations for lunch. Mridula started talking to Lakshmi: 'Can I call you "Sister"? You are older than me.'

Lakshmi found it strange and foolish. Even after many years of marriage, she didn't consider herself to be a part of her husband's family. She had never called her sisters-in-law 'Sister'. She saw them as competitors. Her mother had never advised her on what to expect from her in-laws or how to behave with them. She had suffered humiliation, encountered jealousy and shrewdness in the joint family. She had learnt how to survive through her own experiences.

Lakshmi pitied Mridula because she had never seen the real world where you rarely come across genuine love and affection. She smartly said, 'Sure, Mridula, you can call me Akka.'

Then, she asked her, 'Mridula, where did you meet Sanjay for the first time?'

As expected, Mridula did not hide anything and told her the whole story in detail.

By then, it was time for lunch. There were around fifty guests and hardly anyone was related to Bheemanna's family. The only relatives were Rukuma's brother Satyabodha, his wife and their two children. Sarla was still unemployed and Satish was a lecturer at Hubli College after having completed his master's in mathematics. The four young cousins were around the same age and very close. Lakshmi found it most unusual that there was no competition among the cousins.

By the time lunch ended, the shrewd couple realized that they would be given whatever they asked for. When they sat down to talk after lunch, there was no negotiation at all. Shankar was very clever in putting across his demands; Sanjay had already requested them not to talk about money. So he said, 'We don't need money, nor are we interested in it. But we want a grand wedding. You can give Sanjay whatever is usually given to the groom.'

Bheemanna did not understand the words 'whatever is usually given to the groom'. So he said, 'Please explain. I don't understand.'

'Oh! It is our custom that the boy gets suits, silver vessels for the entire kitchen, a silver puja set, saris for all the women and shirts and trousers for all the men, a gold chain, a watch, a ring . . .' Shankar's voice trailed off.

Bheemanna quietly said, 'That's not a problem.'

Rukuma wanted to ask, 'And what will you give Mridula, your daughter-in-law?' But she was scared to ask this question in front of Bheemanna.

Shankar added, 'We would all like to come for the wedding in a luxury bus and you must take care of it.'

'We don't know how to arrange this. That is left to you. You can hire the bus and we will pay for it.'

Bheemanna ended the conversation. That same night, Lakshmi and Shankar left Aladahalli happily.

The people of Aladahalli were quite disappointed with Mridula's informal engagement to a doctor from Bombay. Each function in the village gathered at least three hundred people and a lot of importance was given to the menu to make the guests happy. In contrast, Mridula's in-laws were very unusual. Only two of them had come and they had not even taken a second serving.

Sarla and Satish had stayed back because they had a holiday the next day. Satish and Mridula were friendly. They had grown up together and during his childhood, Satish had spent all his vacations in the village. Satish teased Mridula, 'You were already a half veterinary doctor and with your first-aid training, you are now a half lady doctor. By marrying an intelligent doctor like Sanjay, you are on your way to becoming a full-fledged doctor.'

Mridula blushed and smiled.

There was a special dhobi ghat on the side of the lake. The day after the guests left, Sarla insisted that she wanted to wash her clothes there. Mridula agreed. She knew that Sarla wanted to play in the water. There was great joy in washing clothes at the big lake. With one foot firmly resting on a big boulder, the clothes were thrashed on the rock with force, which sprayed the water about everywhere. It was very different from washing clothes under a tap in a city home.

Mridula and Sarla walked to the lake. When they reached the shore, Mridula started soaking all the clothes. Sarla forgot everything and played in the water a short distance away. Suddenly, Mridula found something in the pocket of one of the trousers. She put her hand in the pocket and took out a wallet—it was Satish's. Abruptly, she heard a shout and looked around. She saw Satish running towards her. He was some distance away and she could not hear what he was saying. Her attention wandered back to the wallet. She was worried that the money inside would get wet, so she opened it. She found money and a small photograph stashed in a corner. She was happy to have found something to tease Satish about. When she pulled out the picture, however, she was shocked to see a photo of herself from her old college ID. She didn't know what to do. She was not expecting this. She had always thought of Satish as a good cousin. Things may have been different if she had known about his feelings earlier, but now she could only think of Sanjay. Her devotion was to him alone. She turned her back to the approaching Satish and hid the photo.

Soon, Satish reached her. 'Hey, is my wallet here? I left it in my pants when I gave them for a wash. There's an important paper in it.'

Mridula snapped, 'If the paper is that important, then you shouldn't have forgotten your wallet! Here, take your pants.'

Satish took his wallet out quietly and walked away. He turned back to look at Mridula but she pretended to continue washing the clothes. He mulled over the things left unsaid and left the ghat, deep in thought.

9

Partners

By the time Sanjay and Mridula got married, Sanjay had quit his job in Bombay.

Before the wedding, Mridula told Sanjay, 'Why don't you find a job in Bangalore? It'll be easier for us to settle there. At the end of the day, language matters. We both belong to the same region. I have seen a newspaper advertisement for a temporary government job at Bangalore Victoria Hospital. I hope you'll think about my suggestion.'

Sanjay agreed. He was not too fond of Bombay either. He had obtained enough experience there and knew that it was expensive to get a decent apartment to live in. Moreover, Mridula would have to leave her job, which she absolutely loved. She wouldn't be allowed to take a transfer out of state and go to Bombay. However, if he found a job in Bangalore, she could take a transfer there. Besides, he was confident that he would get a postgraduate seat in Bangalore. So Mridula and Sanjay decided to make Bangalore their home.

Sanjay got the job at Victoria Hospital and asked Mridula to join him there after marriage. When Mridula came to Bangalore for the first time, she saw a new world. She had spent most of her life in Aladahalli and found life in Bangalore tough. It was hard for her to understand the local version of Kannada, which was mostly mixed with English. Sanjay and Mridula wanted to stay near the hospital but could not afford the high rent. They looked around and decided to rent a house in Yelahanka. It was far from the city but the rent was affordable.

Mridula took a transfer to a government school in Yelahanka but she found a lot of difference between Aladahalli High School and Yelahanka High School.

Aladahalli High School was very famous and students came from surrounding villages to study there. The school was not just a building. It had a huge playground and an open-air theatre. It had its own kitchen garden which was under Mridula's supervision when she was working there. It was compulsory for all the children to work in the garden for at least two hours every week. The vegetables grown there were used for cooking and the children were given a midday meal with the help of the villagers and without government aid. Obedience was important in the school. So students were polite and listened sincerely to the teachers. It was like a big joint family and it was a joy for Mridula to be a teacher in the school.

But Yelahanka High School was very different. It was not the only school in the area. When the students had a choice of schools, the best often chose not to study in a government one. The English-medium private schools were popular even though they were more expensive. The teachers' attitudes were also different. In a big city like Bangalore, some teachers gave private tuitions at home while others had a small business on the side and were more interested in running the business than in teaching. Most of them did not consider the earnings from teaching to be their main source of livelihood. They thought of it just as an appetizer to the main course. So there was no personal connection between the teachers and the students.

Still, the situation was not that bad. Some teachers like Principal Muniyappa were like Mridula. They considered teaching to be a pious profession and taught the children passionately. Principal Muniyappa was from Kolar and was a warm-hearted person. He also stayed in Yelahanka with his family. On Mridula's first day at the school, he affectionately told her, 'Mridula madam, please don't be nervous. You have two years of good teaching experience. We have four Kannada-medium sections and one English-medium section in this school. Feel free to choose any class and language that you feel comfortable with.'

These small words of encouragement were enough for Mridula to work efficiently.

Soon, Mridula and Sanjay settled into a comfortable routine. Mridula got up early in the morning, cooked and gave Sanjay breakfast. He carried a lunch dabba to the hospital and returned home at night. After Sanjay left, Mridula went to school; she cleaned the house in the evenings. She was left with no time for herself. If there was an emergency or night duty at the hospital, Sanjay stayed back there. Since they did not have a telephone or a vehicle, Sanjay would call up Muniyappa's house and leave a message for Mridula. Their twenty-year-old son Arun would cycle over to Mridula and Sanjay's house to pass on the message to her, irrespective of the time of day. He was a nice and intelligent boy, studying engineering and majoring in computer science.

Mridula had never cooked a complete meal at her parents' home in Aladahalli. She had helped her mother but never made the main course by herself. When there were many guests at home, a cook used to be called from Hubli. So Mridula never had much responsibility in the house. But now, she had to cook and, more importantly, she had to lock the house, which her parents hardly ever did in Aladahalli. Mridula was nervous because she was not accustomed to cooking many different dishes. She did not have anyone to guide her in her cooking. Principal Muniyappa's wife, Kantamma, was a nice lady; she became Mridula's adviser.

One day, Mridula asked her, 'Kantamma, will you help me cook different kinds of food?'

'Mridula, what can an uneducated person like me teach an intelligent person like you? I was sixteen years old when I got married. My mother-in-law was just like my mother and I am grateful to her for that. She taught me everything I know. I will teach you whatever I can.'

Mridula was not as lucky as Kantamma. Ratnamma neither came to Bangalore nor taught her anything. Whenever Sanjay and Mridula invited her for a visit, Ratnamma always said, 'There's a lot of work in the fields. If I'm not there to supervise, then the men don't work at all. They take away the seeds, and the entire year's crop could get wasted. Anyway, you don't really need me. Mridula is not a teenager. Her mother can help her if needed.'

Ratnamma did not invite the newly-weds to visit her in T. Narasipura for any festival or holiday. Lakshmi avoided Mridula too and took the pretext of her child's schooling and said that she was busy and could not visit Bangalore. So Mridula started her new life with Kantamma's help. She tried her cooking on Sanjay. Most times, the results were disastrous. But Sanjay never said anything negative. This made Mridula more conscious about her cooking.

Except for the tight economic situation, they did not have any problems. Mridula earned more than Sanjay. He gave his salary to Mridula and told her to manage the money. His only request was that she send some money to his mother. So Mridula kept the accounts and insisted that Sanjay keep some money in his wallet. Together, they paid the rent, sent some money to Ratnamma and the remaining money was spent on household expenses. Ratnamma neither felt elated when she received their money, nor would she have blamed them if she did not get any. But she never wasted it—she invested it all in moneylending. For her, there was nothing worse than money not fetching any interest. Though Sanjay did not like this attitude, he could not tell her so.

Once, Bheemanna came to visit Mridula and brought her lots of groceries from the village. He insisted that he would send her groceries from Aladahalli every year. But Sanjay did not like this. He said to Mridula, 'We must spend our own money and buy things slowly instead of taking them from your father.'

So Mridula saved money and over time they bought a TV, a fridge and a new scooter for Sanjay. They led a happy and contented life.

Sanjay had very few friends. Soon, he got busy preparing for his post-graduation. Once he entered the hospital, he forgot about everything else. After his shift ended, he did not waste any time: he went to the library to study. He remembered Dr Jog's words: 'If you concentrate and learn, acquire knowledge and skill, then that is real talent. If you run after money more than work, then money will run away from you. If you acquire skill, money will run after you.'

10

The In-Laws

Since Mridula had been brought up in a traditional atmosphere, she felt guilty about not visiting her in-laws' home. She asked Sanjay to take her to meet his mother and sister many times but he did not show any interest in meeting them. A long weekend was coming up now and Mridula insisted that they spend it at T. Narasipura. She asked Sanjay, 'What should I take for your mother? I'm meeting her for the first time after marriage.'

Sanjay was indifferent. He said, 'My mother doesn't expect any gifts. She will accept whatever you give her.'

So Mridula asked her guide Kantamma who advised her not to go empty-handed. Kantamma said, 'After marriage, your mother-in-law becomes as important as your mother. If you keep her happy, then your mother will also be happy. You should get used to your mother-in-law. If she gets upset with you for any reason, you shouldn't be upset. After all, she is older and you are still young. I know that you have patience. Take a sari for your mother-in-law and some fresh fruits and flowers.'

Meanwhile, Lakshmi wrote a letter to the couple saying, 'Belur has many beautiful temples and we may get transferred any day. So come and visit us.' Though Shankar was working as a bank clerk there, he was keen to run his own business. He had a friend who owned a hotel in Belur. Shankar borrowed some money from the bank and invested it in that hotel in Lakshmi's name.

Finally, Mridula and Sanjay left for T. Narasipura on a Friday evening. When they reached the bus stand, there was nobody to greet them. Ratnamma's house was nearby—they walked to her house.

Ratnamma was sitting in her shop and was happy to see them. She stood up when she saw her son and his new bride. Then she asked Mridula to step into her shop with her right foot first. 'I'm sorry that there's no other lady here to escort you inside the house. Even Lakshmi couldn't come. Please don't feel bad.'

Ratnamma lay the mat for them and went to the kitchen. Mridula sat down and Sanjay went to the backyard. Mridula observed her surroundings and was surprised. Though she had been brought up in a village, this looked different from any house in her village. This village was much better developed than Aladahalli. It was also considered a pilgrimage place and was located close to the big city of Mysore. But Ratnamma's house was inferior to any poor farmer's house in Aladahalli.

The only signs of modern civilization were the water taps and the electricity in the house. There was a black-and-white TV, no radio and no gas stove. There was a mud stove in the corner and the dry leaves of the coconut tree provided the cooking fuel. More than poverty, negligence was rampant in the house.

Mridula wondered, 'What will my mother, Rukuma, think about this house? Would my parents have allowed me to marry Sanjay had they seen his family home?'

Almost immediately, Sanjay came in. When he looked at Mridula's face, he understood what was going on in her head. Sadly, he said, 'You know, Amma is alone and very busy. She can't look after the house.'

Ratnamma came back from the kitchen. She brought water in a steel jug and two bananas for her new daughter-in-law. The usually talkative Mridula was dumb before her. She did not know what to say. The silence was unbearable. Even mother and son did not converse much. Sanjay asked Ratnamma, 'How are you, Amma?'

'I'm fine. How are you?'

'I'm fine, too. How's Lakshmi?'

'She's okay.'

That ended the conversation.

Nobody spoke to Mridula; but she asked, 'May I cook tonight?'

'Yes, you may.' There was neither affection nor enmity in Ratnamma's voice. It was an emotionless, businesslike reply.

Many of Sanjay's friends were not in T. Narasipura now. They had moved to other places—but a few remained. Sanjay did not really want to meet them, but he wanted to go around the village and revisit the places where he had spent his early years. So he said, 'I'll go for a walk and come back soon.'

Some customers came into the shop and Ratnamma went to assist them. She talked to the customers and tried to persuade them to buy from her. Mridula found it strange that her mother-in-law was silent at home, but so talkative at the cash register.

Mridula went inside the dimly lit kitchen. After searching for some time, she found rice, tur dal and a little ragi flour, but she couldn't find any oil or vegetables. So she came out of the kitchen. She kept the sari, fruits and flowers that she had brought for her mother-in-law on a plate. By then, the customer had gone and Ratnamma walked back in. Without any pretence, Ratnamma told Mridula directly, 'Don't search for vegetables. There's a small pumpkin in the attic. Red chillies are in the shop and the curry leaves are in the backyard. You have travelled a long distance and you must be tired. I'll make sambar and rice.'

Ratnamma was direct, especially when it came to money matters. She was aware that misunderstandings could lead to unnecessary expenditure. If Mridula saw that there were no vegetables, she would tell her impractical husband to get some. Sanjay would buy lots of vegetables from the market without bargaining; they would lose money.

When Ratnamma saw the gifts from her daughter-in-law, she was disappointed. In her head, she calculated how much money they must have wasted. She exclaimed, 'Oh, Mridula, why did you buy such an expensive sari? I don't have places or occasions to wear it. I don't teach in a school like you either. Whatever was given to me in your marriage is still lying unused. And I don't eat so many fruits—or wear flowers.'

Mridula did not know what to say.

Ratnamma could hear another customer's voice in the shop. Today was Friday and there was more rush than usual. If she did not assist them, they would go to the next shop. She couldn't afford to sit and chat with her daughter-in-law now. She said, 'After Sanjay comes, you can go to the temple. Take these fruits along. Go around the riverbed and come back. Take your time.'

After Sanjay came back, the couple left for the temple. Sanjay recognized many people in the village. Some of the women said, 'Sanjay, at last we see your wife. We hear that your wife is from Bombay. Can she speak Kannada?'

Mridula interrupted and replied, 'Oh no, I'm not from Bombay. I'm from Dharwad and I can speak Kannada.'

She thought, 'In small villages such as this, rumours fly quickly—T. Narasipura is no exception.'

There were some older married ladies sitting in the temple. Mridula remembered her mother and the custom followed in Aladahalli on a Friday evening. Irrespective of the community, Rukuma would give betel leaves, turmeric, kumkum, flowers, fruit and some money to such women. So Mridula gave ten rupees and betel leaves to everyone. Then she did namaskara.

By the time Sanjay and Mridula came back from the riverbed, the news had reached Ratnamma: 'Ratnamma's new daughter-in-law gave ten rupees and betel leaves to everyone.'

Ratnamma felt uncomfortable. She thought, 'What does Mridula know what the value of ten rupees is? Blessings are not proportional to money. If blessings had that power, then the world would have been different.'

She had seen enough nonsense in her life. She wanted to warn her daughter-in-law for the sake of her son. When people wanted money, they told Ratnamma, 'Please give me money. I'll return it quickly. I'll be your slave for ever.'

But when Ratnamma asked for the money back, the same people called her a greedy owl. Ratnamma thought, 'Look at these women. They are from well-to-do families. Why will they say no to free money? If Mridula believes that blessings from such women are important, then I don't mind if she touches their feet, but she shouldn't give them money. If the woman of the house is a spendthrift, then what will my son's future be?'

By the time the couple came back, it was 9 p.m. and Ratnamma had closed the shop. She had made rice, pumpkin sambar, ragi balls and chutney for dinner. Sanjay loved ragi balls. Though Mridula had recently learnt to make them, they did not taste like Ratnamma's.

'Sanjay, what are your plans for the future? Do you still want to study further?'

'Yes, Amma, I am applying for post-graduation this year. My goal is to get a government job and teach. That will give me more happiness than private practice.'

Ratnamma did not understand the intricacies and kept quiet.

'Amma, how do you spend your time?' asked Sanjay affectionately.

'I have plenty of work. Every week, I get supplies from Mysore and I must keep accurate accounts. That takes time. Moreover, there's intense competition among the shops these days. If I close my shop even for a day, I'll lose my customers. Getting workers to help in the field has also become difficult. There's a big sand business on the banks of River Kaveri. You must have noticed it. Most workers go there because it pays more. The sand there is good for use in construction. Since there is a lot of building work going on in Bangalore, the trucks are filled with sand and sent there.'

Sanjay thought about what he had observed on his way to T. Narasipura. He had read in the newspaper that even big rivers like the Yamuna, Ganga and Mahanadi were subjected to this exploitation. Nobody checked whether the sand dealers were legally allowed to take away the sand from riverbeds. The digging caused the water to clog and collect in pits in the rainy season. Because of the stagnant water, many diseases were caused.

Ratnamma continued talking to Sanjay. 'Now, I have started the chits business too. There's a meeting every month. This month's meeting is tomorrow, in my house.'

Sanjay read his mother's mind straight away. The conversation at the meeting was going to be about finances and moneylending. He did not want Mridula to hear all that. He was conscious about what she would think about his mother.

He said, 'Amma, I'm glad that I came and met you. It is difficult for me to get a few days of vacation like this. So maybe Mridula and I will go to Belur tomorrow and meet Lakshmi too.'

This new plan surprised Mridula—Sanjay had not discussed this with her. She could never read her husband's mind. But Ratnamma was not perturbed. She asked, 'How many days of vacation do you have?'

'Three, but I've already used up one day here in T. Narasipura.'

'That's all right. You can leave after breakfast tomorrow. There's no direct bus to Belur from here. So you'll have to go to Mysore and then catch another bus from there. But call Lakshmi before you go.'

'Lakshmi has a phone now? I didn't know that.'

'Yes. Shankar wants to show off and Lakshmi agrees with him. The truth is that they don't need a phone. But Shankar wants it because his brother Mahadeva has one in Mysore. There's so much competition among the brothers and their wives. The competition should be about who earns more money and not about who spends more. Every week, Shankar and Lakshmi hire a taxi and go on a short fun trip.'

'Amma, who gives you this information?'

'Subbaiah Shetty. Lakshmi and Shankar met him two weeks ago at Shringeri. Four weeks ago, they were at Dharmasthala. They don't try to save and don't respect my advice. Since you're going there, why don't you talk to them?'

Ratnamma was tired, probably at the very thought of her daughter spending money like water. She decided to turn in for the night. Later, Mridula said to Sanjay, 'You didn't tell me that you plan to go to Lakshmi's house.'

'I thought that later I won't be able get holidays and I'll get busy preparing for my entrance exam. Lakshmi has invited us and you also wanted to go see her sometime.'

Sanjay easily hid the real reason for the change of plans and Mridula believed him. She said, 'Okay, you're right. But I don't have much money with me now. How can we go to her house for the first time without taking a gift?'

'That's not a problem. Lakshmi won't mind.'

Mridula found it strange that her mother-in-law did not insist that they stay with her for longer. The next morning, Ratnamma gave them breakfast. Before they left, she called Mridula inside and told her softly, 'We don't know when we'll have to face difficult times. Life's good when we have money. People will be friends with us. But when we don't have money, nobody will help us. So try to save some money from your salary. I can't tell Sanjay this but I can share this with you.'

Mridula nodded quietly. Then she touched her mother-in-law's feet; she felt nice about getting advice from her.

When they reached Mysore, Mridula was happy. She said, 'Sanjay, can we stay here for two or three days? After all, it is Saturday today. Then we can see the Mysore Palace, Krishna Raja Sagara Dam and Chamundi Hills.'

Sanjay thought, 'Where will we stay? Lakshmi's in-laws won't welcome us and we can't afford to stay in a hotel. We don't have any relatives with whom we can stay without feeling obliged.' So he consoled his wife and said, 'We'll come again and stay longer next time.'

With the little money Mridula had, she bought a synthetic sari, fruits, vegetables and flowers for Lakshmi from Devaraja Market. After seeing her mother-in-law's house, she could only imagine how Lakshmi's house must be. They called Lakshmi from the Mysore bus stand and she sounded happy to learn that they would be visiting her.

When they reached Belur, Shankar was waiting for them at the bus stand. Sanjay said, 'Why did you come, Shankar? We know your address. We could have come on our own by autorickshaw.'

Shankar smiled and did not say anything. He had a taxi waiting for them. When he took them home, Mridula was taken aback. Shankar was an ordinary bank clerk but his house was better than a manager's. It had all the modern amenities and expensive furniture and equipment, which even a rich person like Mridula's father did not have in Aladahalli.

When Mridula placed her gifts on the table, Lakshmi smiled and said, 'Oh Mridula, why did you bring all these things? We get everything we need in Belur.'

Lakshmi was wearing an expensive Mysore-silk sari and had fresh flowers tucked in her hair. Mridula said, 'You're looking nice, Akka. Are you planning to go out later?'

'No, this is how I usually dress. Shankar likes neatness.'

Mridula was surprised. She had received only one Mysore-silk sari at her wedding. She kept it for special occasions and had worn it only once.

The lunch was excellent. Lots of dishes were served at the table. Mridula was pleasantly surprised. She asked, 'Akka, how did you make so many things in such a short time?'

'Oh, that isn't a problem. I ordered some food from a hotel and our cook made the rest.'

'Do you have a cook for three people?' Mridula was open and direct.

Lakshmi felt uncomfortable answering her. She said, 'No, I call a cook only when I have guests.'

The taxi remained in front of the house—it would be at their disposal through the entire visit. Sanjay told Shankar several times that they could travel by bus, but Shankar did not listen. He said, 'You're our guest. I can't take you by bus.'

On Sunday, Shankar took them to the temples at Belur and Halebid followed by lunch at the Taj Ashoka in Hassan. Mridula was worried that he was spending too much on them. The day they were leaving, Lakshmi gave Mridula an expensive sari and presented a good watch to her brother. Mridula was touched. She thought that she had gained a friend and a sister. Life was beautiful.

When Shankar returned home after dropping Sanjay and Mridula to the bus stand, Lakshmi commented, 'Mridula is really stingy. She's the right daughter-in-law for my mother.'

Shankar was not as smart as Lakshmi. He asked, 'Why do you say that?'

'She gave me a cheap synthetic sari and shamelessly took the silk sari I gave her. She gave me vegetables as a gift—as if I don't have vegetables at home!'

Shankar joined in, 'Sanjay is also very shrewd. He didn't offer to pay the taxi bill. He should've at least had the manners to ask. I don't think he earns well. Even an ordinary doctor in a village earns more than him.'

On the journey back to Bangalore, Mridula was all praise for Lakshmi and Shankar. She was blissfully unaware of what they actually thought of Sanjay and her.

A few months passed and Shankar's niece Usha's marriage was fixed. The groom was an insurance officer.

Usha's mother, Vimla, did not like Sanjay even though she had once thought of Sanjay as a prospective groom for her daughter. At the time, she had been impressed by the fact that he was a doctor—despite his deformity. He came from a good family and was a good-looking and decent boy. More importantly, everybody was aware that Ratnamma had money and the biggest share would go to her son. Though Ratnamma was stingy, she was not a cruel mother-in-law. Keeping this in mind, Vimla and her husband had thought that it was a good match. But Lakshmi was not interested and had not even entertained the idea.

Now, Sanjay was married and Usha had found another groom.

Secretly, Vimla and Lakshmi could not stand each other but no one would ever know it from the way they behaved with each other. Vimla gave a few wedding invitation cards to Lakshmi and told her to call whomever she wanted.

When Lakshmi sent a wedding card to Sanjay, Mridula was enthusiastic. The wedding was in Bangalore. She wanted to attend the entire three-day ceremony since she had not had a chance to attend family functions from the time they had moved to Bangalore. In Aladahalli, her house always had guests and there were plenty of invitations for gatherings. Mridula really missed the social interactions.

After her trip to T. Narasipura, she felt uncomfortable thinking of going to her mother-in-law's house again. Though she liked Lakshmi's company, she could not visit her often. So this wedding card brought her great joy. She asked Sanjay, 'Can we attend the ceremonies on all days?'

Usually, Sanjay did not care about these things. But this time, he categorically told her, 'No, we'll only go for the reception.' Mridula was raised to believe that she should not question the elders in the family when they made a decision. So even though she was disappointed, she did not push the matter.

They bought a gift and went to the reception. This was the first time Mridula was seeing a wedding celebrated with such grandeur. A lot of money had been spent on the decorations, flowers, live music and designer clothes for the bride and groom. There was a separate room full of gifts to be given to the guests. If someone from Aladahalli had seen this, they would have mistaken it for the wedding of a minister's daughter.

Lakshmi's relatives from Mysore saw Sanjay but did not bother to talk to him. There was a big queue of people waiting to greet the newly married couple. Before long, Sanjay and Mridula ran into Lakshmi. She had just come from the beauty salon and was looking even better than the bride. She asked them to wait to greet the newly-weds till the rush of people reduced.

Weddings are a gossipmonger's paradise. There was a group of people sitting in a corner and chatting. Sanjay knew them.

They had not seen Sanjay and Mridula yet but Sanjay could clearly hear what they were saying. One of them said, 'I heard that Vimla's husband, Dinesh, has spent almost five lakh on this marriage.'

'Yes, he had to—because Usha was rejected by many people,' said another.

'Do you know that even Sanjay didn't want to marry Usha?'

'Which Sanjay are you talking about—Lakshmi's brother with the short arm?'

'Yes, the same dumb fellow.'

'I heard something different. I was told that Lakshmi wasn't keen about Usha's proposal and the matter never even went to Sanjay. Lakshmi said that Sanjay wanted to marry a doctor.'

'Well, he's married now. Whom did he get married to?'

'A girl from a remote village agreed to marry him. She must have some handicap too or her parents must be very poor.'

'You're right. Sanjay may not even be a real MBBS doctor. Lakshmi must be boasting. Who is going to check his certificate?'

'Yes, that's true. If he were a doctor, he would have opened a nursing home by now. Look at my son-in-law, Prasad. He has already purchased land to build a nursing home and owns a car too. Shankar is also very smart. He has a car and Lakshmi buys jewellery every month.'

Sanjay felt awkward and Mridula was horrified to hear what the people were saying about them. Just then, they saw Prasad skipping the queue and making his way to wish the bride and groom.

Sanjay and Prasad had known each other fairly well in college. Prasad had taken eight years to complete a four-year course. As a student, he cheated regularly. After his graduation, he had become an abortion specialist. He had married an ugly girl because she was from a rich family and, as a part of the dowry, his in-laws had given him land and a car.

Sanjay felt odd. He thought ruefully, 'How can people compare Prasad to me? We shouldn't have come for the wedding.'

11

Changes

Sanjay got admission to the post-graduation course and decided to go to Vanivilas Hospital in Bangalore and study gynaecology. He quickly became extremely busy. He was awarded a scholarship but their main source of income was Mridula's salary from her steady government job.

In Sanjay's batch, some students had work experience and some were right out of college. The head of the department was Dr Kamala, with whom Sanjay had worked before. She liked him for his hard work, experience, patience and intelligence. He took complete responsibility of all cases assigned to him.

After a few months, Mridula and Sanjay moved out of Yelahanka and into Vijayanagar. Fortunately, Mridula was able to get a transfer to Vijayanagar High School. She felt sad leaving the Yelahanka school. She was going to miss Principal Muniyappa and his wife, Kantamma. They had been family to her in the big city. Principal Muniyappa was going to retire after a year and he and his wife wanted to go back to Kolar where they owned fields and plenty of sheep.

When Mridula joined the Vijayanagar school, she found it quite different from Yelahanka's. Nobody cared about anyone. But by now, Mridula had learnt not to expect to find a meaningful relationship in the school. The government schools were looked down upon. The school buildings were not maintained properly and the teachers felt it was the duty of the local corporation to maintain them. The corporation said that it was the duty of the government—and in this blame game, the school and its students suffered.

Four years passed.

Sanjay had finished his studies and started working as a doctor and lecturer in a government hospital. Mridula's salary had also increased and, together, they bought a flat in Vijayanagar with the help of a bank loan. Soon, they also became parents to a healthy baby boy, Sishir.

In Aladahalli, Krishna had got married to Vatsala who was from a neighbouring village. Bheemanna and Rukuma wanted a village girl because they thought that she would understand the difficulties of an agricultural family.

Sarla had married Prasanna, a software engineer, and settled in San Jose, California. She had started working there. She came to India at least once a year and visited everyone.

Meanwhile, Satish had got married to Shyla who worked in a bank in Hubli.

Alex had married his girlfriend, Anita, in a church in Mangalore, and Mridula and Sanjay had gone for the wedding. It was a big event. Dignitaries from the government attended the marriage. Alex had come from the Middle East and spent money like water. Anita and Mridula liked each other at their first meeting and decided to keep in touch.

Shankar had been transferred to Mandya.

But life in Aladahalli and T. Narasipura had not changed even after four years.

When Lakshmi heard about Sanjay's permanent job with the government, she was upset. 'What's the use of academic intelligence? My brother is wasting his time. He spent two years in Bombay and four years in Bangalore and now he's happily working for a low salary in a government job. If he were practical, he would find a good location to open a clinic.

Then, he would make money. But Sanjay hasn't learnt to be smooth and charming, which is essential in private practice. And Mridula is even worse. She believes everybody. After all, she has been raised in a village. If I were her, I would control my husband and push him to start a nursing home of his own. There's nobody in our family who can advise this impractical couple. My mother is in her own world and I really don't understand why she wants to run a small shop. After all, how much profit can she really make?'

Lakshmi felt ashamed. She remembered how her sisters-in-law made fun of her. Shyamala, Mahadeva's wife, had sarcastically remarked once, 'Oh, Lakshmi! You come from a rich family—your brother's a doctor and his wife's a government schoolteacher. Your mother owns a shop. But look at me. My father's only a revenue inspector and we have just one source of income.'

Lakshmi had known that Shyamala was not really complimenting her. At the time, her veiled comments had hurt Lakshmi like a high-heeled sandal wrapped in a silk shawl. She wondered now, 'How much money can my mother earn from moneylending, the fields and her shop?'

If she asked Sanjay about it, she knew that he wouldn't answer her. Sanjay was impractical. But not her husband, Shankar. She was proud of her street-smart husband.

So she turned to Shankar and asked, 'How much money do you think Amma has?'

Shankar was distressed because the stocks he had invested in were not performing well and his wife's question irritated him. He snapped, 'Why're you asking me? Neither your mother nor your brother shares their financial matters with me. The only way to get any information is from the village gossip.'

Lakshmi realized that if she continued talking, it would end in a domestic quarrel. So she kept quiet. She thought about Mridula. 'She doesn't understand the real world. If someone says nice things to her, she thinks that the person is good. There's a difference between what we say and what we actually mean.

Mridula is transparent and absolutely naive. She thinks about others and how they feel instead of what she herself wants.'

Whenever Lakshmi met Mridula, she praised her saying, 'Mridula, you are fortunate. You give education to poor children and your husband gives medical treatment to poor patients. You are made for each other.' Mridula happily thought that the praise was genuine.

But Lakshmi actually thought, 'These days, Bangalore is growing fast. There are more tuition classes than schools. Many teachers have resigned their jobs and opened tuition centres where they earn much more than they did when they were teaching in schools. Why does Mridula continue to work in a stupid government job? She can take tuitions instead and earn much more money. But I can't tell her that. She's the perfect daughter-in-law for my stingy mother. Mridula doesn't buy anything for herself. She uses every penny for the home. She hasn't bought a gram of gold after marriage. All of Mridula's ornaments from her wedding are heavy. If I were her, I would have bought many sets of thin jewellery. Poor thing, she has only one silk sari. My mother did not give her any gifts when she was expecting her first baby either. My mother is shrewd. She will say, "Oh, we don't have that custom" if it means giving a gift to someone. It doesn't matter whether that someone is Mridula or me.'

The clock struck twelve.

Lakshmi remembered that she had not done any household chores since the morning. Her son, Anil, was still sleeping. Last night, all of them had gone for a late-night movie. She felt lazy and did not want to get up, clean the house and cook. She had an idea. She told her husband, 'I've been getting backaches recently. It pains when I bend forward. Shall we go out to eat today? I want to rest until Anil and you get dressed to go out.'

Shankar had just finished reading his paper. He said, 'Okay, you rest. I will wake you up once we're ready to leave.'

Lakshmi smiled to herself. 'Nobody should be able to read a woman's mind, including her husband. If he gets to know that she is acting or is too lazy to cook, he might pass a sarcastic comment or compare her to his dead mother and say, "See, my mother was a great cook. She could cook for thirty people at a time." A husband must feel that his wife is delicate and has a medical problem. These are techniques to control one's husband. You should never instantly say yes to whatever your husband says. If he finds out that his wife is obedient and a workaholic, then he'll give her more work. Then the wife will have to work in the office and at home. I'm not like Mridula, who can work all the time.'

Shankar told her repeatedly, 'Lakshmi, you are a graduate. Why don't you apply for a job in the bank? Then we'll get additional income. We can take more loans and maybe build a house.'

Though Lakshmi got offended at this, she did not show it to Shankar: the husband must think that his wife is listening to him. Instead, she gently said, 'I wish I could but Anil is too young for me to leave him alone at home. Had your mother been alive, she would've looked after our child and I would have happily found a job. Let Anil become independent. Then I'll surely work.'

This way, she smartly praised her dead mother-in-law and also sent the message to Shankar that he did not have anyone in his family to help look after the baby.

12

Different Values

Minister Nagalingegowda had been in politics for a long time. But he was a quiet and gentle person and avoided giving public statements. Many people did not even know that he was a minister. His family had plenty of land near a town called Kunigal, which was also his constituency.

Nagalingegowda had three sons. The eldest son looked after the farms and the second one owned a business. They were both married and did not interfere in their father's political work. Nagalingegowda's wife, Ningamma, wanted her third son, Suresh, to become a doctor. So she told her husband, 'Many ministers' children study in a government college and then go abroad. You've been in your political party for a long time. Why don't you get Suresh admission in a private college through the government?'

Even though Suresh did not want to become a doctor, he listened to his mother. He completed his MBBS, got a government scholarship, went abroad and returned to India with a foreign degree. He got married to Sushma and now, four years later, he was working as assistant surgeon in a Bangalore government hospital.

Ningamma had grandchildren from her first two sons within the first year of their marriages. But Suresh and Sushma were not so lucky. Sushma had become pregnant a few times but she miscarried every time. So Suresh took her to a lady gynaecologist Dr Kamala who worked in the same hospital.

Dr Kamala was a senior gynaecologist and the head of the department. She recommended a lot of tests. After the test results came in, the doctor carefully gave her opinion, 'Sushma, your uterus is quite delicate. It doesn't have the capacity to bear a child for nine months. So, when you become pregnant, you'll need a special stitch called the Shirodkar stitch. Moreover, you should take complete bed rest for the duration of the pregnancy.'

Suresh was a colleague and Dr Kamala was hesitant to get involved. Sushma was a VIP patient. If things went well, a few words of appreciation may come her way but if something went wrong, nobody would care to find out the truth; instead, there may be an inquiry or a transfer. She was aware that the case itself was not complicated but the consequences were heavy and may affect her working relationships or her future at the hospital.

In her thirty years of experience, Dr Kamala had seen many cases where she had assumed that things would not go wrong, but they had. So she thought that it was better for such cases to go to a doctor with whom the patients felt comfortable. She paused and said, 'If you want a second opinion, please feel free to consult another doctor.'

Suresh had a high opinion of Dr Kamala. He knew that she was not corrupt and was excellent at her job. He had done a year of residency under her guidance. He said, 'No, madam, we don't want a second opinion. I have complete confidence in you. I want you to handle this case.'

When Sushma became pregnant, she came to see Dr Kamala every month. At the right time, Dr Kamala stitched Sushma's uterus and told her, 'Don't lift heavy things. Take complete bed rest. You must come and get admitted in the hospital one month before your due date.'

Sushma was nervous and asked, 'Doctor, do you think that I will need a C-section?'

'That's difficult to predict. Things like that are usually decided at the time of delivery. But don't worry. You will be fine.'

Dr Kamala had two assistants—Lata and Sanjay. Dr Lata's father was a senior IAS officer. She had grown up in Bangalore, came from a rich family and had never been to a village. She was good in studies, spoke good English and could impress anybody. She had done her MBBS in Bangalore, then gone to England for work and come back a few years later. She had joined the hospital as a lecturer. Dr Lata usually did not take any responsibility but pretended to work hard. Her husband

was an income tax officer. Her father had given them a big
bungalow in Sadashivanagar as a gift and she came to the
hospital in a car.

Dr Kamala preferred Sanjay over Lata. When Dr Kamala
went out of town, she made Sanjay the person in charge.
Though he did not talk much, Sanjay was good at his work.
Even the hospital staff liked Sanjay over Lata.

Today, it was Dr Lata's shift at the hospital. At 8 p.m., there
was a call from the minister's house that Sushma was on her
way to the hospital and that she was in labour. Unfortunately,
Dr Kamala was in Chennai. Dr Lata was scared because Sushma
was a VIP patient and there was no senior doctor around. She
went to Sanjay and caught him just as he was about to leave.
She said, 'Sanjay, this is an important case. Madam is out of
station. Please don't go.'

'I'm sorry. They must want a lady doctor. So I may not be of
any use to you.'

Almost immediately, Sushma came in. She was in a lot of
pain. Dr Suresh told Dr Lata, 'Madam had told me to admit
Sushma one month before her due date. I'm sorry that I didn't
do it. There was a by-election in our constituency and we got
busy. We remembered only after Sushma had the labour pain.
She can't feel the baby move.'

Sanjay thought, 'What kind of a husband is Suresh? His wife
had such a difficult pregnancy and being a doctor himself, he
knows the importance of the Shirodkar stitch. How can he be
so busy that he forgot about his wife's medical needs?'

Dr Lata wanted to escape. She said, 'Madam is out of town.
You can take your wife to any other private nursing home. We
don't have any objection.'

Suresh insisted, 'No, we don't want to go anywhere else.
Her case history is here. You're also well trained.'

Lata did not know what to do. She took Sanjay aside and
requested him, 'Sanjay, you have much more experience than

me. I can't manage this VIP case by myself. Will you please help me?'

This was not a difficult case for Sanjay. He had handled similar cases in Bombay. Dr Jog was a great teacher and Sanjay had been exposed to different types of cases while working for him. He thought, 'Lata is well qualified. Why is she so scared? I wonder what she learnt in England.'

Then he thought of the patient and forgot about everything else. He nodded his head and agreed to help Lata. Sanjay realized that Sushma needed a C-section quickly because the cord was around the baby's neck. So he prepared to operate on Sushma; Lata assisted him. They performed a C-section. When the baby was taken out safely, he felt happy seeing the newborn. A few minutes later, he went to wash his hands and change his clothes.

Dr Lata took the newborn and went outside to show the baby boy to the father and grandmother. Ningamma was very happy to see her first grandson and became emotional. A short while later, the minister also reached the hospital. Ningamma turned to her husband and said, 'Lord Shiva has been kind to us. This lady doctor worked really hard and has taken good care of Sushma and the baby.'

Lata took advantage of the opportunity and replied, 'Yes, sir. This was a very difficult case. In the end, I had to do a C-section.'

'How long have you been working here?' the minister asked with concern.

'For the past five years. Sir, you may know my father, Mr Balasubramaniam.'

'Oh! So, are you Chief Secretary Balasubramaniam's daughter?'

'Yes, sir.'

Suddenly, the baby started crying and Lata took him inside. Sanjay was not back yet. He was still changing out of the doctors' hospital uniform. Sushma was under the influence of anaesthesia. Lata was excited that she had hit the iron while it was hot.

Soon, it was the naming ceremony of Minister Nagalingegowda's grandchild. It was a joyous event. The minister had also won the by-election and he wanted to thank everyone who had helped. So a big party was planned to celebrate both the occasions. The minister sent invitation cards to Dr Lata and told her to invite everyone who helped during Sushma's operation. Lata gave the nurses and ayahs the invitation but did not give a card to Sanjay. She was worried that if the minister came to know that it was Sanjay who had performed the operation, then she would not look good.

The day of the function came and went and Sanjay remained unaware that he had also been invited to the party.

A few days later, Sanjay was sitting in his room preparing for a conference. He was feeling low and wondered how his paper would matter in the long run. He loved his work but appreciation was important because it brought a lot of enthusiasm. Dr Kamala entered his room. She was on the verge of retirement and had seen many ups and downs in her life. In her long career, she had helped many people and was happy about it. Seeing Dr Kamala, Sanjay stopped what he was doing and stood up to show his respect. Dr Kamala smiled and said, 'Please, Sanjay, sit down. When do you think you'll complete your paper?'

Dr Kamala was interested in academics. She encouraged hard-working youngsters like Sanjay because there were few people working in government hospitals who wanted to achieve academic excellence. She knew that Lata's knowledge was hollow—she was more interested in publicity than in being a good doctor. The reason Lata was here was because of her father's influence. Otherwise, she would not have been hired by the hospital. Dr Kamala was aware of who had performed the operation and why Sanjay had not got an invite.

'How was the function, madam?' Sanjay asked.

'It was an obligation and a formality. Simple people like you and me can't understand all the reasons behind such parties.'

Sanjay kept quiet. Kamala showed him the sari the minister's family had given her and said, 'You know that I didn't perform the operation, Sanjay. Maybe they gave it to me because I had examined Sushma during her pregnancy. But I was surprised at one thing . . .'

'What's that, madam?'

'I was surprised at the way everyone was praising Lata and the way she was lying through her teeth. She was saying that she has handled many such cases in London. I know it is a lie. But who will take the effort to actually find out the truth? Lata must have got a better gift than me. Sanjay, one thing is true— in government hospitals, it is not only important that you do a good job but also that you showcase it to others.'

Sanjay started thinking about Dr Kamala's wise words and did not reply.

13

The Fall of Idealism

After Sishir's birth, Mridula's life changed completely. She wanted someone to look after the child during the day so that she could return to work. Rukuma and Bheemanna told her, 'You can leave the child with us at Aladahalli. We'll take care of him.'

But Mridula did not agree. Though she herself had been born and brought up in Aladahalli and loved the village, leaving her child there was difficult for her. Sanjay also agreed. Bheemanna or Rukuma could not leave the village and come to stay with Mridula for a long period either.

By now, Mridula knew very well that her mother-in-law wouldn't help her. Sanjay had indirectly told his mother, 'Amma, Mridula is worried about where she'll leave the baby when she returns to work.'

Ratnamma had kept quiet. She was not willing to come and take care of the baby. Still, Mridula was grateful to her mother-in-law. At least, she did not trouble her like other mothers-in-law. She did not taunt her with sarcastic comments or take her daughter's side or discriminate against Mridula. Ratnamma lived in a completely different world.

Mridula could leave her job and stay at home, but that would not work. Sanjay and Mridula had taken a loan for their flat. Unless both of them worked, they would not be able to repay the loan. Mridula was saving every paisa. She did not take an autorickshaw or spend money on stitching blouse pieces to match with her saris. She wanted the loan to be repaid at the earliest. But Lakshmi made fun of her. Behind her back, she said, 'What's the use of all the salary and education when Mridula can't even dress properly?'

Mridula tried to get somebody from Aladahalli to stay and work in her house but after they stayed in her Vijayanagar apartment, they quickly got bored. They left within three months because they missed the village.

One day, Mridula was thinking about this problem while she was buying some vegetables when she ran into Muniyappa and Kantamma. She was happy to see them. Kantamma told her, 'Mridula, we didn't go back to Kolar. We're staying in a rented house in Vijayanagar too.'

They gave her the address and told her to visit them soon. Since Mridula was attached to them, she took Sishir and went to their house the next Sunday. She told them about her difficulties in getting a good daytime babysitter and said, 'I don't think that I can continue to work if I don't find someone reliable.'

The husband and wife looked at each other and excused themselves. They went inside their bedroom and came back in five minutes. Kantamma told Mridula affectionately, 'Look, if you and your husband agree, you can leave your child with us. I'll look after him like my own grandson. Please don't leave him alone with some unknown help.'

Mridula could not contain her joy. Tears flowed down her cheeks in gratitude. Later, she talked to Sanjay and he did not have any objection either.

Despite the baby and the lecturer's job, Sanjay spent most of his time in the library. One day, the hospital informed the doctors about a three-week AIDS training programme in the USA arranged by the World Health Organization (WHO). All doctors working in government hospitals were eligible for this training but preference was to be given to the gynaecologists who were also teaching there. Sanjay thought that it was a good opportunity for him since he did not have the kind of money to personally go and attend the training on his own. So he filled out the application and went to Dr Kamala's room.

Dr Kamala was busy reading a medical journal. When Sanjay came and sat in front of her, she asked him, 'What's the matter, Sanjay?'

'Madam, I need a favour. I'm applying for the training programme in New York. Will you recommend me?' Sanjay asked hesitantly. He found it hard to ask for favours.

'Sanjay, I attended the training last year. You'll meet many people there. The library may help you acquire knowledge, but attending a seminar or training is much more useful. This is a good idea.'

'Madam, do you think I have a good chance of being chosen? You know my work style and my nature.'

Dr Kamala was quiet for a minute and then replied, 'I'm aware of the situation. I've worked with you for years now, but I don't know whether you'll be able to go.'

'Why not, madam?'

'Even after so long, I don't understand the basis on which the hospital panel selects a person. Every year, the criteria are different. They modify the selection process based on the candidate they want to send. I really don't know the rules for this year.'

Sanjay turned pale. Dr Kamala consoled him, 'Sanjay, I'm not discouraging you. The truth is that I don't want to give you false hope. A best friend is one who tells you the bitter truth. It is not necessary that you go through the government. There are some medical companies which can also sponsor this training.'

Sanjay smiled gently and said, 'I heard that Dr Lata went on such a drug company sponsorship to Malaysia. Is there any way that I can also get that sponsorship?'

Dr Kamala kept quiet. Sanjay could not get that sponsorship. Lata worked part-time for a private nursing home. The drug company sponsored private-hospital doctors and not government ones. Lata had another advantage. Her husband was in the Income Tax department. She ensured that people who didn't help her had their income tax audited and their house raided. Everybody was scared of her. Dr Kamala remembered that a few years ago, Lata had wanted to go to Singapore and asked for a six-week vacation. Dr Kamala had refused because the department was short-staffed. The next week, the income tax department had audited her. There was nothing wrong with her income tax filing, but the multiple visits, verifications and waiting had caused a lot of irritation.

When Dr Kamala had gone to the income tax office, the inspecting officer Louis had felt awkward. His daughter Mary had been Dr Kamala's student and had great regard for her. Softly, he had told Dr Kamala, 'Madam, your reputation precedes you. My daughter was your student.'

Then he had got some coffee for her. After the verification, Louis had said, 'Madam, please know that we're only junior officers.'

Dr Kamala had asked him, 'Can you please tell me who sent you instructions to audit me?'

'Madam, please don't ask me that. Here, even the walls have ears. I hope you understand.'

When she had returned to the hospital, she had met Lata who had smiled and innocently asked her, 'Madam, you're looking exhausted. Have you come to work just now? Are you unwell? Do you want to go home?'

Dr Kamala had replied, 'I don't harass others just because I have power.'

Lata could not face Dr Kamala after that. She had looked at the floor and walked away. Afterwards, she had behaved as if nothing had happened.

Though Dr Kamala had given her only a week's vacation, Lata had sent a medical certificate of ill health through her father and stayed six weeks in Singapore for a family holiday. She had brought gifts from Singapore and given them to the people who would be of use to her in the hospital. That included the lower staff such as clerks and the cleaning ladies. She wanted to keep them happy so they would not complain about her long vacation or her laziness. Dr Kamala knew all this but had been forced to keep quiet because she had no support from the hospital.

She thought, 'How can Sanjay understand all this? It's difficult to explain. Twenty-five years ago, I was just like Sanjay—contented with work and believing in idealism. Life has taught me big lessons. If a person is intelligent and an idealist, then he will be a good teacher. And if a man is intelligent and selfish, then he can go to any extent to get money. In the end, it is a personal choice about how closely we follow our own principles.'

Sanjay was unaware of what was going on in Dr Kamala's mind. He was thinking about the sponsorship and how he could get it. He wanted Dr Kamala to recommend him to any drug company. Dr Kamala knew what he was thinking. She also knew that no drug company would sponsor Sanjay because now, nobody would listen to her. All the company medical representatives were aware of her impending retirement and were concentrating on pleasing the next head of the department, Dr Saroja.

Instead of talking about sponsorship through drug companies, Dr Kamala said, 'Our Health minister is the chairman of the WHO fund in our state. Why don't you go and meet him? I can put in a word for you.'

Sanjay nodded. He thought he should try that route too.

A few days after Dr Kamala's suggestion, Sanjay decided to go to the Health Secretariat. He entered the building. It was a sultry afternoon and Sanjay was sweating despite the numerous fans around. There were people standing in front of the Health minister's personal assistant. Others were standing in the hallway, smoking and talking. Everybody seemed to have a problem. Some wanted a transfer while others wanted a promotion. Sanjay felt lost. It was the first time that he had entered a minister's office asking for help.

Hesitantly, Sanjay went and stood in front of the PA. The PA looked at him but did not say anything. Even though there was an empty chair in front of him, he did not tell Sanjay to sit down. He was talking on his cell phone and completely ignored Sanjay. Finally, the call ended. Still standing, Sanjay greeted the PA with a namaskara. The PA did not reciprocate. 'What do you want?' he asked directly.

Sanjay showed his file to the PA. The PA said to himself, 'People greet me only when they have work—otherwise they don't even recognize me. Why should I be nice to them?'

He was rude. 'Give me one reason why the government should sponsor you. You must think that the government is a bottomless treasury. You should first understand the rules of the sponsorship and then come here. You're wasting my time.'

'I'm not asking for funds from the government. I'm asking for help from the WHO funds.'

The PA became even more angry. 'Who gave you the information about those funds? Bring that person here. Even if I accept that they exist, why should they be spent on you? There are people more senior to you. We must give them an opportunity too.'

'May I meet the Health minister?'

'If you want to meet him for this reason, then . . .'

Before the PA could finish his sentence, his phone rang again. The PA's tone became pleasant and he started speaking politely into the receiver. 'Brother, please don't misunderstand me. I have told our Health minister already. She is very strict. When she is in a good mood, I will give her the file . . .'

The conversation continued and the PA picked up the cordless phone and went to the hallway so that he could speak in private. Sanjay did not know what to do.

Meanwhile, a man had been observing him. He walked over to Sanjay now and greeted him. Sanjay looked at him. He was around thirty-five, with a slightly chubby face, and was wearing plain and simple clothes. Sanjay did not know him. The man started chatting. 'You may not know my name, Doctor. My wife was your patient. When we came to your hospital, Dr Kamala Amma was on vacation. So you operated on my wife and looked after her very well. You didn't even ask us for money. We sent you fruits and flowers to convey our gratitude. But you didn't accept those either.'

Sanjay could not remember him. Many patients came to a government hospital and it was difficult to recall all their names. Had the man told him what kind of an operation it was, Sanjay may have remembered his wife. He did not take gifts for his services, even if they were fruits and flowers. Sanjay said, 'I'm sorry, I still don't recognize you. What's your name?'

'My name is Chikananjappa and my wife's name is Kempamma.'

Chikananjappa smiled, showing his paan-stained, red teeth. He asked, 'Doctor, why're you here?'

Sanjay explained the situation to him and showed him the file. Chikananjappa said, 'Doctor, I'm a clerk—but let's not talk here. Everybody is listening to us. Come to Chalukya Hotel at 5.30 p.m. We'll chat over a cup of tea.'

Without saying anything more, Chikananjappa walked away.

Shortly, the PA came back. Many people were still waiting for him. The PA announced, 'Madam is on a trip to north Karnataka. From there, she'll go to Delhi. So there are no appointments available until late next week.'

Sanjay left the building disappointed. He decided to wait and meet Chikananjappa.

At 5 p.m., Sanjay started walking towards Chalukya Hotel. He was dejected and depressed. He thought about his selection for the lecturer's post. It had been absolutely effortless. Dr Kamala had been in the selection committee and he had got the job without even a recommendation. But things had changed a lot in the last two years. Even though he was sincere, Sanjay found it difficult to ask for rightful credit and promotions.

On the way to the hotel, Sanjay remained deep in thought. In the outpatient department, almost 180–200 patients came in for treatment every day. Nobody was mollycoddled like in a private hospital but at the same time, nobody was turned away either. Usually, four to six doctors were working at any given time. It was difficult to handle so many patients and their unending questions. All the doctors were taught that their highest duty was to serve the patient even if he was his enemy. But when such doctors came to government offices, the people in power, who may be less educated than the doctor, treated them very badly. Sometimes, Sanjay found it tough to continue.

By the time he reached Chalukya Hotel, Chikananjappa was waiting for him and had already ordered two coffees. Chikananjappa said, 'Doctor, I want to tell you the truth. You won't get the sponsorship. Only people with connections get them. However, I want to take all your relevant details. Give me your home phone number so that I can call you if something works out. Are you aware that there are very few doctors like you in government hospitals? When a patient comes and is recommended by a minister, he gets VIP treatment. For people like us, even though the drugs are available in the store, the answer is no when we ask the staff. There are fixed rates for every operation—and you aren't even aware of it. Similarly, we also have certain rates in our office for things like transfers, no objection certificates and so on. This unwritten rule can't be changed by anyone. In short, I scratch your back and you scratch mine.'

Sanjay did not know what to say. Chikananjappa continued, 'Doctor, if you keep working for the government, you'll make many visits to our department. You can't get a transfer, promotion, NOC or sponsorship without our department's cooperation. You should also know who's who here. Our people help the doctors. That's the reason many doctors consider the people from our department to be VIPs. If you've ever noticed, several of your colleagues come to our department often.'

Sanjay had not noticed it. Had Chikananjappa not enlightened him, he would have remained ignorant about it. The waiter brought the coffee bill and even though Sanjay insisted on paying, Chikananjappa did not let him.

Getting up, Sanjay asked him, 'May I call you after a couple of days?'

'Please don't do that. In our department, people are more interested in finding out what others are doing rather than doing their own work. When I get a telephone call during office hours, my boss thinks that I'm making money on the side. If somebody finds out that I'm trying to help you, they'll think that I'm giving out all the inside secrets to you. They'll punish me and transfer me to a place like Bellary or the Tourism department. Please keep our meeting a secret.'

Sanjay promised to do so and left. Chikananjappa kept sitting, probably in wait for his next visitor.

The next day, Dr Kamala called Sanjay and advised him, 'Sanjay, just last year, I met a doctor from Bombay. Her name is Varsha and she got a sponsorship from Tata. She told me that every year, the Tata Foundation gives some sponsorships to doctors. Forget about getting assistance from the government, you'll face a lot of hurdles. Try to get assistance from private NGOs. They're usually fairer and rely only on merit. Apart from Tata, you can also apply for sponsorship to some good NGOs in Bangalore. Remember—don't rely only on one. Send your application everywhere.'

Dr Kamala gave Sanjay Dr Varsha's address and phone number.

For the next seven days, Sanjay was busy drafting request letters to different organizations for sponsorship. The first negative response came from the Tata Foundation. They replied, 'Your credentials are excellent. We would have definitely considered you for a sponsorship but we have a fundamental rule that the doctors whom we sponsor must currently be working in Bombay. After the training, the doctor must serve the Bombay citizens for three years. Hence, we regret that you aren't eligible for our sponsorship. We wish you all the best.'

The remaining replies that followed also had some reason or the other to reject Sanjay. Some said, 'We cannot sponsor the entire amount. We can give you only Rs 10,000.' Others said, 'We can give you half the amount for the training. You must provide for the other half.' Yet others replied, 'We have invested our funds in another project, so we are unable to sponsor you at this time.'

Sanjay felt depressed.

One evening, when he came back home with a heavy heart, Mridula was feeding Sishir; she looked excited. Before he could ask, she said, 'Alex and Anita are here in Bangalore. Anita phoned me just now. They will be here for four days.'

Alex and Sanjay had continued to remain in touch. Alex had not wanted to do his post-graduation. He had gone to the Middle East and made plenty of money. Mr Pinto, his father-in-law, was very happy.

Alex and Anita visited India every year; this time they had come with their baby daughter, Juliet Pratibha. Alex was staying for only two weeks but Anita was staying for four; they planned to spend most of their time in Goa, Bangalore and Mangalore. Anita was open and transparent and both the women got along very well despite the difference in their backgrounds. Anita always brought a gift for Mridula.

It was getting dark. Sanjay parked his scooter and went to wash his face. Mridula started talking as she put his dinner plate on the table and served him: 'I'm going to call them for dinner. Let's go out tomorrow. Their baby isn't here; they have left her in Mangalore.'

Sanjay did not say anything.

'What should we call the baby—Juliet or Pratibha? I like Juliet. What do you think?'

Sanjay was still quiet.

'Do you know that they want to buy a house here? But I don't know why they chose Bangalore. Neither of them is from here. Did Alex talk to you about it?'

Without waiting for Sanjay's answer, she continued enthusiastically, 'Anita wants a Kasuti sari from Hubli. She insists that I take her there at least once. Do you know the Gomantak hotel on the traffic island crossroad? The owner of that hotel is related to Alex. Anita has seen Hubli once when she was only a child. I told her that if you want to go there just to buy a Kasuti sari, then let's not. My mother has sent me a black one for my birthday and I have still not used it. I can give that to Anita. Also, a new Kasuti sari shop has opened in Hosur. I can get it from there too.'

Sanjay was having his dinner quietly but his mind was somewhere else. Now, Mridula realized that Sanjay was not listening to her. She asked, 'Why aren't you saying anything? Is there a problem at the hospital?'

Sanjay continued eating silently.

Mridula tried again: 'What happened to your sponsorship to go to the USA? I'm sure that you will get it. You're a rank student and intelligent. Satish and Shyla are also coming to Bangalore for work but by then, you'll be in America. Shyla is smarter than Satish. She has taken a loan to build a house in Hubli. She even visited the USA last year to help Sarla with her child. She loves to help people but doesn't get personally attached. Can I invite Shyla to stay with us for two weeks? She always brings something for us. Oh, that reminds me. Here is more news for you—next year, Sarla and Prasanna may shift base to India. But I don't know whether they'll settle down in Bangalore or Bombay.'

Before she could finish, Sanjay got up and washed his hands. Mridula followed him. 'May I tell Shyla that she can stay here?'

'Sure.' That was Sanjay's only reply—short and sweet.

'I knew that you won't refuse. At Aladahalli, we constantly had guests at home and it was fun. I like having people around. Otherwise, I feel lonely. You enjoy reading and your work. But for me, people are important.' Mridula continued, 'Oh! I almost forgot. Anita had given me a gold chain the last time she visited us. I don't like expensive gifts but she just doesn't listen. She's fond of Sishir too and I really love Juliet. I want to buy something for Juliet this time. Is that okay with you?'

Mridula started washing the dishes. Scrubbing a vessel with a nylon scrubber, she followed Sanjay to the bedroom. Sanjay said, 'Give her whatever you feel like. Have I ever stopped you from spending money?'

'No, never. But I never spend a rupee without informing you. I believe that a husband and wife should be honest with each other and take decisions together. If you spend money without informing me and I spend without telling you, then life will become tough. Isn't that true?'

Sanjay wanted to be left alone. So he said, 'Yes, it is.'

Suddenly, Sishir called out for his mother from the dining hall. Forgetting everything, Mridula left the vessel by the table lamp in the bedroom and ran to Sishir.

Though the fan was on, it was hot. Sanjay started thinking about life. 'Change is the only constant. Changing according to one's circumstances is essential. Mridula hasn't changed much except for a few things. She has learnt Bangalore Kannada very well, her cooking has improved and she dresses better. But her heart remains the same. I remember seeing her in the wedding hall years ago. Her mind is still an open book. Sometimes, like now, she doesn't even understand whether the other person is listening to her or not. She's so naive.'

Sanjay was unable to read or sleep. A storm was brewing in his mind. If he shared his problem with Mridula, she would not understand the delicate situation. She was in her own world of happiness and was looking forward to meeting Anita. He could not understand how Mridula could tell Anita everything. She just could not keep a secret. The worst thing was that Mridula thought that everybody was like her.

Sanjay recalled the time, soon after their marriage, when they were travelling from Hubli to Bangalore. On the way, Mridula had told him, 'I want to tell you a secret—Satish's secret.'

Sanjay could not remember who Satish was. Mridula had explained, 'He's my cousin.'

'Oh, yes, I remember him.'

'What did you think of him?'

'He's nice.'

'You know, he wanted to marry me.'

Sanjay's ears had perked up. He could not contain his curiosity. 'Who told you that?'

'Nobody.'

'Then, how did you learn about this?'

'I saw my picture in his wallet.'

'When?'

'After our engagement.'

Sanjay had immediately asked, 'What did you do?'

'I didn't like it and took the picture away.'

'What did he say?'

'Nothing. I felt very strange. I never had such feelings towards him. I didn't share this with anyone.'

Sanjay had laughed at her innocence. He had thought, 'Mridula and Satish grew up together—any boy will like Mridula. It must have been infatuation. There was no reason for her to tell me this.'

Mridula had continued, 'I want to be open with you. If you liked any girl before me, please say so. I will be a good sport. But tell me the truth.'

Sanjay had paused for a few seconds and said, 'Nobody. You're the first and the last girl to whom I have been attracted.' Somewhere in his mind, he had thought about Vasudha but then had immediately dismissed her image from his mind.

There was a storm in the Bay of Bengal due to which there were furious rains in Bangalore. There was a strong wind and a few dried coconuts flew up from the ground; one of them broke the light bulb in their small garden. Sanjay came out of his reverie and opened a window. The cool breeze gushed inside. Though it was pleasant, Sanjay was not at peace. He knew what Alex would tell him the next day: 'Sanjay, think. How much will you earn working at a government hospital all your life? You can earn that much money within a year of private practice. After retiring from the government hospital, you'll work as a professor and probably get minimal old-age pension.

The greatest headache in government service is transfers. It just isn't worth it.'

Though Sanjay's mind agreed with Alex, his heart did not want to accept it. If he continued in the government hospital, he could teach the next generation and easily keep himself updated with the latest information about surgery, drugs and other medical breakthroughs. He recollected his father's words: 'Sanjay, the foremost duty of a doctor is to take care of his patients. As a doctor, you should understand a patient's suffering and serve him the same way that you serve God. God doesn't stay in just T. Narasipura's temple. He also comes in the form of a patient.'

Sanjay would ask, 'Appa, how should the patient behave?'

'Child, patients also have their own code. They must see God in their doctor. Only then can they have faith in him. If the patient believes in the doctor, then a good relationship is built. Our ancestors say that even if you give water to the patient, his faith will transform it into medicine.'

Sanjay thought, 'I wonder what my father would have to say if he was alive today.'

As expected, when Sanjay met Alex the next day at dinner, Alex laughed at him. 'Come on, Sanjay, times have changed. Once upon a time, the priest in the church was considered a doctor. Before that, even barbers were doctors. But today, there's no way that a barber can be considered remotely close to a doctor. I see our priest's face only on Sundays if I go to church. The medical profession is no longer a service. It has become a commercial business. And in any commercial organization, you require administration, systems, payment methods and the need to be professional. Our society has changed over a period of time in every aspect, whether it is in terms of dress, lifestyle or language. Then why don't you expect a change in attitude in the field of medicine? Just observe the things around you. We can't be like your father any more. If a person has cancer, no amount of goodwill or faith in the doctor can cure the patient.

It requires surgery. That kind of an emotional society doesn't exist any more. So I don't agree with your father at all.'

Sanjay was quiet.

Alex was an aggressive and powerful speaker. He continued, 'I'll tell you a story from Goa. You know that there are many streams in Goa that flow towards the sea. In the old days, small boats were used to cross them. There were no bridges and no government doctors then. A village doctor visited many villages using these boats. The doctor's source of income was the money given to him in the boat by the patient's relatives on his way back after treating a patient. Once, a patient was ill and his family came to fetch the doctor. After treating the patient, the doctor was coming back in the boat along with the patient's relatives. There was a big storm. The boatman asked the passengers to reduce the weight of the boat by throwing one person into the river. Immediately, the patient's relatives chose the doctor. By doing this, they killed two birds with one stone. They didn't have to pay the doctor and his work of treating their relative was also over. So Sanjay, the point is that there is nothing called "gratitude". You are an idealist—you are intelligent and caring and you take complete responsibility for your patients. Listen to me. Let's start a nursing home. Bangalore is growing and software companies are starting offices here. We'll do well.'

Sanjay did not answer him. His mind was still having trouble accepting Alex's words.

14

Family Visits

Sishir continued to go to Muniyappa's house whenever Mridula was not at home. Meanwhile, Muniyappa and Kantamma's son,

Arun, joined a software company and married his colleague Anuradha, who was from Bihar. At first, his parents refused the alliance, particularly Muniyappa. But Kantamma knew that they could lose their son if they objected too much. So she took the lead and convinced Muniyappa to give his consent.

Now, both the son and the daughter-in-law were working. They were happy that the house was being taken care of by the elders at home. That was the reason they were staying with their parents. Though Muniyappa wanted to go back to Kolar, Kantamma did not. She said, 'We've been away from Kolar for the last thirty years. What'll we do there at this age? There is a shortage of water there and the weather is hot. On top of that, we have a lot of relatives there and will unnecessarily get into obligations and money issues. It is better to be in Bangalore with our son and daughter-in-law.'

Arun also wanted them to stay with him. Anuradha was indifferent; she was always busy listening to songs on her MP3 player or playing games on the computer. She did not know Kannada, nor did she try to learn the language. Arun had learnt Hindi and the conversation between the couple was either in Hindi or English. Anuradha thought, 'It's better to stay with my in-laws because then I needn't worry about a baby-care centre later.'

Sishir was used to staying in Muniyappa's house for a few hours every day. They had become his surrogate grandparents. He called Muniyappa 'Tata' and Kantamma 'Ajji'. After school, the school van dropped him at Muniyappa's house. He ate his lunch there, did his homework and came back home only at night. Arun and Anuradha were also fond of him. Sometimes, Anuradha would take Sishir to Brigade Road or MG Road in their new car and buy him toys. He loved eating ragi just like them. He would tell Mridula, 'Amma, you can't cook like Ajji. She makes excellent food with ragi.'

Meanwhile, things had changed drastically at Aladahalli. Krishna and his wife, Vatsala, had a baby boy. But Vatsala and

Mridula were not good friends. Surprisingly, Vatsala was street-smart despite being from a village and considered Mridula her competitor. Once, Champakka had softly told Rukuma, 'Vatsala is neither good at work nor friendly like Mridula. She is selfish and calculating.'

Vatsala was short-tempered and discontent with her life. She preferred the city to the village. She would say, 'What's there to do in this village? It's the same agricultural activity over and over again—sow the seeds, reap the harvest, store the grains and get the fertilizers. At other times, there's a religious occasion like Hanuman Jayanti. There's no change at all! If it were Hubli, there would've been so many things to do. I'm tired of this place.'

She constantly complained to Krishna. Krishna was quiet and less aggressive and at most times, he did not answer her. But sometimes, he would tell her, 'Why do you grumble all day? You were aware of what the village was like when you married me. Mridula never felt bored here. She was busier than all of us. You can learn a lot of things from Champakka. She knows various kinds of cooking and rangoli. You can tend to her garden like Mridula used to do.'

During such times, Vatsala's anger would know no bounds. 'Don't talk about your sister!' she would say. 'She didn't know anything else so she learnt all this useless work. She knew that some day she would get married and go away to the city. That's the reason she enjoyed Aladahalli—it was a short stay for her. Your sister hardly comes to Aladahalli any more because she likes Bangalore. And don't talk to me about Champakka. She always compares me to Mridula and talks too much.'

Vatsala just needed a reason to fight and could not stand hearing Mridula's name. She wanted to stay in Hubli and visit Aladahalli only during weekends. When she looked at jewellery shops in Hubli, she felt like buying similar ornaments, but the elders at home did not allow her to do so.

Mridula came to the village once or twice a year. Now, Rukuma had arthritis and Bheemanna had become hard of hearing. Mridula did not feel comfortable with Vatsala. Vatsala would start taunting her and pick a fight with her as soon as she arrived. Because of the unfriendly atmosphere, nobody would eat that day and Vatsala would cry. Then she would take her son and go to her mother's house. It made Mridula feel sad. So she would spend a maximum of two weeks in Aladahalli.

Sanjay would make fun of her: 'Oh, Mridula, you're so talkative that you can befriend a stone. Why not Vatsala?'

Mridula would think sadly, 'Yes, I can make a stone talk, but not a stone-hearted person.'

From Aladahalli, she would go to Satish's house in Hubli and spend a week there. Shyla was very hospitable. But Sishir would get bored in Aladahalli and Hubli. He would insist on coming back to Bangalore. He liked to stay only in his home and in Kantamma's house.

Sanjay's brother-in-law, Shankar, had also got promoted to assistant manager and had bought a car. But they hardly ever visited Mridula and Sanjay. Lakshmi was not close to Sanjay. Ratnamma never came to Bangalore either. Sometimes, Sishir went to T. Narasipura. Ratnamma would give two bananas from her small shop to her grandson every day. She advised him, 'Sishir, you shouldn't spend too much money. If someone gives you money, invest it so that it increases. Don't buy sweets and spend everything. Anyway, sweets are not good for health.' Then she would say, 'Child, whatever I am earning and saving right now is for you after I die.' Still, there was no emotional connection between Ratnamma and Sishir.

These days, Anita was in Bangalore and Mridula went out shopping with her regularly. Anita was not happy in the Middle East. She said, 'I get bored there.'

'Why can't you work?'

'Women can't work there. When we go out, I have to wear a burka. All women must wear burkas irrespective of their religion. Women are allowed to have restricted professions only, like working as a teacher, doctor or nurse. I don't know how to spend time there.'

'Do you have a lot of work at home?'

'No, there's hardly anything to do at home. We never have guests there either. Alex is always busy. You know that I'm fond of the choir and church. But the only thing you can do there is shop for gold.'

'Oh, are there many gold shops?'

'We have gold shops there the same way that you have fancy stores here. There are varieties of ornaments and all of them shine yellow. All the shopping malls are centrally air-conditioned and lit with bright lights. The jewels dazzle under those lights. But Mridula, I don't feel like wearing any gold. When I wear jewellery, I like my friends to compliment me. That possibility is so low there. So I don't wear any.'

'Anita, why don't your in-laws visit you?'

'My in-laws don't want to leave Goa. They have a house on Miramar beach, a cashew farm, and they get plenty of fresh fish. Their house is a paradise. The church is also near. Feni flows like water in their house. Tell me, why would they want to go elsewhere? My parents are not interested in visiting me either. Mridula, if I send you tickets, will you come for three months?'

'That may cost a lot, Anita!'

'It'll be my gift to you. If I had a sister and had she come there, I would have done the same. You are more than a sister to me. But if it makes you feel better, I will leave the shopping to your account.' Anita continued, 'Mridula, we want to come back to India within a few years. I've told Alex that if we come back, we'll settle in Bangalore. It is a big city with better schools and it is more cosmopolitan. And I can still talk in Kannada here. More than that, you are here.'

Anita was straightforward, generous and very affectionate. Whenever they talked, she touched Mridula's heart. There was a good understanding between the two of them. Mridula did not feel the same way about Lakshmi, Vatsala or anybody else.

Meanwhile, a phone call from Chikananjappa brought disappointment to Sanjay. He said, 'Doctor, I have checked all the confidential files. There are three people who are getting the sponsorship. One candidate is from Gulbarga. He's related to someone in the Opposition party. If they don't give the sponsorship to their candidate, there'll be too much noise in the Assembly. The next candidate is somebody from Kolar. From what I have gathered, his uncle supplies machines to the government. The third one is Dr Suresh. He's been selected because his father's a minister. Doctor, please don't tell anyone that I have shared this with you. I don't have the power to remove any of the candidates and give you the sponsorship instead. I can just give you the information.'

'Thank you, Chikananjappa, for the trouble that you've taken for me. I won't mention your name at all.'

Sanjay put the phone down. He thought, 'All the candidates are neither gynaecologists nor teaching staff. Their training will be of no use to the government. They've been chosen because of their connections and not because of their merit. Alex would say "I told you so"—merit alone is of no use. A person must be at the right place at the right time.' He felt grateful to Chikananjappa. 'At least, he told me that I haven't been selected. Otherwise, I would have waited with hope.'

Alex and Anita came to Sanjay and Mridula's house for dinner that night. Alex looked at Sanjay and knew that something was wrong. He asked, 'What's the matter, Sanjay?'

Sanjay did not feel like sharing the news with him, so he said, 'Oh, it's nothing.'

'Come on, Sanjay, don't hide anything from me. I know you well. Is there a problem in your department? Have you been transferred or penalized for something you haven't done?'

'No, Alex. That's not it. Even if I tell you what's bothering me, the solution isn't in our hands. And I already know what you'll tell me.'

'Sanjay, my logic is different. Let's assume that you get a salary of ten thousand rupees. Half of that is to accept the injustice around you and the other half is for your actual work. If you still don't understand that, then you're foolish.'

'According to you, I'm always foolish.'

'Sanjay, my intention isn't to hurt you. You know that you have to make some decisions regarding your career.'

Politely, Anita left them and went to the kitchen to help Mridula.

Sanjay told Alex everything about the sponsorship. At the dinner table, Alex said, 'Mridula, I've given Sanjay my opinion about his career. I know that both of you have taken a loan to buy this apartment. At the rate that you're going, you'll be busy repaying the loan for the next twelve years. By then, Sishir will be in college. Both of you are educated and give preference to education. If Sishir wants to study medicine and if he doesn't get admission even with merit, then what will you do? You must realize that the days when only merit and talent were respected are gone. Today, the competition is high and there are reservations in every field. As a good friend, I must tell you the facts—even if they hurt you. Look at yourselves. Sanjay, you're still running around in a scooter. Your students themselves own cars within three years of private practice and build their houses within five years. Within eight years, they have their own nursing homes. Isn't that true?'

Sanjay knew that Alex was right. Alex continued, 'Along with talent, a strong sense of practicality is essential. There's nothing wrong in earning more money. If you want to help people, keep aside a percentage of your earnings for philanthropy or treat some poor patients for free.'

Sanjay had always thought that poor patients went to government hospitals, which was why he had wanted to work in one. But listening to Alex, he realized that he could in fact help the poor through a private practice too. Alex said, 'Look at me now. I've made enough money working in the Middle East. I help our church in Panaji and Anita helps an orphanage in Mangalore. I've purchased a cashew farm for my brother. My family is happy. Money is a useful tool. It's like a knife— you can either kill a person with it or you can cut an apple. It's up to you to decide how to use it.'

Alex turned to Mridula. 'You have a permanent government job. So if Sanjay leaves his employment, life won't be difficult for you, though it may hurt while repaying your loan. But there's no gain without pain. I plan to return to India after a few years. But for now, I'm looking for a business partner. I want to make the first offer to Sanjay. I won't mind if he refuses. But I think that it's a great opportunity. I'm not saying it just because I want Sanjay. This also benefits you and your family. Think about it. Sanjay shouldn't leave his job and regret it later.'

After Alex and Anita left, Mridula asked Sanjay, 'What do you think about Alex's proposal? It's a big decision. If you aren't happy with what you're doing, then you should consider it. There are many hurdles in working for the government. Getting transferred is a big issue. I know how difficult it is to stay in Bangalore even in my job. We aren't well-connected people. My nature is different and I don't take life so seriously. But you don't share your feelings with others and you take everything earnestly. So maybe you can resign and start something of your own.'

'But Mridula, it isn't easy. Private practice doesn't mean that money will pour in immediately. It takes years to establish oneself. Until then, our only source of income will be your salary. We may not have the same enthusiasm after a few years either. Of the two of us, you'll be the person carrying the maximum load.'

'Sanjay, don't worry about me. I don't have a habit of buying things or spending too much money. Your satisfaction and joy in work is more important to me than my difficulties. I have never given private tuitions at home. But Sishir is growing up now. If needed, I can start giving tuitions at home in the evenings too.'

Sanjay was overcome with emotion. He thought, 'Mridula's from a better family than mine. She's good-looking and could have married anybody. By marrying me, she knew that she would lead a middle-class life, but she was still happy. Her cousin Sarla is financially much better off than us. But money has never been important to Mridula. If it was, then she wouldn't have married me.'

Yet, Sanjay was hesitant to start his own practice. He told Mridula, 'Give me some time to decide.'

15

Disillusionment

There were numerous changes in the hospital. Dr Saroja had become the new head of the department. She gave a speech when she came on board, in which she said, 'I need to improve my department. This department should be vibrant with enthusiasm. Energetic and dynamic people will get priority.' Sanjay was known to be loyal to Dr Kamala and Dr Saroja did not like her. Moreover, Dr Saroja thought that Sanjay was not dynamic. So he was sidelined at work.

During Dr Kamala's tenure, there had been a set of strict rules to be followed. Every assistant doctor had to take a night shift and no doctor would get the night shift more than once a week; everybody had at least one Sunday off every month; and nobody could take their consultation fees from the donation money reserved for the poor—that money was used only for procuring blood for the poor.

During Dr Saroja's tenure, things started changing. Sanjay got two night shifts per week and he was the only one on duty every Sunday. When he asked Dr Saroja about this, she smiled and said sweetly, 'Oh Sanjay, you're honest. I have great respect for you. If I give Sunday shifts to someone else, they may make money under the table since there's no one to monitor them that day.'

Sanjay knew that this was just an excuse but did not know how to respond or argue with her; he continued to perform his duties sincerely.

One day, after his night shift, Sanjay was about to go home. Dr Saroja was on her rounds. She was talking to her assistant loudly about her connections. As soon as she saw Sanjay from a distance, she signalled him to come and talk to her. She said, 'Two patients are in the labour rooms. They're related to some VIPs and are important. They may have delivered by now. The junior doctors are attending to them. There's no problem but I want you to check in on both of them. Let me know if you think there's going to be an issue. You can go home later.'

Dr Saroja knew that Sanjay was a sincere doctor and that she could depend on him. When Sanjay went to see the patients, he found that both of them had delivered. There were two junior doctors sitting there—a young boy and a young girl. They were sitting with their heads close together and talking softly. It was obvious that they were in a romantic relationship. As soon as they saw Sanjay, they leapt apart. Sanjay examined both the patients. They had both had normal deliveries with no complications. There was nothing to worry about.

One patient's name was Nanjamma and her husband was a gardener in a minister's home. The other patient was called Kempunanjamma and her husband was a cook in another minister's home. So they were both VIP-recommended. Kempunanjamma's husband, the cook, arrogantly told Sanjay, 'Please look after my wife well. Otherwise, I'll complain to the minister. Then he himself will come and give you a piece of his mind.'

Sanjay got upset. After all, he was a well-qualified and experienced doctor. He replied, 'What do you mean? We look after all our patients here. Your wife has had a normal delivery and there's no need for any medicine to be given to her. You can call anyone else in the hospital. The treatment will be the same.'

The cook was offended. Sanjay ignored him and reported back to Dr Saroja. He told her that everything was fine. Then he left the hospital.

After three days, Dr Saroja saw Sanjay passing in front of her room. She yelled, 'Sanjay, come here. I thought that you were a responsible doctor. I'm terribly disappointed in you. You've spoilt a VIP case.'

Sanjay did not understand. The hospital got VIP cases every day. 'Which case are you referring to, madam?' he asked politely.

'Kempunanjamma's case.'

Sanjay thought, 'That's not my case. That's her case.' He said to Dr Saroja, 'But both the patients were fine.'

'They may be fine, but I'm unwell because of them.'

'What happened?'

'Didn't you read today's newspaper? Kempunanjamma's husband told the media that their child got switched at birth. Even the Health minister phoned me.'

Dr Saroja's phone rang. She did not want Sanjay to listen to her conversation and signalled him to leave. Sanjay came out of the room; he was confused. The labour room ayah Mariamma followed him. She said, 'Doctor, it isn't your fault. Dr Saroja wants to blame you for someone else's error. The babies haven't been switched. The truth is that one of the babies fell sick and died. The dead baby is a girl. The mother of the baby boy is Nanjamma. She had seen her son as soon as he was born and knew that she had given birth to a boy. However, Kempunanjamma's chart is wrong—the young doctors on duty wrote the incorrect gender on her chart. She had given birth to a girl child but the chart incorrectly says that the baby was a boy. So she alleged that the boy baby was hers. That's why there is a fight for the boy now. This is the mistake of the young doctors who spent most of the time looking at each other instead of correctly filling out the charts. It isn't yours. Dr Saroja is their supervisor and she's to blame.'

Sanjay realized that Mariamma was telling the truth. He thought, 'Nobody can switch babies easily. It's a big offence and everybody knows it. As soon as a baby is born, it's kept next to its mother. Forty years ago, every newborn was taken for a bath immediately after its birth. At that time, that baby's hand was tagged with the mother's name and the height and gender of the baby were noted. Today, that procedure has disappeared because of the shortage of water . . . Why am I being pulled into this controversy? I haven't taken care of the two deliveries nor have I filled out the charts.'

Dr Saroja called out to him again and asked him to step into her office. She said, 'Sanjay, there may be an inquiry into the matter tomorrow. You must be careful.'

'Madam, how am I connected to this?'

'You were the senior doctor. You managed the deliveries.'

'No, I didn't manage them. I only checked their health once after you asked me to. The shift doctors were the ones who filled out the charts.'

'But the shift doctors are juniors. Wasn't it your responsibility to check what they had written?'

Sanjay was really upset now. He quietly said, 'No, madam. The duty doctors are postgraduate students. The standard rule is that the doctor who delivers should fill out the chart. Why would I not follow the standard rule? After all, I'm only an ordinary lecturer. I know my limitations.'

Saroja became livid. 'Dr Sanjay, don't give me a lecture. Please remember that I'm your boss. You'll face the inquiry tomorrow.'

Dr Saroja's phone rang again and Sanjay slipped away. He was worried. He wanted to see the charts but they were not available now. He knew that it was unjust to drag him into this. He couldn't do anything because Dr Saroja was the head of the department. He felt helpless.

As he was walking away, he met Govindanna, the office superintendent. Govindanna was a shrewd manager; he was cunning but had a soft corner for Sanjay. He could not stand Dr Saroja. Govindanna and Saroja were distant relatives but, more than that, they were bitter enemies. Govindanna told Sanjay, 'I knew that you'd be the sacrificial lamb. This lady has connections everywhere.'

Sanjay worriedly said, 'Govindanna, I'm not connected to this case at all. She's dragging me into this. May I see the charts?'

Govindanna lowered his voice. 'Dr Saroja is keeping them under lock and key because they are evidence. However, I have a copy.'

Govindanna opened his steel cupboard and showed the copies to Sanjay. Sanjay recognized Dr Saroja's handwriting. She had added his name to the charts. Sanjay was shocked. 'Is this the reward for my sincerity?' he said to himself. 'Had I been making money practising in a government hospital and skipping my duties, I wouldn't have been thrown under the bus like this. Dr Lata is insincere and skips work but she keeps talking about her connections so people are scared of her. She says, "Today my daddy and I had breakfast with the Health minister," or "I was playing golf with Daddy and I met the CM there." Because of this, nobody questions her even when she comes late. There's no justice in the world.'

He asked, 'Govindanna, what will happen now?'

Govindanna was seasoned. He had handled many offices in his time and could take care of any complicated situation, by hook or by crook. He did not believe in values such as truth, sincerity and honesty. But he was good to Sanjay. He said, 'Doctor, don't get scared. Dr Saroja is feeding on your fear. Tell her that your shift was over at 8 a.m. and since the time of delivery shows 8.30 a.m., you aren't responsible since you weren't even here. Don't keep quiet. This lady can go to any extent. You can also drop big names like Dr Lata does.'

'But Govindanna, I don't know any ministers and Dr Saroja knows that.'

'In that case, say that you know the chief editor of a big newspaper. One of my cousins is a chief editor. Doctor, please remember that you don't have to be truthful in such circumstances. Nobody's going to check whether you actually know a chief editor. When the other party lies and can harm you, you needn't behave like the Buddha. Even Lord Krishna told a lie in the Mahabharata. You should know—you read much more than I do. But don't tell anyone about my advice. Give me back the copies. I'll keep them inside.'

Suddenly, they heard footsteps. Govindanna turned his back to Sanjay and started talking about the weather. Soon, Sanjay left for home with a heavy heart.

When he reached home, he found Mridula in the bedroom. She was preparing for the school's Annual Day. She had bought a lot of crêpe paper and was busy cutting it into various shapes. Sishir was sitting right next to her and helping her. When Sanjay came into the room, she wanted to talk about her work. First, she brought him coffee and said, 'Our school's Annual Day is the day after tomorrow. But tomorrow is Debate Day. The judge is Sri Dasharati, the editor of a local Kannada newspaper. I've chosen a topic for the debate—"Should a person be idealistic or not?" Do you think the topic is good for children?'

Sanjay was feeling disillusioned and said, 'I don't know.'

'I think that it's important for children to be idealistic.' Then Mridula looked at Sanjay's face. She could see that he was disturbed. She asked, 'What's the problem, Sanjay? Are you feeling unwell? Do you have a headache?'

Sanjay did not want to talk about his problem or face Mridula's questions. So he said, 'Yes, I have a headache.'

'Then please rest. It's hot outside and you must be tired. The noise and pollution may have aggravated the headache too. Sleep for an hour and you'll be all right. I'll take Sishir outside to play so that you don't get disturbed.'

She picked Sishir up, closed the bedroom door and gave Sanjay some time alone.

When Sanjay went to the hospital the next day, he was asked to meet Dr Saroja immediately. When he entered her room, Dr Saroja smiled and said, 'Sanjay, I'm glad you're here. Kempunanjamma has realized her mistake and apologized to the hospital. The entire inquiry has been closed.'

She did not apologize for her false accusations and rude behaviour the day before. She behaved as if nothing had happened.

When the list of candidates to be transferred from Bangalore appeared on the hospital noticeboard, Sanjay was surprised to see that he was first on the list. He had been transferred to Bellary. There were other people who had been in Bangalore far longer than him but they were still assigned to Bangalore. His colleague Lata has been in Bangalore for a long time but she had never been transferred. He knew that he had been reassigned because he did not have connections like Lata.

When he reached his desk, the transfer letter was lying on his table. The letter contained the sentence, 'For the benefit of the people and service towards them, you've been transferred to Bellary.'

As he was taking it all in, Dr Saroja walked into the room and said, 'Sanjay, I'm so sad. You're my right-hand man. I don't know how I'll run the department without you. But your services are needed more in Bellary. It's a beautiful place. I wish you all the best. You'll enjoy your stay there.'

Dr Saroja knew that the transfer would not be cancelled unless a bribe was paid. She herself had got her transfer cancelled the last time by paying a bribe to someone through Lata. Lata was the one who had initiated Dr Saroja's transfer to keep her in her place and had later pretended to help her by cancelling it. But Sanjay was not aware of these secrets. Before leaving, Dr Saroja said, 'You're relieved of your duties from today. Go home Sanjay, and prepare for Bellary.'

Lata also showed her sympathy: 'Sanjay, you're an honest person. Had they transferred me to Bellary, I would have gone. But the government requires your services. A sincere person like you will serve the poor people with focus. You work there for a year. After that, I'll tell my daddy to get you back to Bangalore and I'll go there instead. Mutual exchange is allowed in government service.'

Dejected, Sanjay headed home. What would they do about their apartment? Sishir was going to school in Bangalore. Mridula's job was also here. He did not know what to do.

Mridula consoled him, 'Shall we go to the minister and meet him? He should know that other people who have been in Bangalore longer than you have haven't been transferred. It's unfair.'

Sanjay had not forgotten his previous encounter at the Health Secretariat. He said, 'No, Mridula. It doesn't work that way. Moreover, we don't even know the minister. There are hundreds of people like me who want the minister's help with their problems. You have to be recommended by an MLA to meet a minister and we don't know any MLA.'

Mridula asked, 'Do you remember if any MLAs or their relatives have come to you for medical help?'

'When I deal with my patients, they are only patients to me. I don't ask who they are. I know only Chikananjappa, a clerk in the Health department.'

Mridula was good at converting every negative to a positive. That was her nature. She said, 'That's excellent. Sometimes, people in lower positions are more useful than bigger connections. Why don't you ask Chikananjappa? He may tell us how we can get to talk to the minister.'

Sanjay called up Chikananjappa and explained the situation to him. Chikananjappa said, 'Doctor, it's difficult to get an appointment with the minister at this busy time of the year. A small person like me can't help you. It's better that you go through an MLA. But don't join your work at Bellary immediately. Give yourself at least one week.'

Mridula suggested, 'Sanjay, why don't we go and visit Principal Muniyappa? I think he had told me once in passing that he knows an MLA from Kolar. He'll definitely help us if he can.'

Sanjay had had very little interaction lately with Principal Muniyappa and Kantamma. So he was hesitant, but Mridula insisted that they go.

They visited the old couple on a Friday evening. Arun and Anuradha were not at home. Kantamma welcomed them and went to the kitchen to bring them some coffee. Sanjay explained his problem to Principal Muniyappa in two sentences and then fell silent. Mridula said, 'Without an MLA's recommendation, it's difficult to get an appointment with the Health minister. We don't know any MLA. It'll be nice if you can introduce us to an MLA.'

'Mridula, I've taught many children and today, a lot of them are in high positions. But when we ask them for help, people respond differently. Some people refuse to even recognize us. Some of them say that they'll help us but they want a favour in return. Sanjay's a doctor and everyone will think that he must have made money under the table. So they'll want to extract money from you. Nobody will know that your husband is an honest doctor.'

Sanjay knew that there was truth in Muniyappa's words. Muniyappa continued, 'Even if you meet the Health minister, there's no guarantee that she'll fulfil your request. All the ministers say "yes" in front of you but they may not actually do as you ask. This is exactly the reason my son has never wanted to join any government job. He is happy with a private company.'

Kantamma brought the coffee out. Muniyappa said, 'Anyway, I do know an MLA from Kolar. Her name is Thayamma and I've taught her son. He remembers me and always thanks me for teaching him. It's quite rare for students to do that these days. I'll talk to him.'

Mridula said, 'Sir, we won't ask Thayamma to cancel the transfer; if she can only get us an appointment with the minister, it'll really help.'

After two days, Muniyappa called Mridula and confirmed an appointment with the Health minister at her house at 9 a.m. Since Sishir did not have school that day, Mridula and Sar left him at Muniyappa's house for a few hours. Then the co went for the appointment.

When they reached the Health minister's house, the that it was full of visitors and there was no place fo to sit. Somehow, they both managed to squeeze into There was an old man sitting next to them. He polit the peon, 'Is Madam at home?'

The peon said loudly and arrogantly, 'No, Madam has gone to Tumkur. She'll be back at any moment. You just sit there and wait.'

Sanjay wondered, 'Why did the Health minister give an appointment at 9 a.m. when she hasn't returned from her trip? How can she help people when she doesn't value their time?'

Everybody kept waiting. Even at noon, there was no sign of the minister.

The old man asked another peon, 'When is Madam coming?'

The peon took pity on the old man and answered, 'Madam's at home. There's a phone call from the high command and so she is busy.'

'When will she meet us?'

'Please wait. I'll let you know as soon as she gets here.'

People waiting outside in the hall felt restless. Some of them got hungry and went to have coffee and snacks at a tea shop in front of the Health minister's house. The shop was doing brisk business that day. Mridula started talking to some people around them. Sanjay felt frustrated. He said, 'Mridula, I'm going to get myself a cup of tea. Do you want anything?'

'No. You go ahead. I'll stay here. If the minister calls your name while you're out, I can go and talk to her.'

The elderly gentleman sitting next to them was listening to their conversation. He said, 'I'll also come with you.'

While walking to the tea shop, Sanjay asked him, 'You don't look like you are working for the government. Why are you here?'

'I have come to ask for help for my daughter and son-in-law. Both of them are doctors and they've been transferred elsewhere.'

Sanjay told the old man that he was there for the same purpose. The old man said, 'Oh, this is very common. Most people are here for the cancellation of their transfers.

Everybody's reasons are different. Some people lie and say that their spouse has cancer—and Bangalore has an excellent cancer hospital. They even get a false certificate. Some people are about to retire in a few years and are settled here. So they don't want to leave Bangalore. People from north Karnataka come here for five years and then they don't want to go back. Even people from different states come here and don't want to return because of the nice weather here. Everybody wants to settle down in Bangalore.'

Sanjay thought, 'That's true. Bangalore has hi-tech hospitals for cancer, heart, eyes, neurosurgery and so on. It's a good city for education too. Nobody would like to leave Bangalore.'

They bought tea and walked back. The old man wanted to talk more. He said, 'Bangalore has around fifty-three engineering colleges and ten medical colleges.'

'Do you know the minister?' Sanjay asked.

'Sort of. When the minister was young, she was a substitute teacher in our village school. Later, she got into politics and slowly went up the ladder. She is not very educated but has good experience in politics.'

'How does she manage to do her job with so little education?'

'Who says she manages? She has people under her to help manage everything. But I really appreciate her courage and aggressiveness, especially since she's a woman. She doesn't get perturbed even in stressful situations. There are many people more educated than her but they're standing in front of her in a queue to request for the cancellation of their transfers. None of them has the guts it takes to be a minister. I tell my daughter— every year this transfer epidemic affects you. Both you and your husband are doctors. Why don't you resign and start a nursing home? But they don't agree. They say that there is so much security in a government job and private practice is difficult. So they send me every time to request for a cancellation. They don't have the courage to even spread their wings.'

Sanjay thought of Alex. He was a man of courage. For a minute, Sanjay sadly wondered why he was not more like Alex.

When they got back, they saw that the crowd had increased and there was still no trace of the minister. The security man said, 'Madam has tremendous tension. So she's resting. I don't know when she'll be available.' After some time, another peon said, 'Madam is having a bath. Then she'll do her puja and have lunch.'

It was one excuse after another. One thing was certain: the Health minister was not bothered about other people's time. At 4 p.m., she finally came out. She was plump and in her mid-fifties. She was wearing an expensive silk sari and a lot of jewellery. The air-conditioning was on, but she was sweating profusely.

People crowded around her. The security men asked everyone to form a queue. Sanjay and Mridula stood at a distance. They noticed that everybody gave a written application and almost all of them were asking for cancellations or promotions. Mridula realized that if they continued standing there, nobody would see them. The Health minister may go back inside at any moment and then the whole day would be wasted. Mridula insisted that Sanjay go and give his application. By the time their turn came, the Health minister was at the end of her patience and looked tired. Without even looking at the application, she asked, 'Which MLA sent you?'

'Thayamma. She is an MLA from Kolar.'

'Tell me, what do you want?'

'I have been transferred to Bellary.'

'And you don't want to go there. Well, if nobody wants to go to Bellary, then how will our state progress? Karnataka doesn't mean that you'll only be in Bangalore. Moreover, this is a government order.'

Sanjay did not know what to say. The Health minister continued, 'You're young and energetic. At your age, there are usually no physical problems either. You should be bold and adventurous. If you were about to retire, I would have understood why you don't want to move. But it's better that you go to Bellary. Come again next year and I'll relocate you back to Bangalore. I'll also update Thayamma about our conversation.'

Her personal assistant came in with a cordless phone. The minister was happy to take the call. She took the phone and, without even turning back, went back into her house. Sanjay and Mridula did not have much choice and came out. Mridula said, 'I've talked to other people here about our situation. Most have bigger problems than ours. In government service, you can't refuse your transfer. We are young and Sishir is in a lower grade at school. Even the minister has promised us that you'll be transferred back to Bangalore next year. I can manage to stay alone with Sishir for a year. We'll try again next year.'

Mridula loved peace and did not have the capacity to bear conflicts. She believed everybody. If someone said a few nice words to her, she thought that they were genuine. As soon as she heard the minister's decision, she made up her mind to live without Sanjay for a year.

A few hours passed; Thayamma phoned the Health minister. She said, 'Madam, I've sent a candidate to you because of pressure from my son's teacher. The candidate's name is Sanjay. You can decide whatever you want to do in his case. The decision is completely yours. I don't have a personal interest in the case.'

This was politics. All MLAs gave recommendation letters but that did not mean that they actually cared. Sometimes, they themselves called and told the minister not to do the work. If the work was done successfully, then they got the credit. If it was not done, they would simply say, 'I tried my best. But nobody listens these days. Even God needs pujas and bells to remind him to do our work. A minister's job isn't easy. She gets pressure from party workers and the local and central government. That's why she has high blood pressure.'

And the drama went on. In today's politics, everything was an act but no actor was permanent. The only constants in politics were money and power. You needed money to be in power and you had to be in power to make more money. Why would anyone help Sanjay, who was never going to be in a position to return the favour?

Sanjay decided to go to Bellary for a year. The maternity hospital was in Satyanarayana Pet in Bellary. Sanjay rented a small room nearby with a kitchenette and an attached bathroom. Since he intended to stay just for a year, he did not buy many household items. Mridula continued to stay in Bangalore with Sishir. Rukuma and Bheemanna came and stayed with Mridula for fifteen days, but then they got bored. The pollution in the city did not suit them either. So they went back to Aladahalli.

On most weekends, Sanjay would come to Bangalore by the Hampi Express and go back after two days. During school holidays, Mridula and Sishir visited him in Bellary. People there were friendly and nice. Sanjay's honesty was noticed and he became popular. Sometimes, Sanjay thought, 'Why should I ask to be transferred back to Bangalore? If I tell Mridula that I want to stay here, she'll agree. But Bangalore has its own attractions. It has good colleges. People like to send their children there for education. I shouldn't make Sishir shift to Bellary. Education is much better in Bangalore.'

A few months later, the Health minister was named in a corruption case and criticized by the media, so she was replaced. The new Health minister was different—he wasn't corrupt and had entered politics with the sole intention of giving back to the country. He was in his mid-sixties and had a lot of experience. He delivered what he promised. But people still criticized him saying, 'He isn't a dynamic person.'

Meanwhile, Anita and Alex had bought an expensive penthouse near the Cantonment railway station in Bangalore.

Anita had shared the details of the transaction with Mridula but she hadn't bothered to remember them. It was a large four-bedroom apartment. Though they had relatives in Bangalore, Alex did not want to rent the place out to them. He said, 'If you rent a flat to your relatives, you lose the house as well as the relationship.' So the apartment lay vacant. Mridula went with her maid and got it cleaned every month. Despite Mridula's reluctance, Anita insisted on paying her for the cleaning expenses.

A year passed by quickly and it was time for transfers again. Sanjay went to visit the new Health minister at his residence. This time, there were fewer people in the house. Sanjay met the minister and explained his situation. The minister carefully listened to him and said, 'Doctor, I can't transfer you back to Bangalore after one year without a specific reason. People will tell you what you want to hear. But the truth is that you'll have to stay in Bellary for at least three more years. If someone has promised you a transfer to Bangalore in exchange for money, then they are lying.'

Sanjay understood. He felt like a baby who has come out of his mother's womb and cannot go back there again. He longed to be back in Bangalore. But he thanked the minister and left. By the time he reached home, his head was spinning. He remembered Chikananjappa's words: 'Unless you pay money, you won't be transferred back to Bangalore.'

Sanjay realized that it was time for him to make a decision. He thought, 'I'm not like Dr Lata or Dr Saroja. I'll never be sponsored for any programmes even if I'm eligible. I'll eternally be the department scapegoat and the first person to be thrown out of Bangalore. What have I achieved after all these years? My students themselves don't recognize me once they are out of college. My colleagues in Bombay have opened their own nursing homes. Santosh left his job in the Middle East and went to the USA after doing a computer course. Arun was a teenager when I first met him and he is now building a house in

JP Nagar. What have I done? My wife is a government servant and both of us work hard. Despite that, we had to take a loan to buy a small apartment. I'm sending money to my mother every month too. I haven't saved any money.'

Then he thought of Shankar. 'Shankar is courageous. He's bought a site in Mysore and is running a company in his wife's name. Most of my family looks down on me because I haven't earned enough money.'

When Dr Kamala was about to retire, she had told him, 'Sanjay, times have changed. Now, we have to keep the consumer act in mind. Gone are the days when we used to take decisions on behalf of the patient. Today, the patients can sue us to get money. Even students have changed. They're more interested in knowing how to get more marks with minimal studying. I can't adjust to this new environment. You can either take voluntary retirement or you can adapt yourself to the new system.'

Now, Sanjay could relate to her words. He thought, 'Mridula is no problem. She'll support me in any decision I make. This time, the decision is completely mine.'

Then, he recollected what Alex had said: 'It's better to get out of the system and fight than stay in the system and struggle.'

He called Alex.

16

The Decision

Alex came to visit from the Middle East that week. He had decided to settle in India. Anita was moving back first and Alex would join her later. At dinner, Alex said, 'Mridula, you should take the initiative this time. Convince your husband to do something on his own.'

For the first time, Sanjay interrupted him, 'Alex, it's our decision and not just mine. I'm ready to quit government service but I want to understand the struggles of starting a private practice.'

'Sanjay, you can't become rich overnight. Most people start fighting when the money starts rolling in. So we must be careful if we become partners—we must keep an account of every rupee. That's the secret of a long-lasting partnership and friendship.'

'Where do you think we should open the nursing home?'

'It should be in a crowded area. We must keep it neat and clean. And we'll need to invest twenty-five lakh each to start.'

'That's a lot of money!' Mridula got scared.

'Don't worry, Mridula. You can get a loan for fifteen lakh. That way, you'll need to put in only ten. We can divide the work into two streams—technical and administrative. I'll look after the administrative side and Sanjay can take care of the clinical part. Both of us will draw a salary of ten thousand in the beginning. I have a building in mind.'

'Where?'

'On Bannerghatta Main Road. We can see it tomorrow. The area is good. The building has two floors and we can rent it.' Alex looked at Sanjay and continued, 'Sanjay, you'll have to buy a car. Even if it means that you have to take a loan. If you come on your scooter, people will think that you have less knowledge and experience. I want to tell you something more but I'm a little hesitant.'

Sanjay said, 'Tell me, Alex. What is it?'

'With your immense knowledge, you don't have much to learn. Still, you should go to England for at least six months and then work in the Middle East for another six. If people know that you've studied and worked abroad, then you'll get more respect.'

'But I don't have the money to go to England.'

'That's why I suggested the Middle East. I can arrange everything for you. Male gynaecologists are not allowed there. So I'll arrange for you to work as a general practitioner. Please don't feel bad. These moves are essential.'

Alex stood up and was about to leave. Then he turned around and said, 'I can help you financially, Sanjay, but that won't be right if we're going to become partners. It can lead to misunderstandings later. I know that you'll understand.'

After Alex left, Sanjay started getting worried about the pace at which his life was changing. Mridula was also concerned. Life was about to become stressful. Till now, it had been flowing smoothly like a quiet river. But now, there would be waterfalls and whirlpools that they would have to weather.

Mridula was confident. She said, 'Sanjay, don't worry. It's better to be out of the frying pan. Alex is with you and I support you. Even if you don't earn anything, I can manage. We have our house and I have a steady government salary. It'll be enough for the three of us.'

'Mridula, there are still a lot of loans to be repaid.'

'Sanjay, I have gold jewellery that my parents gave me during our wedding. I don't wear much gold anyway. I can sell it. I'll ask Appa for some money too. We can borrow the remaining amount from a bank. But we won't take any money from Alex.'

'But Mridula, all this will be really inconvenient for you.'

'I don't mind. As long as you earn money legally and ethically, I'm with you. I'll help you in your struggle. You can earn money illegally too, but I'll never approve of that.'

'Mridula, should we ask Amma?'

'Please don't.'

Mridula did not say why, but Sanjay knew. Ratnamma liked Mridula but she did not give them any money even for festivals or occasions. She sent her blessings but not money. They could not ask Shankar either because Lakshmi and he were spendthrifts. Ratnamma regularly complained to Mridula about Lakshmi's spending habits.

Mridula had never asked her father for anything since she got married. Every year, her parents gave her a gift and she was happy with that. Now, she had no choice. She thought that it was better to ask for money from her father than from Sanjay's family. So she decided to visit her parents.

When she phoned her father to inform him that she was coming alone, Bheemanna found it a little strange. But he did not ask any questions. Usually, whenever Mridula visited her family, she went with Sishir and Sanjay. Sanjay spent most of his time in Aladahalli reading or sleeping. He hardly talked to anyone. Now, she was going to Aladahalli alone for the first time after ten years of marriage.

When Mridula entered the house, she realized that the family home had gradually changed a lot in the last decade. When Mridula was a young girl, they had an embroidered tablecloth, a painting that she had made, an old radio and other things. Today, the old things had disappeared. The dining table had a glass top and the gadgets in the house included a Siemens phone, a fifty-one-centimetre television and the latest Sony music system. The garden had also changed. There were no jasmine creepers any more. Instead, there were wood roses and croton flowers. However, the kitchen remained almost the same and Rukuma was still in charge of it.

Everybody welcomed Mridula lovingly. Only Vatsala did not greet her or smile at her. Mridula thought of Lakshmi. Lakshmi always smiled at her and invited her in pleasantly. After lunch, Mridula decided to talk to everybody, including Vatsala. She said, 'Can all of you please come and sit down? I want to discuss something important.'

Vatsala replied sarcastically, 'I don't have any authority in this house. After all, I'm an outsider. You can discuss whatever you want with your brother and parents.'

Mridula was hurt. How could she ask for money if someone was unhappy with her before she had even initiated the discussion? She said calmly, 'To be honest, I'm the outsider now. You're the one who takes care of my parents. Please come.'

Vatsala shook her head and walked away to her bedroom. But she stood by the door to listen to the conversation.

Mridula turned to her parents and her brother and said, 'Sanjay wants to start a private nursing home and we have to chip in twenty-five lakh. We're already taking a loan of fifteen lakh from the bank. But we don't have enough savings. If you give us a loan of five lakh, we'll return it within three or four years with interest. I don't know anyone else whom I can ask. Please know that even if you don't give us the money, I won't be upset. I understand that you may have problems too. My relationship with you won't change.'

Vatsala was livid when she heard Mridula.

Meanwhile, Krishna was silent. Rukuma looked at Bheemanna and said, 'Five lakh is a lot of money. These days, things aren't going smoothly for us. Sometimes, there's no rainfall and then there's no profit. Our tractor is old and has to be replaced. Besides, Vatsala wants us to buy a house in Hubli.'

Mridula sensed that Bheemanna was wondering what they should do. She wanted to give her family time to talk about the matter. So she said, 'I'll visit Champakka for a few hours.'

As she walked over to Champakka's house, Mridula thought about the village school. She had seen the change in the village too. Everybody thought like Vatsala now. They wanted their children to study in Hubli or Dharwad so that they could learn English and get admission in better colleges later. Only people who could not afford to send their children to Hubli or Dharwad sent them to the local school in Aladahalli. Good teachers took transfers to city schools. Nobody thought of the school as an asset to the village. The school had become an orphan.

Champakka was ecstatic to see Mridula. She had become very old but her mind was as sharp as ever. Champakka said, 'Mridula, I thought you had forgotten Aladahalli and that you don't go out of Bangalore any more. You used to love this village. How can you live in the city? It's crowded and people are indifferent there.'

Mridula knew that Champakka was not serious, so she did not even answer her. She noticed that Champakka had developed a hunch. Champakka continued, 'Mridula, I don't have the energy to walk today. Yesterday, I made special laddoos for you after your father told me that you were coming. Take them from that *dabba*. Don't sit on the floor. It's cold today. Take a mat and sit on it.'

Out of habit, Mridula peeped at Champakka's garden. Then she brought the laddoos and sat in front of Champakka. She asked, 'Champakka, what happened to your garden? It's full of weeds. All the colourful flowers are gone. Only the mehendi tree is still blooming.'

'Don't talk about the garden, Mridula. It hurts me. After you got married and went away, no one cared for it any more. You used to tend to it like it was your own child. But your sister-in-law Vatsala doesn't bother. Do you know what she said to me?' Mridula did not reply but Champakka continued, 'She said that she wasn't my servant to look after my garden and that I should keep a servant for a hundred rupees who can clean and water it. Vatsala prefers to buy the kakada flowers from the Hubli market. She keeps them in the fridge so that she can use them for days. She doesn't want to work in the garden and grow fresh flowers. She's lazy.'

Somehow, Champakka and Vatsala had become enemies. Mridula knew that Champakka was soft at heart and forgave easily. But Vatsala was different. Mridula did not want to talk about her and changed the topic. She asked, 'Aunty, who tends to your garden now?'

'Peerambi. But she has a lot of work at home. She takes care of the garden as often as she can. She's fond of mehendi. That's why the mehendi tree is taken care of very well. She takes flowers to the Hanuman temple every day. Mridula, you used to make such beautiful mehendi designs. There was no bride in the village who didn't have your mehendi on her hands.'

Mridula remembered Surekha's wedding and the way she had met Sanjay. The memory made her happy and she forgot about Vatsala. Champakka asked her, 'Why have you come alone? Is everything all right?'

Mridula told her everything. Champakka commented, 'They won't give you money. Your sister-in-law will ensure it. Peerambi told me that Vatsala has already booked a two-bedroom flat in Hubli for eight lakh.'

In Aladahalli, Peerambi and Bheemanna were like All India Radio. Nothing remained a secret. Champakka lowered her voice and said, 'I hear that there's a new law that gives married daughters entitlement to their parents' property. Use the information and scare your sister-in-law to get your money.'

'Champakka, I don't want a single rupee using legal rights. I want my brother's family to live happily and prosper. My mother used to pray to God for her brother and she has taught me to do the same. When we start talking about legal rights, I may get the money but I'll lose the relationship. I care more about the relationship with my brother and my parents.'

Champakka smiled and nodded in approval.

After Mridula came out of Champakka's house, she did not go home. She went instead to the Hanuman temple and sat on the swing there. The cool breeze from the lake made her joyful. She started singing. She had her parents, a brother, a son and a husband, but more than anything else, just being in Aladahalli gave her enormous happiness.

It was Ugadi time, in the month of February or March. Summer had just arrived. The mango trees sported soft reddish-green leaves and the cuckoos were making lovely coo-coo sounds. Everyone in the village was busy preparing for the festival. Yet, there was a pin-drop silence near the temple.

But for Mridula, nothing mattered. She was swinging without any bondage and with a free mind. From the swing, she could see her house. She was happy.

Mridula was not like everybody, she was different. She had enormous enthusiasm for life and unlimited energy for reading, cooking and sketching. She wanted to spend every minute of the day fruitfully. It seemed that the sun rose for her and the rainbow colours were meant only for her. Every day was to be lived to its fullest and every beautiful minute to be enjoyed.

After dinner, Bheemanna called Mridula to his side and said, 'Mridula, you're our daughter. We can't give you a loan. Your mother and I thought about it. We want to give you three lakh with our blessings. You'll prosper with this money.'

Krishna and Vatsala peeped out from their room and listened to every word.

Mridula had tears in her eyes. Her parents had kept this money for their old age. They did not want to upset their daughter-in-law, so they must have taken the money out from their emergency fund. Mridula said, 'Appa, you're very generous. But I feel odd taking money from you. You don't have to gift me such a huge amount. I want to return this money later.'

'Mridula, let's not talk about it. Rukuma, bring kumkum and give it to Mridula along with this cheque. Well, I have things to do. Mulla Sabi is unwell. He had gone to Hubli today for a detailed health check-up and I want to know the results.'

Bheemanna walked out of the house, smiling at Mridula.

17

The Beginning of the End

Four years passed.

There were quite a few changes in Mridula's life. She had become the principal of Vijayanagar High School. Sanjay and Alex had started the Sushruta Nursing Home. Mridula also worked hard and helped to get the nursing home up and running. She had mortgaged her wedding jewellery to invest in the nursing home. When they started the nursing home, Anita was new to Bangalore and did not know much. So Mridula got things done from the carpenter, the dhobi, the tailor and other people. Though Alex was supposed to look after the administration, he was busy searching for another site for the nursing home. So Mridula even did all the bank work and took care of the income tax formalities too. The nursing home became popular quite quickly.

During a visit to T. Narasipura, Ratnamma's sharp eyes immediately noticed that her daughter-in-law was not wearing any ornaments. She asked Mridula, 'What happened to your jewellery?'

Mridula told her that she had mortgaged her jewellery. Ratnamma advised her to get it back as soon as they could but did not offer to help. She simply said, 'Your father has given you pure-gold ornaments. Experience has shown me that once people mortgage gold, they usually don't get it back. Instead, they sell it off. Don't do that.'

After Sanjay and Mridula made some money from the nursing home, they paid off the mortgage and got the jewellery back.

The nursing home did well and money started to come in. Sanjay felt happy and confident about his work. Now, he drove a car and Mridula owned a Kinetic Honda scooter. She had repaid the loan for their home but they had not moved out of the apartment. Mridula wanted to build a house in Jayanagar or JP Nagar but they did not have that much money yet. She was aware that Sishir would go to college in a few years and then they would need money for his education. So she did not want to spend all their money on a new home. Mridula took care of their finances and Sanjay insisted that she operate all the bank accounts and keep control. She continued to give Sanjay pocket money.

Meanwhile, Anita and Alex remained regular visitors to Sanjay and Mridula's home. Alex had initiated a new venture in the Middle East and so he travelled a lot, while Anita loved living in Bangalore. She joined the church choir. Her daughter, Julie, went to Baldwin Girls' High School on Richmond Road.

Anita hired a girl named Maggie from Mangalore to work for her. Maggie had studied till high school and was usually well dressed and presentable. Sometimes, she looked even better than Anita. Maggie was the eldest of five daughters in her family and she had taken up the job due to financial reasons; she stayed in Anita's house. Anita treated her well and opened a bank account for her so that she could deposit her salary and start saving money. Maggie and Anita got along well with each other and they were happy.

Sanjay now understood how a private nursing home worked. It was not just about giving the best treatment. It was about cleanliness, talking politely and inspiring confidence in patients. When Alex had told him about it before, Sanjay had not taken him seriously. But now, he realized the importance of Alex's words. In government hospitals, the treatment of the patient was the only essential thing. Assistant doctors did everything else. In private practice, however, the doctors had to closely watch and take care of everything. If a patient died due to any reason, the hospital's reputation immediately got affected. Sanjay learnt that once a nursing home became famous, patients would automatically come to their door. But he had to be careful to protect the nursing home's name.

Shankar had been transferred to Mysore and had built a big house there. Mridula had gone to Lakshmi and Shankar's house-warming. Ever since Sanjay had started his private practice, he hardly went anywhere because he was so busy. He did not have anything to say about what gift should be given to Lakshmi at her house-warming. Everything at home was decided by Mridula. Lakshmi's house was beautiful. It had four bedrooms, an Italian kitchen and marble floors. Lakshmi had spent twenty-five thousand rupees on flower decorations alone for the house-warming. Mridula gifted her a silk sari and gave Shankar a silver bowl. But Lakshmi's return gift was better than her gifts. Ratnamma came to the house-warming at lunchtime and did not give any gifts; she did not understand why two gifts should be given from the same family. A few months later, Shankar took voluntary retirement and fully involved himself in the business in Lakshmi's name.

After a year of no contact, Lakshmi came to visit Sanjay and Mridula from Mysore. It was Sunday and Mridula was at home. Sanjay was in the nursing home. Mridula was surprised to see Lakshmi. Usually, she was dressed well even at home but today, she was wearing a cheap sari and looked rather unhappy. Mridula said, 'Akka, come inside. When did you come from Mysore?'

'I took the 6 a.m. bus.'

Mridula was surprised to hear that Lakshmi had come by bus. She said, 'Freshen up and have breakfast first. Then we'll talk.'

Lakshmi went to take a bath. She entertained guests very well and Mridula wanted to reciprocate. But today, things were different. Mridula understood that Lakshmi had a problem and she wanted to help. Even though they were not rich, their financial position was better than before. Lakshmi had never asked for help from her brother before this.

Lakshmi finished her bath and gave a basket to Mridula. It had brinjals, Mysore jasmine flowers and bananas. Mridula asked affectionately, 'Akka, why did you bring me all this? Tell me, how are you?'

Lakshmi started crying. Sobbing, she said, 'Mridula, my husband got some money after his voluntary retirement and we used that money to take a loan and invested it in the business. At the time, our hotel business was doing very well. But our business partner cheated us. We are innocent people and we believed him. We even mortgaged our new house to expand the business. Now, we are incurring heavy losses and are in a financial mess. We have lost our house and our business.'

'Akka, Shankar's brothers are in Mysore with you. Aren't they helping you?'

'They are of no use. We are facing tough times and instead of helping, they're refusing to talk to us. Not only that, but they also make fun of us. We've lost everything. Anil is a young boy and he can't help his father yet.'

Mridula was taken aback. Sanjay and she had just finished repaying their loan and it was beyond their capacity to help Lakshmi much. She felt sorry for her. She asked Lakshmi, 'How much money do you need to come out of this?'

'About thirty lakh.'

'Stay here for a few days. I'll talk to Sanjay about this. He'll be back for lunch.'

'No, Mridula, I can't stay that long. I have to go and meet a friend in Rajajinagar now. He has taken a loan from us and is yet to return it. I'll be back at night.'

Lakshmi ate her breakfast and left for the day. Mridula was worried. She felt like she herself had a problem.

When Sanjay came back early from the nursing home, Mridula was surprised. She asked, 'How did you manage to come back early today?'

'Rosemary is now managing a lot of the work. So I can take some time off from my administrative duties.'

When they had first started the nursing home, Sanjay had found it awkward to ask for consultation fees since there were no such fees in a government hospital. Alex had sat down with Sanjay and persuaded him to start charging for his work. He had helped him decide the fees for consultations, normal deliveries, C-sections, tube testing and other procedures.

Some smart patients would say, 'Doctor, we don't have money to pay you today. Can we pay on our next visit?'

Sanjay could never refuse and then he would forget all about it. When the patients came in the next time, he would not remember to charge them for their previous visit and the patients never paid on their own. So the nursing home's income suffered. After a few months, Alex had told Sanjay, 'You can't conduct business in this way. I'm travelling frequently on business trips and can't be here to track such patients down. Let's hire a smart secretary. We'll pay her three thousand rupees a month. She can sit at a table outside your office and ask for money without hesitation.'

Sanjay had agreed with a sigh of relief. He never liked asking patients for money. That was how Rosemary had been employed. Alex had known her family for a long time. She had a bachelor's degree in science and came from a poor family. She would not have been able to complete her graduation without the church's help. After graduation, she had started a two-year nursing course. But her father had died when she was in the first year. Rosemary did not have any other choice but to discontinue her studies and find a job so that she could take care of her family. Alex had hired her and arranged for her to stay on the first floor of the nursing home. Over the years, Rosemary had worked her way up to head nurse.

Now, she managed all accounts very well. With her intelligence and honesty, she would have made an excellent doctor.

Mridula explained Lakshmi's problem to Sanjay but he did not say anything. Then he got called for an emergency at the nursing home and left. Mridula decided to call her mother-in-law. Sanjay and Mridula sent her money every month but Ratnamma still did not have a phone in her house. Sanjay did not tell his mother to get a phone either. Nobody knew where the money went, and they could not ask her. Though Ratnamma had no phone, the shop next to hers had one, and the people there were nice enough to call her whenever she got a phone call.

Mridula phoned her mother-in-law and said, 'Amma, Akka has come here. She's facing tough times and needs thirty lakh.'

Mridula told Ratnamma about Lakshmi's visit. There was silence at the other end. Mridula thought that the line may have been disconnected. She said, 'Hello, hello, Amma, can you hear me?'

'I can hear you, Mridula. But what are you talking about? She came here just yesterday and yes, she told me that she didn't have any money. But she didn't mention the thirty lakh. Ever since she got married, I've told her to reduce her expenses and not to worry about status. But she doesn't listen to me. Anyway, you decide if you want to help her or not. I don't want to interfere.'

Ratnamma kept the phone down. Mridula found it strange that Lakshmi had visited her mother's house the day before but had not told her. She felt sorry that Lakshmi and Shankar would have to sell their new home.

When Sanjay came back from the nursing home, Mridula found that he felt the same way as his mother did. He said, 'If I help Lakshmi financially, it's of no use because Shankar and she are addicted to spending more than they earn. But because she's my sister, I have to do something for her.'

'Sanjay, we should decide what help we can give Lakshmi before she comes back.'

'Mridula, we don't have that kind of money. I've lived in their house for two years and seen how they live. They show off too much. I don't want to give them a loan because they'll never return it. If Shankar agrees, I can give him a job at the nursing home with a monthly salary. But they must stay separately and not in our house. I can't help them more than this. That's my final say.'

Mridula kept quiet. She was upset because Sanjay had not asked her for her opinion and had made a unilateral decision. For the first time, she felt uneasy in her marriage. It was not wise to bring a person like Shankar into their nursing home and expose their finances to a relative. Moreover, if they started staying in the same city, then it may lead to misunderstandings later. Mridula retreated to the kitchen and started cooking so that she did not have to think about it any more.

18

Money Brings Changes

Fourteen years had passed since the nursing home had been started and Sushruta Nursing Home had now become one of the leading maternity homes in Bangalore. Many people had written Sanjay off before but now, he had become a role model. He had progressed in leaps and bounds, amassed a fortune and made a name for himself.

Anita and Alex had shifted to a home in Palace Orchards in Bangalore; Julie was in her final year in high school. Maggie had got married to Joseph who had started working as Anita's driver. Anita and Alex had given them separate quarters.

Mridula and Sanjay had sold their Vijayanagar house and were now living in a beautiful four-bedroom house in JP Nagar. They had three cars. Mridula continued to work and had become principal of a high school in Jayanagar. Sishir was now in medical college and had a large circle of friends. He was intelligent but stubborn, and pampered by his father. Their driver, Nanja, and his wife, Chikki, worked for them. Mridula helped them to buy a house in Puttenahalli. The cook, Sakamma, came every day at 6 a.m. and left at 10 p.m. The three servants were honest. Mridula did not want to keep a stay-at-home servant.

Sometimes, Sanjay made fun of her job. He said, 'Mridula, why do you still work? I spend more money than you earn on our cars, cook and driver. If you stay at home, it'll be cheaper for us!'

'That's impossible. You were able to start the hospital because of my salary. My pay has helped me in our difficult times and I enjoy and respect my work. I'll never leave it. It is oxygen to me and not just a source of income.'

Things had changed a lot in Aladahalli too. Rukuma Bai and Champakka were no longer alive. Krishna stayed in Hubli with his family and Bheemanna was left all alone. Krishna visited his father twice a month but Bheemanna was not doing well health-wise. The yield from the fields was not good either because there was nobody to till them. The villagers did not want to work there and preferred to go to work in the garment factory on the outskirts of Hubli, even if they got paid less. They looked down upon working in the fields.

Champakka had willed all her property to Chandrakant Jog. When she died, Chandrakant came to Aladahalli, but he was not interested in the land because he was settled in Bombay. As he was leaving, he told Bheemanna, 'Sell this property to good people. I don't mind if they buy it at lesser than market value. I want to use that money to renovate the Hanuman temple.'

There were many contenders for the house because of its good location. The rich Basavantappa Patil wanted to buy the house but Bheemanna rejected the offer on moral grounds. He thought, 'Basavantappa and his friends will use the house for playing cards and other such activities. I don't want Champakka's house to be used like that. Her soul won't rest in peace.'

One day, Sanjay had gone for a minister's daughter's wedding. As he was about to make his exit, he ran into his ex-colleague Dr Lata. She seemed happy to meet him and wanted to talk to him. She said, 'Sanjay, how are you? Do you remember me? We're seeing each other after at least ten years.'

'I'm fine.' Sanjay did not want to talk about the past and fell silent.

'Sanjay, I can't believe the way you've grown. Just the other day, I was attending a seminar where you were presenting a paper. Your presentation was absolutely fascinating. I wanted to congratulate you but there were so many people around you that I didn't get a chance.'

Sanjay sponsored and attended medical seminars since they helped advertise the nursing home and him. He usually attended them for just ten minutes—either at the beginning or at the end. His talks were short and powerful. Hence, he was quite popular. Sanjay tried to change the subject: 'You must have become a professor by now.'

'No, not yet. It isn't easy in government service. You're lucky. Your name is famous in Bangalore. I've heard that people wait for as long as two months to get an appointment with you.'

Sanjay knew that she was exaggerating. He said, 'Maybe, I don't know. My three secretaries manage my appointments.'

Sanjay remembered how Lata had used her father's connections at work and asked her, 'Tell me, is your father still working?'

She said sadly, 'Oh, he retired a long time ago.'

'Where all have you been transferred to till now?'

'Once to Mysore and once to Hubli.'

'You must not have liked leaving Bangalore.'

'I had no choice in the matter. I would have had to quit this easy job if I didn't go. But you don't have transfer troubles like us.'

'Yes, that's because I didn't have a godfather to protect me. I had to stand on my own. That's how I learnt to take calculated risks and become successful. I have to go now. See you, Lata.'

Lata wanted to talk some more but Sanjay turned around and left. It was the same Lata who had played games with him during his transfer and Sushma's delivery. Lata used to make fun of his honesty and sincerity. Now, she wanted to talk to him, but he was not interested. He had seen and learnt many things in the last fourteen years on the path to success.

A senior gynaecologist in Bangalore, Dr Rao, owned a big nursing home in an expensive neighbourhood but his son chose to work for a software company. So Dr Rao decided to sell his practice. By then, Sanjay and Alex had made enough money to buy the nursing home.

Sanjay had no hesitation in taking a loan. He had taken several loans in the past, and expanded the nursing home and acquired the most modern equipment. Repeated success had made him confident. Though Alex was Sanjay's partner, he rarely came to the nursing home. He was busy establishing new pharmaceutical companies on the outskirts of Bangalore. But the two of them split the profits and did not have any problems. Their friendship remained the same.

Shankar lived in Malleshwaram now. Sanjay monitored him closely, so Shankar worked diligently at the nursing home. His son, Anil, had taken many years to complete his bachelor's degree in commerce and was now working in Alex's pharmaceutical company's sales department.

Sanjay had learnt a lot—things that one can never learn from any management book. When he was a child, he had been fascinated by his father's words but with experience, he had developed his own philosophy about running a business. This philosophy contradicted everything that he had learnt from his father. People who came to private hospitals were different from those who visited government hospitals. Affordability was a major factor. Every patient had their weakness and Sanjay knew that their weakness was his strength.

When Sanjay and Alex had first started the nursing home, Sanjay's initial consultation fee was fifty rupees. One day, he overheard a conversation between two patients. One of them said, 'SRK Nursing Home is very good. Their doctor is excellent.'

'Why do you say that?'

'The doctor there charges one hundred and fifty rupees per consultation and you have to wait for appointments. The doctor is always busy. He spends just fifteen minutes with every patient.'

Sanjay figured that if he took more money and said that there was a long waiting time to get an appointment, people would think that he was a better doctor. The very next day, Sanjay increased his fee to a hundred rupees—and just as he'd expected, the number of his patients also increased at once. He decided to revise his consultation fees every year. But he spent more time with his patients and that made him popular.

When Sanjay was teaching at the government medical college, he used to tell his students, 'A normal delivery is the best. That's how nature wants it. We should do a C-section only if there's a problem. Don't listen to the patient or ask if they have a preference. Decide using your expertise and skill.'

Years later, after starting a private practice, Sanjay had changed his stance. VIPs preferred a C-section. Now, Bangalore had many software companies and young engineers earned at least fifty thousand rupees a month. So when they came to a maternity home, they did not mind spending more, but they expected a five-star facility and Sanjay's nursing home catered to them.

Sanjay had also learnt a lot about money management. Every patient did not pay by cheque; many businessmen paid in cash. Sanjay figured that he did not need to declare all his earnings to the Income Tax department. So he had black money as well as white. Shankar was good at handling this. He was strictly instructed not to talk about money matters at home or outside and was paid handsomely for his discretion. Shankar ensured that only the white money went to the bank. Sanjay also had a share in Alex's new factory. Black money was used to buy the site and get the factory up and running. All bribes were paid using black money. Mridula was unaware of this and Sanjay did not want to tell her. She kept track of the money in the bank.

Sanjay knew that if Mridula learnt about the black money, she would oppose it and say that it was immoral. Besides, she could not keep a secret and shared everything with Anita. Sanjay did not know if Anita was aware of the black money. Even though Alex and he were good friends, they did not discuss personal matters. Sanjay wondered why some women shared all their secrets with other women. His mother and sister were not like that. But there was nothing called privacy for a simple girl from Aladahalli like Mridula.

One day, Sanjay told Alex, 'We don't value what nature gives us for free. We whine about the rainy season, but in the Middle East, there are people who have never seen rains. Why don't we introduce a monsoon package? We can advertise it in the papers in the Middle East. People with small and not-so-serious ailments can come to India in the monsoon, see the rains, shop, visit the forests and take medical treatment in our nursing home. We can make loads of money.'

Alex was surprised at how Sanjay converted every idea now into a moneymaking scheme. He sometimes wondered whether he was the same old Sanjay who once felt too shy to even ask for a consultation fee. Time could change anybody.

A few days later, Sanjay decided to buy a Mercedes-Benz, but Mridula opposed it. She said, 'Let's not form unnecessary and expensive habits.'

'Mridula, I have earned money with my hard work. When I didn't have money, I rode a scooter. Now, I want a Mercedes. Please don't try to stop me.' Sanjay kept pressurizing Mridula with such words until she accepted his decision.

One afternoon, Anita came to Mridula's home. She was looking stressed. Mridula kept her hand on Anita's shoulder and asked, 'Anita, what's wrong?'

Anita ran into Mridula's bedroom. Mridula followed her and Anita closed the door. Then she started crying. Mridula got worried. She asked, 'Is Julie all right?'

'Yes.'

'Did Alex say something?'

'No.'

'Is everybody okay in Goa and Mangalore?'

'Yes.'

Mridula did not know what else to ask. After some time, Anita stopped crying and said quietly, 'Mridula, I want to tell you something personal. But promise me that you'll keep it to yourself.'

'Of course, Anita.'

'You know that I went with Julie to my cousin's wedding in Mangalore.'

'Yes, you had invited me too but I couldn't go.'

'Alex did not come for the wedding because he's busy with the new factory.'

'But that's okay, Anita.'

'I know that it is. But when I came back from there, I wanted to have a bath—you know where my bedroom is.'

Mridula knew Anita's house very well—she had stayed there several times. Anita's heart was in her house. She spent all her days decorating and cleaning her house. Anita's bedroom was large and had a huge bathroom with a marble tub. She also had a big dressing table.

Anita continued, 'I was hot and went to the bathroom to have a bath. After that, I wanted to comb my hair and I pulled open the dressing-table drawer to take the hairbrush out. But by mistake, I pulled out Alex's drawer. Do you know what I found?'

Anita started crying again. Sobbing, she said, 'Condoms.'

'I don't understand. What's wrong with that?'

'Mridula, don't be stupid. We don't use them. Moreover, for the last two months, I've been bleeding continuously and Sanjay has been treating me. Didn't he tell you?'

'No, he didn't. Sanjay doesn't tell me anything about his patients and I respect that.'

'Now, put yourself in my shoes. What should I think? What would you have done?'

'Anita, have a little patience. Let's not jump to conclusions. Was Alex in town?'

'Yes, I asked a few people and they told me that he was here in Bangalore. We always lock our bedroom when I'm travelling. Alex has one key and I have a duplicate. Maggie doesn't have any keys.'

'Was Maggie here in town too?'

'Yes, she was.'

'Anita, do you suspect Maggie or do you think it's someone else?'

'Mridula, I really don't know. I'm confused. But my intuition says that something's not right.'

'Did you ask Alex?'

'Of course. He swore on St Maria and said he doesn't know anything about it.'

'How many condoms were there?'

'It was a strip of ten, but two slots were empty. Mridula, tell me honestly, what's your opinion?'

Mridula was quiet. She was aware that whatever she said next may have a profound effect on Anita. So she carefully said, 'We shouldn't think that we know exactly what happened without knowing the details and without proof. Think rationally. Your future will get affected if you take a wrong step. Anita, have you observed any changes in Alex's behaviour?'

'I don't know. He travels a lot. But I've never known what he does in other places. My mind says that there's something wrong here but my heart doesn't want to believe it. Tell me, have you ever suspected Sanjay that way?'

'Not at all.'

'Mridula, I've lost my peace of mind. A woman can go through anything but not this. I can't share this fear with anyone. Alex's sister, Barbara, is of the same age as me. If I tell her, she'll blame me. She already says that I don't dress well. Mridula, infidelity, deceit and lies are like close-knit brothers. All liars don't deceive. But all deceivers are liars. All deceivers are not cheaters. But all cheaters are deceivers. I've seen Alex lie many times for his business. So I don't know what to think about him any more. Has Sanjay ever lied to you?'

For the first time in a very long time, Mridula thought about Sanjay's personality. She believed that he told her the truth. Why would he lie to her when she had been honest with him? Just the thought of Sanjay lying made her uncomfortable.

Anita continued, 'Mridula, do you know that when men get more money than they need, their wife starts looking ugly to them? They think that they could have done better. They forget that they were nothing when their wife married them and that she has stayed loyal to them through their ups and downs.'

'Where's Julie?'

'Fortunately, she's still in Mangalore. I don't want anyone else to know about this.'

'Anita, be careful with your servants and behave exactly like you did before. Don't let them get suspicious.'

'No, I won't. I still can't believe that Alex might have cheated on me. Sometimes, I feel that all these problems are because of money. If we had a fixed income, then I would know everything. But now, I don't know where the money comes from or where it goes. Mridula, you're more intelligent than me. Do you feel the same way? Don't you think money is affecting our children? I feel that Julie is becoming a little too headstrong.'

Mridula knew that she was right. She had noticed that Sishir was also becoming very stubborn. She asked Anita, 'Do you think Alex has changed with money?'

'I think so. I don't know where he goes or what he does. He's permanently on the phone, even when he's at home. When I was crying about this incident and talking to him, he didn't show any emotions at all.'

Anita started crying again and said, 'I'm really worried about my marriage.'

'Anita, don't worry. Things will work out in the end. Please don't cry. I feel so helpless.'

'Mridula, you are a sister to me and that's the reason I can cry in front of you. I feel much better now.'

Though Mridula insisted that Anita have lunch with her, Anita refused and left without eating. Mridula became jittery, nervous and unusually quiet. She did not tell the cook, Sakamma, what to cook for the day. Instead, she told her to make whatever she wanted to and went to her room. Sakamma saw Mridula's worried face but told herself that it was not her business to think about her employer's issues.

In her room, Mridula thought about Anita. She was shocked to see what Anita was going through and did not know how to react. She examined her own life and analysed it—something that she had never done before. Had Sanjay changed with money? Was this affecting Sishir and changing him too? She was aware that money had brought a lot of comfort into their lives but she had never thought of the difficulties and changes that had come with it. When they had less money, she would take Sishir with her to buy groceries and they had a lot of fun at the store. Now, the servants went to buy the groceries. Even otherwise, their family time together was minimal. If Mridula had a school holiday, Sanjay came home for lunch. Otherwise, everybody met only in the evenings. They had separate televisions, computers and friends.

19

A Silver Spoon

Sanjay's nursing home had expanded to a hundred-bed institution. There was a canteen and a pharmacy in the nursing home. Mridula had opposed non-vegetarian cooking in the beginning but Sanjay had snubbed her and said, 'This is not a temple. We have to give our patients whatever they need. After all, they're paying us. Please don't try to teach me moral science.' Sometimes, Sanjay himself ate in the canteen.

There was a rumour that Sanjay performed all the operations in the nursing home, but it was not true. He had a team of highly paid doctors who were as efficient and as good as him. But Sanjay checked in during every operation. He was good at talking to patients, making them feel safe and boosting their morale. He had an office in the nursing home too. He knew that in government hospitals, you learnt through experience and by treating poor patients, but in private hospitals, you had to keep yourself updated with the latest research and findings. After his consultations in the evenings, Sanjay checked the accounts. He did not trust anybody with money matters, even though Rosemary was very trustworthy.

He came home and joined his family for dinner. This was the only time he spent with Sishir. He talked to him about everything and advised Sishir on his future. Mridula did not play an important role anywhere in Sanjay's life. Rosemary assisted Sanjay in the hospital, Shankar managed the accounts, Sakamma did the cooking and Sishir entertained him. Sanjay hardly ever took a holiday and when he travelled abroad, it was only for business. Sanjay didn't ask Mridula what she did during the day or about her family at Aladahalli. As far as he was concerned, this small talk was a waste of time.

At home, Sishir had a modern bedroom on the first floor and a small gym as well. He had everything he needed in his room—an air conditioner, a television, video-game stations and a music system. He went downstairs only for meals.

One day, Sanjay was talking to Sishir during dinner. He said, 'Sishir, when you start practising medicine, you must have an infertility centre and a test-tube baby centre. There is a lot of money to be earned from these. Childless couples are ready to spend any amount of money to have their own baby. But please remember—a childless mother consults many doctors and you shouldn't get upset. It is the desire to have a baby that makes them take multiple opinions. You should exploit their weakness and make money.'

Mridula did not like conversations about money and such advice being given to her son. But she kept her thoughts to herself.

Sishir was intelligent and secured a merit rank in the medical entrance examinations. But he lived in his own world. After a few days, he asked his parents for a car. Mridula was against the idea because Sishir was still a student and she wanted him to use public transport and live the life of an average boy. But Sanjay said, 'Mridula, we went through such a tough time because we didn't have money to make our lives a little easier. At this age, children have lots of desires. Our desires disappear when we grow older. So let him buy a car. Why do you want to stop him?'

They argued this way about everything and Sanjay always ended the argument with, 'Why not? We can afford it.'

Mridula was worried that there was no discipline in Sishir's life. She tried to talk to Sishir: 'I was young once and my parents were wealthy and could afford everything I wanted. But I listened to my mother and learnt to keep things simple.'

'Oh Amma, that's your old thinking of Aladahalli. It doesn't work here in Bangalore,' Sishir said. Sanjay agreed with his son and that hurt Mridula tremendously.

Mridula's cook, Sakamma, made different and delicious things every day. Mridula was indifferent to the variety but Sishir was fussy about food and his father indulged him. Sanjay told Sakamma to make whatever Sishir asked her to. Mridula advised Sishir, 'You should adjust and not complain about food. It isn't good to be stubborn.'

But Sishir did not listen to her. Often, Sakamma would cook something complicated on Sishir's instructions, but after it was made, he refused to eat it and instead had only cereal and milk.

Sakamma wondered, 'There are only three people in this house but I have to cook so many things. Sishir's a difficult child. But Madam is kind and looks after me well. Sometimes, Sishir brings many friends home for a meal—and sometimes he eats alone. When Sishir brings his friends for a late dinner, Madam sends me home and serves them herself.'

One day, Mridula was waiting for Sishir. Sakamma had made several dishes, all of which were Sishir's favourites. He was supposed to come home with his friends for dinner. Sanjay was also waiting for Sishir. At 10 p.m., Sakamma left and Mridula called Sishir. He said, 'Sorry Amma, I forgot to tell you that today is my friend's birthday and we're celebrating at The Leela. I've had dinner and am leaving right now.'

Mridula objected, 'But we've been waiting for you. Your father's also here and he hasn't eaten anything either.'

Her son interrupted her, 'Amma, I've said sorry already. I can't help it.'

He disconnected the phone.

Mridula was upset. She was worried about what she would do with all the food. There were only two people at home. She could store it in the refrigerator but Sanjay wanted fresh food every day and he would not eat the same food tomorrow. She thought, 'Sishir is not a child. He's a young man. I'm unhappy with his negligent attitude.'

Sanjay looked at her and said, 'Mridula, please don't start anything. He's only a kid and he wants to enjoy himself. He's even apologized to you.'

This made Mridula all the more upset. She said harshly, 'You always support him. If he's not disciplined now, he'll never be disciplined.'

'Mridula, times have changed. If you try to control him, he may leave the house and go live separately. He's our only child. You should try to learn and adjust with him.'

'I've been married to you for twenty-four years. Have I not adjusted to everything you wanted? Have you ever tried to adjust with me? You think that whatever you want is right and he's learnt this from you.'

'Yes, whatever I think is right. That's the reason for my success. What do you know about real life? Your world is limited to your school. Look at my colleagues. They're still rotting in government service. But look at me. I made the right decision at the right time. I've been successful without anybody's help.'

Mridula became angry. But before she could answer, Sishir's car entered the driveway. So she kept quiet. They tried to minimize their arguments in front of Sishir. It was an unwritten rule.

Sishir came in whistling a tune. He had bought some fifteen expensive shirts. He said, 'Dad, how do you like the shirts?'

'They look good. You have excellent taste.'

Mridula, however, was still upset. Angrily, she said, 'Sishir, why do you have to buy more shirts when you already have hundreds at home? I see many poor students in my school wearing the same shirt every other day. Don't become a spendthrift.'

'Amma, you can give them my old shirts. I don't have a problem with that.'

'Sishir, that's not the point. Don't get used to buying unnecessary things. Once the fashion changes, you'll just put the clothes aside. Try to buy a few things at a time and enjoy them. You must learn to save. You don't know when life may become tough for you.'

Before Sishir could reply, Sanjay raised his voice saying, 'Mridula, don't keep arguing about small things. Sishir's a child and wants to enjoy life. I work hard and earn money from morning till night. I earn the money for him too. Don't spoil his mood. I just want to come home and spend some time with my family but you always start something.'

Mridula felt like she had been slapped in the face in front of their son. She turned around so that the men in her life could not see her tears and walked to her bedroom. Sishir went to his room upstairs, still whistling a tune, and Sanjay started surfing the news channels on the television.

The relationship between a son and a mother is very different from that between a daughter and a mother. When the daughter becomes a young woman, she becomes a friend to her mother but the son becomes a stranger. Sishir looked like his mother but his voice, mannerisms and thinking were Sanjay's. He was not too attached to anyone and not idealistic at this young age.

In her bedroom, Mridula wondered, 'How is it that this young generation is so practical?'

She recalled a conversation that she had heard between Sishir and his friend. Sishir was advising his friend, 'There's really no profit in medical science these days. And on top of that, we have to work really hard. But if we study engineering and find an IT job, then we can make money easily. After a few years, we can start our own company. It'll be to our advantage to marry a software engineer. My mother's cousin Sarla's husband, Prasanna, earns almost two lakh a month.'

Mridula could not help but notice that they were focused only on money and how to earn more of it. There was no emphasis on the nobility of the medical profession. Mridula did not talk about these things with Sishir. When his friends came home, they told him, 'You're lucky that your dad has a great practice and that you're the only child. You needn't struggle like us. You are a born prince.'

Sometimes, Sanjay joined Sishir and his friends' conversations. Sishir was proud of his famous father. The young boys treated him like their friend without hesitation and Sanjay liked that. They greeted Sanjay and said, 'Hi Uncle, how's it going?'

The only conversation they had with Mridula was about food. They said, 'Please don't give me too much rice, Aunty' or 'Why did you make dessert for us? It has too many calories'. Mridula missed the days at Aladahalli when everyone talked at the dinner table about a variety of topics.

She recollected what she had read long ago: 'At twenty, if you are not an idealist, then you don't have a heart. And if you continue being an idealist at forty, then you don't have a brain.' She thought that these children had no heart while Sanjay thought that she had no brain.

One day, Sanjay advised his son, 'People respect successful people. You keep your focus on your goal and work towards it. Remember, there are no permanent friends in life. Instead, the more successful you are, the more enemies you have.'

'Dad, is it possible to remain at the top?'

'It's difficult. The only way to stay at the top is to learn about the latest developments in your industry and stay one step ahead. It's easy to get to the top, but much harder to stay there.'

'Dad, how do I recognize and judge people correctly?'

'Don't believe anyone straight away. Trust very few people and check on them regularly. If you expect everybody to take advantage of you, then you'll be aware of what's happening around you and you won't be disappointed. Money is the most important thing. Almost everybody has a price.'

'How can you say that, Dad?'

'Sishir, everybody has a price at which they are ready to compromise their principles. For some, it is ten thousand rupees and for others, it may be ten lakh. Money is most people's weakness. When I was in school, children made fun of me because of my arm. Today, the same people call me "Sir".'

Somehow, Mridula could not control herself when she heard this. 'You shouldn't say such things,' she burst out. 'Children are young and innocent. Their intention was not to hurt you. You were just different and that's why they talked about you. When I was in school, I had long and thick hair and everybody made fun of me and called me a snake-girl. I used to get upset at the time but now, I laugh about it. If money's so important, then all rich people should be happy. But that's not the case. Don't teach wrong things to our young son.'

Sanjay looked at Sishir and replied, 'Mridula, the helplessness of being without money causes a lot of suffering. You have never known it because you were always protected. You are the principal of your school and you have all the power. That's why everybody listens to you in school. Actually, your views are impractical.'

Mridula felt humiliated and went to her room. There, she realized that Sanjay and she were about to complete twenty-five years of their marriage in less than a year—but she felt unhappy. She could not pinpoint why she was feeling restless. She remembered that Sanjay had told her that he would ensure that a part of his earnings was donated to the poor. But he had done nothing about it. Whenever he donated money, he wanted his name to be associated with the charity. Only the rich could afford his fees. He charged as much as twenty-five thousand rupees for a normal delivery. What had he done to help the poor?

———

Sishir's typical day started at eight at night. He did not care for his mother's words when she told him that he should go to bed early and wake up early too. Instead, he got irritated and said, 'Amma, stop it. You and I have different opinions.'

Sishir told his father and friends, 'My mother's like a broken record. She keeps repeating the same things over and over.'

Sanjay sometimes joked about it and said, 'Well, then think about how I'm living with her.'

At times, both father and son talked about Mridula like this, but Mridula believed that they thought the same way too. She was extremely sensitive to their comments and their words hurt her terribly. Sometimes, Sishir realized that his mother was feeling bad and said lightly, 'Amma, be a sport like Dad.'

Sanjay laughed at Sishir's words. He was aware that he could be rude to others but not to his son. A son is a shady tree in old age and parents must take care of the tree when it is a sapling.

One day, Sishir was idling in his bed. The cuckoo clock indicated that it was midnight. Sanjay had bought the clock for him from Geneva. Sishir reminisced about his first trip abroad when he was in the final year of school. As usual, Mridula had objected to his travelling. She had said, 'You shouldn't send a child alone for a holiday abroad when he's still a dependant.'

But Sishir did not care. He thought that that was precisely the reason why he should go alone. He would see different countries and be able to absorb more of the culture at a younger age. He thought, 'Travelling is also a form of education and we can afford it. Dad is well travelled and he knows the world better than Amma.'

His phone rang. It was Neeta. She was in his class and her upbringing was modern. His mother did not like Neeta's modernity but his Dad did not mind. Neeta said, 'Hi Sish, what's the plan for tomorrow?'

Sishir already knew that Neeta must have something on her mind. So he replied, 'Why?'

'Do you want to go to the disco at The Leela Palace?'

He paused and said, 'I wish I could but I have something else to do.'

'What're you doing that's keeping you busy? Come on, Sish, can't you spare an evening for me? Shall I come and help you?'

'Yes, you can. I'm going to a temple with Mom. Will you come too?'

Sishir knew that Neeta did not like to go to temples and he could escape this way. He thought, 'I rarely go out with Amma. When I was a child, I went with her to a temple often. But Dad was always busy and never came with us.'

The tunes of Metallica wafted out from his music system and Sishir started headbanging. He recalled spending very little time with his father during his childhood. His mother was his true companion then. He thought, 'When Amma went to school to work, Kantamma Ajji's family looked after me.'

He lovingly remembered Kantamma, whom he affectionately called Ajji. She was a generous woman with grey hair. She had a big kumkum bindi on her forehead, flowers in her hair and red glass bangles on her wrists. She was dark in complexion and smiled all the time. He could never forget her red bangles because she used to make him sit on her lap and would prepare ragi balls with her hands. He had sat on her lap like that for many years. She wore little jewellery but looked charming. Even now, when he visited her, she embraced him with the same affection, as if he was still a toddler. He had never felt that affection from any friends or relatives.

Despite the cold winter, he was filled with warmth. It had been a long time since he had seen Kantamma Ajji. He regularly visited Muniyappa and Kantamma annually on Ugadi and Deepavali, except this past Deepavali: he had gone to Singapore with friends and missed the festival this year. He thought, 'Next week, I must go and see them and take a gift for Kantamma. I should ask Amma to buy a nice sari for her. The last time, I told Dad that I wanted to give her a pair of gold bangles. But Dad said, "Sishir, when you give expensive gifts to people less rich than you, their expectations increase and you may not be able to match them every time. I agree that they have looked after you extremely well. So you should give them a gift that they'll appreciate and, yet, not think of as a burden. However, if you still insist, I can ask Rosemary to buy a pair of gold bangles today." Dad must be right because he has seen the world. I can't understand why Amma can't think like him.'

Metallica changed to Yanni and Sishir felt hungry. Though he liked the food at home, he wanted a change every few days. Mridula always said, 'Home-made food is the best and the healthiest. I get upset when you don't eat.'

So Sishir did not know what to do. His father told him, 'Eat a little bit in front of your mother and make her happy. Then go out and eat whatever you want.'

For his birthday, his father had given him a new credit card. Now, he had all the freedom in the world.

When he had first started asserting his independence as a teenager, his mother would get scared and cry. He felt bad for her but then he thought, 'I'm not responsible for anybody's happiness. I have the right to live the life I want.'

He would rebel against his mother but not his father. His father was a friend with whom he could talk about anything, including girls. But his mother was so different. He thought, 'Maybe it's because she was brought up in godforsaken Aladahalli, where obedience is considered a virtue. I think she spent her entire childhood obeying everybody.'

The next day, Sishir wanted some money for petrol and when he asked his mother, she told him to take it from her purse in the drawer. When he opened her purse, he found a lot of money in it, but he took only as much as he needed. He told his mother how much money he was taking. Many of his friends argued about why he needed to tell his mother but Sishir looked down upon that attitude. His mother had taught him about honesty and hard work and he shared those values with her.

As he was about to close the drawer, he saw a photo album. Though he had seen it many times before, something seemed different as he opened it now. He said to himself, 'Amma was so beautiful when she was young. Had she been taller, she could have entered the Miss India pageant. She's wasted her beauty by becoming a teacher and a housewife. Had I been in her place, I would've pursued modelling and probably made more money than Dad and taken less time than him. She could have become a lady doctor and joined Dad and they could have built many more nursing homes together. Amma would have also been famous. She's spent so much energy on teaching children in government schools.'

Sishir closed the drawer and took his car to the gas station to fill petrol. His classmates Neeta and Naren were partying at a bar. Since they had been drinking, they asked him to pick them up and drop them home. When he went inside the bar, he was surprised to see Sarla Aunty, Prasanna Uncle and their daughter Dolly having beer. The last time he had met Sarla Aunty was at a temple where she was dressed in a traditional nine-yard sari and wore exquisite gold jewellery. Though he had nothing against women drinking, the two images of Sarla Aunty were jarring.

Sarla Aunty became pale on seeing him. But she smiled and said, 'Come, boy, join us.'

'No, Aunty. I don't drink.'

'Then your first peg will be a whisky,' Prasanna Uncle joked.

'Well, that time I'll call you for company.' Sishir quickly said goodbye and walked away.

When he came home and told his parents about it, Sanjay happily said, 'You set them right.'

His mother, however, was worried. She said out loud, 'It's wrong. Sarla comes from a conservative family. If her mother gets to know about this, she'll faint.'

Mridula's words annoyed Sishir. He argued, 'Amma, what exactly is wrong? Is going to a bar wrong or is drinking with your daughter wrong?'

'Well, she's a woman and she shouldn't drink.'

'Who said that you have to be a man to drink?'

Sanjay wanted to support his son and said, 'Sarla's worked hard and made loads of money. She has a right to enjoy it too.'

Mridula got irritated. 'What do you mean? Haven't I earned money with hard work too?'

Both men knew that this might lead to a scene, so they got up and went to their rooms. Sishir thought, 'Amma and Dad have lived together for so many years, but they are poles apart. Maybe their upbringing and professions have influenced their thought processes. Thank God they aren't similar. Otherwise, I would've had a tough time. This way, I can take advantage of Amma or Dad depending on the situation.'

20

The Ways of the World

While Sanjay was driving to the nursing home the next day, he thought about Mridula. He knew that she was upset about the previous night. Recently, he had observed that she often talked about impractical issues. She told him that he was not helping poor people as he had earlier promised. He said to himself, 'Yes, I'm aware of my promises, but I was inexperienced at the time and I don't have to fulfil the promises I made then. Mridula doesn't understand this. In fact, she's blunt and speaks her mind freely. In today's sophisticated society, it isn't necessary to tell people what's on your mind. When someone comes to invite us for a wedding, sometimes she immediately tells him or her that we won't be able to attend the event because we'll be out of town. It's so rude. She defends herself and says that she's being straightforward and honest. But honesty isn't needed everywhere. She just doesn't get it.'

When he reached the hospital, Rosemary greeted him with a warm smile and handed over a list. When Sanjay saw the list of patients and their scheduled operations for the day, he remembered his father's words: 'See God in your patients.' Yes, he did see God—Goddess Lakshmi in fact. Every patient was a source of income to him. In government hospitals, the patients were dependent on the doctors. But in private practice, if he and his doctors were not good to the patients, they would go to another doctor and spread rumours about the nursing home. That would be enough to spoil the reputation of the nursing home. It took several years to build a brand but you could lose it very quickly. He kept his personal relationships and money separate. That was why he also kept Shankar at a distance and Shankar understood that.

His phone rang. The receptionist told him that Dr Vasudha was on the line and wanted to talk to him. Sanjay recognized who she was. He told the receptionist, 'I'm busy. Tell her to call back in the afternoon.'

A queue of patients was waiting for him. Mechanically, he got up and washed his hands. Since he had become famous, patients from other states also came to see him. Some people said that he had a magical touch, but Alex said it was his super-salesmanship.

Sanjay's thoughts continued to trouble him. Bheemanna had said long ago that Mridula's horoscope would bring her husband riches. Today, Ratnamma wholeheartedly agreed and proudly told everybody, 'My daughter-in-law has brought luck to our family.'

It was rare for a mother-in-law to pay her daughter-in-law such a compliment.

Lakshmi, however, had a different opinion. She said, 'My brother, Sanjay, is a hard-working and brilliant doctor. That's why he's successful.'

Surprisingly, Mridula agreed with Lakshmi, despite the fact that the sisters-in-law did not get along too well.

Soon, patients started walking in and Sanjay forgot about Mridula. By the time he finished his rounds and OPD, it was 2 p.m. He thought that it was better to eat in the canteen and check the quality of food there. Rosemary arranged for his diet meal. Sanjay was conscious about his diet. Though he was fifty and had a few grey hairs here and there, nobody could guess his age correctly. Most of his friends were jealous about his youthful looks and pestered him to share his secret. Sanjay diplomatically said 'your friendship' but he knew that regular exercise and diet were major factors.

Rosemary ate in the canteen every day. She knew the difference between Sanjay's and her position and ate at a different table. Sanjay appreciated her gesture.

She was the head nurse and knew instantly when patients tried to fool her.

During her first year, she had once asked for fees from a patient who said, 'I've given the money to the other nurse.' Rosemary assumed that it was true but after checking the accounts, she realized that he had never paid. Some patients would tell her, 'Oh, we know the doctor well. He told us not to pay.'

So she thought about what to do and came up with an idea. She decided that she would give pink and green paper slips to Sanjay. If he signed on the pink slip, the consultation was free and if he signed on the green, the patient would have to pay half of the total charges. No matter what the patients told her, she charged them based on the colour of their paper slip.

A few years later, patients had started playing new games. They would get their operation done elsewhere, come for the dressing and say, 'Your nursing home has forgotten to take out the unclean cotton swab from the wound. That's why my wound isn't healing. I'll sue you.' Rosemary had discussed these things with Sanjay and introduced a new computer software where the details of the patient, operation and everything else was recorded and the patient's signature taken.

In the afternoon, Dr Vasudha phoned again and Sanjay asked the receptionist to put her call through. Vasudha said, 'Dr Sanjay, I hope you remember me. I was your classmate at BMC—Bangalore Medical College—thirty years ago.'

Sanjay had not forgotten her. It was the same Vasudha who had said that she had sympathy for him but not love. He said, 'Sorry, I knew three Vasudhas in college. Which one are you?'

'I was in your batch and also Santosh's relative. I used to come to your house too.'

'Yes, I remember now.'

'You've become so popular in Bangalore. I'm proud that we're good friends.'

Naturally, she remembered him because he was successful today. He purposely did not call her by her name. He said, 'Yes, Doctor, what can I do for you?'

'My husband is a member of the Rotary Club. They are starting a health camp and you're the perfect person to inaugurate it.'

Sanjay knew that this was a lie—she either wanted a donation or a professional favour from him. He was not upset. Though he knew that he wouldn't go for the inauguration, he asked, 'When is it?'

Vasudha knew that if she gave him a date, he would refuse saying he was otherwise occupied that day. She smartly said, 'You can pick any date convenient to you.'

Without even opening his diary, Sanjay paused and replied, 'Sorry, my secretary says that I'm completely booked for the next two months. Please call up later to confirm.'

He did not want to seem rude, though. He asked her, 'How many children do you have?'

'I have two daughters. One is in her final year and is studying computer science at RV College and the other one is a first-year student studying commerce at Christ College.'

He could sense pride in her voice. She was telling him the names of the colleges as a status symbol. In return, she asked, 'How many children do you have, Doctor?'

He noticed that she did not use his first name either.

'I have one son—Sishir. Haven't you seen the name of the topper in the medical exams? He's my son, S. Sishir.'

Vasudha had, of course, but she said, 'I'm sorry. Since both my children are not in the medical line, I don't follow the latest updates in that field. What does your wife do?'

'She's very intelligent. Sishir has taken after her. He is not like me.'

Sanjay did not say what Mridula did and before Vasudha could ask him any more questions, he said, 'Okay, Doctor, keep in touch. Take care.'

He disconnected the phone. Sanjay felt bad. Though Mridula was a good-looking girl when they got married, she was not a doctor. Had she been one, they may have had fewer differences. Now, he strongly believed that it was better if a couple worked in the same profession. He was advising Sishir to get married to a lady doctor too. A husband–wife team could build a great business empire together. But Sishir did not seem to care.

At home, Sishir was waiting for a pizza delivery. To pass the time, he stood in front of the mirror and looked at himself. He knew that he was handsome and that there were many girls who liked him. He had everything—money, good education and a great future. Naturally, any girl would love to marry him. Neeta was one of them. She called him all the time and got his mother worried. One day, Mridula advised him, 'Sishir, don't get too friendly with any girl. You're a boy and if something happens, nobody will blame you. But the girl's name and future will get spoilt. We aren't living in a Western society.'

This really upset him. He did not say anything to his mother but he thought, 'If the girl herself isn't bothered and when her parents themselves send her with me, then why does Amma care? Times have changed but she has stayed behind. Sarla Aunty also pushes Dolly towards me and Prasanna Uncle is no less. Sometimes, he calls me for lunch, leaves Dolly with me and disappears after giving a lame excuse. But I'm aware of their intentions. There are many girls more intelligent and beautiful than Dolly, so why should I bother about her?'

The doorbell rang. It was the pizza-delivery man. Sishir went downstairs in his T-shirt and shorts to get his pizza. Mridula was already paying the bill and looked disapprovingly at Sishir.

21

Shades of Grey

Ambuja, Mridula's colleague in school, distributed her nephew's wedding invites to the staff and insisted that everybody must attend. As soon as she left the room, another colleague, Leela, commented, 'Do you realize how shrewd Ambuja is?'

Mridula replied, 'I don't understand.'

'She invites us for her nephew's marriage but not her niece's because for a boy's wedding, the lunch expenses are borne by the bride's side of the family, but in a girl's wedding, they themselves have to bear the expenses.'

Mridula had never thought of it this way and, at times, she wondered why she could not think like other people. She asked Leela, 'Are you planning to go?'

'I don't want to. But I will.'

'If you don't want to, then why will you go?'

'That's etiquette.'

Again, Mridula was unable to understand the word 'etiquette'.

Ambuja's nephew's wedding was on a Sunday. The girl and the boy both belonged to rich business families and there was a long queue of people waiting to congratulate them. Mridula decided to sit in a corner until the rush subsided. Suddenly, she saw Lakshmi; she was a little surprised to see her there. Before she could get up and go to her, Lakshmi had got lost in the crowd. She was dressed nicely and was wearing a diamond set which was shining in the bright lights. She had not seen Mridula yet.

Usually, whenever Lakshmi visited Mridula, she wore only one plain gold bangle. The lady sitting next to Mridula saw her looking at Lakshmi and said, 'Do you know that lady?'

Mridula stayed silent. The lady continued, 'Look at her jewellery. It's beautiful. I saw her buying something at a jeweller's shop just the other day.'

'How do you know her?'

'We are members of the same chit group. Lakshmi pays the highest chit. She invests twenty thousand rupees every month.'

'I see. Is she that rich?'

'Haven't you heard of Dr Sanjay from the Sushruta Nursing Home? She's his sister. Twenty thousand rupees is nothing for her.'

Chit groups were not unknown to Mridula because Ratnamma was also a part of one. Lakshmi was her daughter after all. Mridula thought, 'How can Shankar and Lakshmi afford such a huge chit? They stay in a rented house in Malleshwaram. Lakshmi doesn't work either. Though I'm younger than her, my heavy silk brocade sari and minimal gold are still too much for me. But Lakshmi's dressed like a bride.'

By then, the queue had shortened and Mridula went up to congratulate the young couple. She ran into Lakshmi on her way towards the newly-weds. Lakshmi was shocked to see Mridula there. But she composed herself and said, 'Oh, Mridula, I didn't know that you were going to be here. Are you from the bride's side or the groom's?'

'The groom's.'

'Oh, I'm from the bride's side. I didn't want to come, but they insisted. You know how it is.' Then Lakshmi lowered her voice and said, 'Mridula, you know that I don't have much gold. So I feel awkward whenever I have to attend weddings and functions. These days, you get a lot of fake jewellery that glitters more than the real thing. I bought one fake diamond set to wear during weddings. Everyone thinks that it's real. Look at it. Don't you think it looks real, too?'

Mridula did not know what to say and kept quiet. She thought, 'I should give her the benefit of the doubt. Since I'm not sure, I won't say anything.'

When Mridula reached home, the phone was ringing. It was Ratnamma. Sanjay picked up and spoke to her on the speakerphone. Ratnamma said, 'MLA Adikeshavaiah wants to start a women's cooperative bank in our village. The government also helps in such projects. Because of my experience, they want to elect me chairman. I need to deposit ten lakh rupees for this. Please send a DD for that amount in my name.'

Sanjay said, 'Give me some time. I'll get back to you.'

Mridula found it strange. She had always thought that Ratnamma did not care about position or status. Sanjay was quiet after the call. Mridula asked him, 'What do you think? What should we do?'

Sanjay replied, 'I don't think Amma should accept this position. I'll call her back and talk to her later.'

Mridula felt happy that Sanjay was thinking on the same lines as her.

Every year, Mridula's cousin Sarla held a big Satyanarayana puja at home. After that, she arranged for a luxury bus to Tirupati and invited all her close relatives to the trip. It was something similar to the Purnima celebrations in Bheemanna's house. Bheemanna normally joined the festivities. But now, he did not want to leave his home and go anywhere. After Rukuma Bai's death, he had lost interest in life. In recent years, Mridula's brother, Krishna, and his wife, Vatsala, had started coming to Bangalore for this function. They came a week in advance for sightseeing and shopping. Every year, they stayed with Sarla in her house and that hurt Mridula. They visited Mridula only once for a few hours—like she was a mere acquaintance.

This year, Mridula could not control her grief. She tried to share her thoughts with Sanjay. 'Vatsala and Krishna should stay with us. I'm Krishna's sister. Isn't our relation to them closer than Sarla's?'

Without lifting his head from the newspaper, Sanjay replied, 'Relationships are maintained not just because you are related by blood, but also by keeping in touch.'

'But I'm his sister.'

'Even Lakshmi is my sister. I haven't done anything wrong to her. And yet, she never comes and stays with us for a holiday.'

Sanjay was shrewd enough not to take his mother's name, who refused to come to Bangalore.

Mridula did not know whether Sanjay was saying this to blame her. He acted polished in front of others but in front of his wife, his words could be brutal. Mridula replied, 'I've never ever told Lakshmi not to come. She's involved in activities like ladies' clubs and chit group meetings. Unfortunately, we don't share common interests. We are neither enemies nor friends.'

'Sarla and you were best friends once. But even she doesn't come to our house. What happened?'

'Sarla is busy working or travelling. How can I expect her to come and spend time here?'

'Sarla isn't like you. She's practical. She works hard and makes money and understands the ways of the world.'

This upset Mridula even more. Sanjay appreciated everyone except her. She snapped back, 'I think I should have been more like your sister and spent all of my husband's money and brought him to the streets.'

Sanjay did not bother replying. He had wanted to push Mridula's buttons, and he had. He started whistling. Mridula continued, 'Lakshmi puts all her money in chits. Her friend told me. I saw her at a marriage last week. She was wearing at least ten lakh's worth of jewellery and she told me that it was artificial.'

Calmly, Sanjay said, 'Mridula, you must meet Dr Ramaiah.'

Mridula was taken aback at the change of subject. She asked, 'Are you talking about the famous psychiatrist? Why should I meet him? I don't have a health problem.'

'Yes, you do. That's why you should get yourself checked. Just because someone told you that Lakshmi is involved in chits, you believed that person. I have known my sister longer than I've known you. She doesn't care about money. In fact, she wants to help people and loses money in the process. Why will she lie to you? Had she had your inclination to save money, she would've been wealthy today.'

Mridula felt bad that her husband had more faith in his sister than in his wife. He was not ready to think for a second that his sister could have also done something wrong. On top of everything else, he taunted Mridula for saving money. Lakshmi was known to spend all the money on herself without a thought for her family. Mridula cried, 'What a reward I get for saving for our future! I should've been a spendthrift instead.'

Sanjay did not want to deal with a sobbing wife and left the room. Suddenly, Mridula felt that there was an intense vacuum in her life. The huge nursing home, this big house and its servants were of no consequence to her. Money had taken away her happiness. She could not even raise her son the way she wanted to. Her husband did not understand her. What was the use of this life?

Later that night, Sanjay was unable to sleep despite the cool air-conditioning. He thought to himself, 'Mridula disagrees with me about everything. She has a good house, servants, plenty of money, a great son and a famous husband. Both the men in her life are intelligent and we don't have bad habits. People must envy her.'

He thought about Lakshmi and felt sad for his sister. Her husband was not in a top position and their son, Anil, was not academically inclined. Sishir had told him confidentially that Anil was a chain-smoker and frequented bars. But still, Lakshmi was happy. She was enthusiastic even when she made a small gold purchase or bought a silk sari.

He recalled the last time he went to Chennai for work. He had brought back two silk saris and given one to Mridula. She had told him, 'I don't feel like wearing silk saris these days. When I think of how the silk is made, I feel sorry for the silkworms. Such a waste.'

So Sanjay had hidden the other sari and given it to Lakshmi, whose happiness knew no bounds. She had thanked him many times and talked about its excellent colour and texture. She had promised to wear it during the next festival.

Sanjay thought, 'Mridula must learn how to live life from Lakshmi.'

22

Sweet Revenge

Sanjay's phone rang. He thought that it may be an emergency and reached for his phone. But it was not a call from the nursing home. It was Prakash Kamat, the sales director of a pharmaceutical company. He was not unknown to Sanjay. When Sanjay was working in the government hospital, Prakash was a medical representative and used to frequent the hospital to give literature and samples to Dr Saroja. Prakash had never paid attention to Sanjay then. Over a period of time, Prakash had reached a senior position and he was calling Sanjay to discuss the next contract.

Sanjay knew that big deals and contracts must be a win-win situation for both sides. He thought, 'By recommending Prakash's products, I must also gain something. If two similar products from two different companies are equally good, then I should think of what's advantageous for me. In any business, a win-lose situation equals exploitation. And if it is a lose-win, it's plain foolishness. Mridula won't understand these complicated issues.'

Prakash said, 'Sir, today's the last day. Please let us know your final decision.'

'Let me think about it.'

'Sir, our product is good and the field results are favourable. You don't have to worry.'

'That's easy for you to say. If something goes wrong tomorrow, the patient will catch hold of me and not you.'

'Sir, we have tested it thoroughly.'

'Then I want to see the field trial results.'

Prakash Kamat realized that things were not going to be easy with Sanjay. He began his sales pitch: 'Sir, how many drugs from our company do you use every year? We'll work to get you the best discount. We can't give discounts directly but we can arrange to get you four international trips or something like that.'

'Your company isn't the only one that can send me abroad. Other companies are willing to give me a direct discount. I want to know the final discounted amount. Please send it to the nursing home.'

Without waiting for a reply, Sanjay kept the phone down. He recollected his past, 'Once, I was desperate to get a sponsorship and my case was a genuine one. I had approached many people—Chikananjappa, the Health minister's PA and others. I remember waiting helplessly in the corridor of the government office. But ultimately, Dr Suresh got it because of his father's ministerial connections. I could have resigned immediately and started a private practice. Why didn't I have the courage to do so earlier? Wasn't I aware of my own potential?'

Sanjay felt ashamed of himself. He realized that the real courage of a person lay within himself or herself. 'I'm my best friend and my worst enemy. I know that the courage I have today didn't come overnight. As I started getting successful, I became more and more confident. Alex gave me my first break but the ultimate success is mine. Yet, my wife doesn't respect me. Had she been a doctor, she would've been proud to have a husband like me.'

Sanjay sighed and went back to his routine.

The next morning, while he was shaving, the maid told him, 'Dr Saroja is waiting to meet you downstairs.'

He recognized the name. She was the same Dr Saroja who had humiliated him in front of everyone. She had added his name in Kempunanjamma's case even though he was not responsible for it. She had been ruthless about his transfer. The incidents flashed before his eyes. He thought, 'A sensitive person in my position might have committed suicide at the time. How dare she shamelessly come to my house?'

He knew that she wanted a favour. He told his maid calmly, 'Tell her to wait in the veranda. I'll have my bath and then meet her.'

He took his time shaving, bathed unusually slowly and finally came out of the bathroom. Mridula came in and said, 'Why are you taking such a long time to get dressed today? An elderly lady has been waiting for you for a while now.'

Sanjay did not answer her. He knew that she would not understand. Mridula's world existed only in books. In textbooks, idealism occupied one line and took a minute to preach. But real life consisted of different kinds of selfish people. An intelligent person was one who managed all of them and got his work done with minimal conflict.

He finished his breakfast in his room and came out and found Dr Saroja eating at their dining table. She stood up when she saw him. Mridula explained, 'She was waiting for you in the veranda. I called her inside and gave her breakfast even though she was reluctant to eat.'

Sanjay felt sick of Mridula's foolish hospitality. He thought, 'If Dr Saroja had come to the nursing home, I wouldn't have offered her a drop of water. There's no place for hospitality with her. But if Dr Kamala ever comes to see me, I'll never make her wait.'

He did not show his true feelings, however. He smiled and said, 'Mridula, you did the right thing.'

Then he looked at Dr Saroja and said quietly, 'Please feel free. I was your assistant once.'

Mridula excused herself and went to the kitchen. Dr Saroja started talking to Sanjay. She said, 'Sanjay, I'm proud of you. You were in my unit once and it's my honour to have had you in my team.'

Both of them knew that it was not a heartfelt statement. Sanjay did not waste any time. He asked her, 'Doctor, why did you think of me now?'

Sanjay did not call her 'Madam' and Dr Saroja noticed it. She said, 'My niece has delivered in your nursing home.'

'What's your niece's name?'

'Kamalakshi.'

'Then I'll go and see her. I must give her more attention now that I know that she's related to you. Doctor, names and people play an important role in life. I haven't forgotten Kempunanjamma's name.'

Dr Saroja had either forgotten or pretended to have forgotten. She asked, 'Who is Kempunanjamma?'

'Do you remember the case where two babies were switched and my name was suddenly added in the case without reason?'

'Oh, sometimes these things happen in government hospitals.'

'But I learnt a great lesson from it—the name of the doctor who takes care of the patient before, during and after delivery must always be written down.'

'That's an excellent practice.'

'Okay, Doctor, see you.'

He cut off the conversation because he did not want to talk to her any more. As she watched, he drove off in his Mercedes-Benz. Hearing the car leave, Mridula came out with a gift and a coconut for Dr Saroja and helped her get an autorickshaw. She thought it was rude of Sanjay not to offer to drop Dr Saroja to an auto stand at least.

When Sanjay reached the nursing home, Rosemary was arguing with a patient about money; he called her to his room. He did not discuss money matters in front of patients. Rosemary explained, 'This patient called Kamalakshi says that her aunt met you and you agreed to give her a discount. I told her that I couldn't give any discount until I saw a slip. So she's arguing with me.'

'That's smart, Rosemary. The case was complicated. Please charge them more than the usual.' This was the best way that he could vent his anger and make Dr Saroja pay for her breakfast.

Rosemary nodded and left his room.

When he returned home that evening, Mridula said, 'Prakash Kamat has called three times for you. He says that it's important and you must return his call.'

Sanjay pretended not to hear. So Mridula said loudly, 'Why don't you respond? He'll think that I haven't told you about the call. What's happened to you?'

Without getting upset, Sanjay replied, 'Nothing's happened to me. You just don't have any sense. I don't know how you got an academic rank.'

'What did I do?'

'Please know that neither Prakash Kamat nor Dr Saroja are personal acquaintances. They had business with me. Prakash wants business from me and for that, he'll call me thirty times; you, on the other hand, serve them breakfast and lunch as if they're your relatives.'

Mridula kept quiet, went into the kitchen and brought coffee for Sanjay. She said, 'They may be your acquaintances outside this house but when they come here, they're our guests and I have to do my duty. I overheard your conversation with Prakash yesterday. Isn't it wrong on your part to take financial benefit from a drug company as an incentive to prescribe their medicine?'

Sanjay slowly sipped the hot coffee. He said, 'Nothing is black or white in this world. The cow gives milk for its calf. But we drink that same milk. Isn't that wrong? Trees have life. But we cut them down and use their wood. Isn't that wrong too? Mosquitoes and bugs are also living creatures. Don't we kill them because they trouble us? A big fish always eats the small fish. Is that right?'

'I can't argue with you. I just know that it's wrong to prescribe medicines like this.'

'Prakash Kamat doesn't help me out of the goodness of his heart. If he gives me a discount of one rupee, he still makes a profit of thirty rupees. Once the business is over, Prakash won't look at me until the next deal comes along. If you're an idealist, emotional and sensitive, then you can become a schoolteacher and nothing more. You need toughness to succeed in the real world.'

Sishir came down the stairs. He said, 'Dad, my friends and I have decided to go to Kodaikanal in our car. Is that okay with you?'

'Of course, you must enjoy yourself. But don't take our car.'

Mridula added, 'I don't like the thought of you boys driving the car for that long to Kodaikanal.'

Sishir did not bother to answer her. He looked at his father for approval. Sanjay said, 'Sishir, I'm not refusing to give you money for the trip. I'm not stopping you from driving a car either. But your friends shouldn't think that they can get everything from you. Never allow them to take you for granted. You should pool in money, take a train to Kodai Road and hire a taxi from there and share the expenses. That's the practical thing to do. However, the decision is yours.'

Sanjay knew that whenever he left a decision to Sishir, he did what his father told him to do. But if Sanjay forced him, then Sishir did the opposite.

Sishir thought for a second and said, 'Dad, you're right as usual!'

Sanjay paused and continued, 'Sishir, I know that in a few months you'll be going to England for higher education. There, you'll have to manage everything on your own for the first time in your life. You should be simple, but not a simpleton. In a sacrifice, it is a goat that is always chosen—not a tiger. That's because the goat is a small and meek animal. Nobody dares to touch the tiger because it's powerful. In this world, every relationship depends on its usefulness. If a person is useful to others, people will mourn the death of that person. Getting an academic rank is good but it doesn't ensure success. If you don't have common sense and aren't shrewd, people will walk all over you.'

Mridula did not like Sanjay's advice to their son. When a child leaves home for the first time, it is important to give him love, teach him compassion and the value of good habits. She could not hold herself back. 'Sishir, when it comes to family, you need to give and receive love to have peace in your life. In any relationship, compassion binds people together. A successful person dominates others and people obey him only to keep the peace. That's the reason great emperors were headstrong. They were powerful and people were scared of them. But the Buddha stood out from the rest because of his selfless and compassionate nature.'

Sishir was confused and irritated. He said, 'Amma, I can't understand your lectures. I don't care for a history lesson, so please don't try to teach me. Dad, will you drive me to Neeta's house? She'll drop me back later.'

Sanjay and Sishir left like two friends and Mridula was left standing all alone on the porch.

23
A House of Cards

A few months passed. Anita had stopped visiting Mridula. She had become depressed, quiet and moody. Mridula was worried for her and tried her best to reach out to her. But she failed to bring her back to normal. Anita spent most of her time reading the Bible or going to church. She had turned vegetarian and lost all interest in the upkeep of her home. Julie had finished her twelfth grade and got admission in LSR College in Delhi. So Anita moved to Julie's room and did her prayers there. Alex and Anita hardly talked any more. Conveniently, Alex spent more time on his new company and travelled a lot. Even when he met Sanjay, they did not talk about their personal lives.

Meanwhile, Lakshmi and her family continued to live in Bangalore. But Lakshmi hardly ever met Mridula. Mridula did not know if this was on purpose. But whenever they did meet, Lakshmi did not wear any jewellery at all. Frequently, Mridula would tell Sanjay, 'Lakshmi and Shankar are getting old. They may have their shortcomings but they must own a house in Bangalore. Or maybe an apartment. Sanjay, you may not give them the entire amount for buying a home. But let's give them at least 75 per cent. Anil and Shankar can take a loan for the remainder so that they'll be forced to save and pay it back. They can't continue spending all their income on vacations and gold. God alone knows how much is real and how much is fake!'

But Sanjay never showed any interest. He would say, 'Anil has a good job and they must learn to help themselves. We mustn't make them too dependent.'

One day, Shankar came on a scooter to take Sanjay's signatures on some official documents for the nursing home. Mridula felt bad and said, 'Sanjay, I don't know when they'll be able to buy their own house. Why don't you buy Shankar a car? The hospital is quite a distance away from his current residence.'

'Well, why don't you buy him a car and gift it to the family? They'll be delighted.'

Mridula did what Sanjay told her and it made Lakshmi ecstatic. She said, 'Mridula, you're more than a mother to me. My mother doesn't care about me this much. I don't know how to thank you. Now, Anil can use the old scooter.'

It is human nature that when you help someone, a few kind words in return make you very happy. Mridula was easy to please and she was overjoyed at Lakshmi's response.

One day, Mridula was waiting for her driver at the Jayanagar 4th Block shopping complex. Unexpectedly, she saw Anil driving a car that she did not recognize. Anil had not seen her.

When she came back, she told Sanjay, 'I saw Anil in a different car today. I didn't know that he had a car. Lakshmi didn't tell me.'

'It must be the company car. That's between Alex and him. I asked Alex to hire and keep Anil if he works well. I don't want Alex to feel any pressure to retain him just because Anil is my nephew. You know how I am in business. But Lakshmi may not know about it.'

Mridula thought that this must be true and dropped the topic.

Life went on. Sanjay was away for four days attending an international conference in Malaysia. Mridula received an urgent call from the nursing home regarding some documents for the new pharmaceutical company. She told the clerk, 'I don't know anything about the documents.'

'Madam, this file is usually with Shankar sir or Anil. When both of them are unavailable, it is with Doctor sir who keeps the file in the nursing home. May I get it today? It's important.'

'Well, in that case, you can ask Rosemary and take it.'

'Madam, Rosemary is not allowed to open Doctor sir's cupboard. She has the keys but doesn't operate it on her own.'

Usually, Mridula did not go to the nursing home except on Ayudha Puja day. But she felt sorry for the clerk and said, 'Don't worry. I'll go to the nursing home and search for the file.'

A few years ago, Anuradha had had a baby in their nursing home. After trying to conceive for a long time, she had finally become pregnant and had a normal delivery. Everybody was happy. Sanjay had assisted in her case. Mridula had told Sanjay, 'Please don't charge Anuradha anything. When we had no money, they looked after Sishir without any expectations. I never felt hesitant to leave my child with them.'

'Of course, Mridula. Whatever you say. I won't charge them a rupee even though a normal delivery costs fifty thousand rupees. I respect your feelings.'

Mridula was happy that Sanjay was listening to her, at least this time.

At the baby's naming ceremony, she had given a gold chain to Anuradha's baby boy. Kantamma had welcomed her and made ragi balls especially for Sishir. When Mridula was about to leave, Kantamma had thanked her and said, 'Your husband's a nice person. In spite of being such a senior doctor, he came for the delivery in the middle of the night. He also gave us a concession of ten thousand rupees.'

Mridula had been taken aback. To reconfirm, she had asked, 'How much did you pay?'

Muniyappa had said, 'The actual bill was fifty thousand but Sanjay gave us a green slip with ten thousand written on it. So I paid forty thousand rupees.'

When she sat in the car, Mridula had felt disgusted. She had thought, 'How can Sanjay take money from them? At this stage of life, forty thousand doesn't mean much to them. It was just to show them our affection. Doesn't Sanjay understand?'

When she had come home, Sanjay was talking to Rosemary over the speakerphone. Rosemary was asking, 'Doctor, how much discount should I give the Transport Secretary's daughter? She's getting discharged tomorrow.'

'Rosemary, don't charge them anything. Write a complimentary slip and send them a nice bouquet. He may be of great use to us later.'

Mridula's anger had known no bounds. After he had finished his call, she had asked him, 'Why did you charge Anuradha for her delivery?'

Without batting his eyelids, Sanjay had said, 'Because Anuradha wanted the bill.'

'Of course, she would've asked for it, but you should have refused. You have done wrong.'

'What's wrong in taking money from them? Anuradha and Arun have senior-level jobs and each of them takes home at least one lakh rupees. And their company will reimburse them this cost. I have still reduced ten thousand rupees.'

'Then why did you lie to me?'

'Because you would get upset.'

'Well, I'm even more upset now.'

'That's your problem.'

Sanjay had gone to the other room and started making his office calls again. After that day, Mridula had stopped going to the nursing home except on Ayudha Puja day. She felt that the nursing home could run without her help. Neither her words nor her presence had any consequence.

Today was a first after a very long time. Though Rosemary was just the head nurse, she was Sanjay's right-hand person. She knew how to invoice, whom to bill and how much to charge different people. She knew which doctors to call in Sanjay's absence. But Rosemary was aware of her limitations. Sanjay did not allow her to touch his personal documents in the cupboard.

When Mridula reached the nursing home, she asked Rosemary for the keys. Rosemary said, 'Here you go, madam. But I don't know what's in the cupboard. I've never opened it.'

Mridula opened the cupboard and searched for the file. She found a bank passbook first. She was surprised—all the passbooks were supposed to be at home. When she opened it, she found that the passbook was from Sanjay and Lakshmi's joint account in a bank in Malleshwaram. Mridula did not know about this account. She was under the impression that she was looking after all of Sanjay's accounts, at his own suggestion. The account balance was close to fifty lakh rupees. It was not the money that astonished her, but the fact that she blindly believed that nothing happened in her house without her knowledge, particularly since it was an unwritten understanding that money matters were her domain.

At that moment, something inside her just shattered into pieces. When the foundation of trust cracks, how can a marriage remain the same? Mridula felt like she was drowning. Her thoughts haunted her. 'How can Sanjay open an account without telling me? The date of the first transaction is five years ago. I've been cheated for the last five years and I was not even aware of it. Isn't this infidelity too? Alex cheated on Anita in one way and Sanjay has cheated on me in another. He's the one who said, "I don't want to handle money. You manage it and I'll manage the nursing home." I guess the apple really doesn't fall far from the tree. When my mother-in-law is desirous of money even at this age, what else can I expect from her son?'

Mridula wanted more information about the account. She saw the counterfoil of a Rs 10 lakh DD sent to Ratnamma. Sanjay had sent the money to his mother but he had told Mridula that he would not send it. Mridula realized that he was a practised deceiver. She found a gift deed of a car given to Anil. She recalled how easily Sanjay had told her that it was a company car. Apart from that, there was a joint fixed-deposit for fifty lakh in Sanjay and Lakshmi's name.

But the most important paper was lying at the bottom of the cupboard. Four years ago, Sanjay had bought a house for Lakshmi and it had been rented out. Lakshmi was probably collecting rent every month and was staying in a house paying lower rent instead. Mridula also found numerous cheques made out to Pratibha Jewellers in Chickpet that came to around five lakh a year. Now Mridula realized that all the gold that glittered on Lakshmi's body was real. Every year, she had been giving Lakshmi ten thousand rupees on Gowri festival without knowing that Lakshmi was collecting five lakh from her husband on the side.

For a second, Mridula was upset with Lakshmi; then she thought that when her husband himself was manipulating her, why should she blame anyone else? Was it her ignorance, foolishness or Sanjay's cunning nature that had encouraged all these activities? Mridula did not even care to close the cupboard and walked out without speaking to Rosemary. As soon as she could, she ran to her car.

In one moment, Mridula had lost all her confidence. She reached home without tears and did not let her driver know that anything was wrong. She went inside her bedroom and closed the door. She was so hurt that she could not even cry. She was filled with shock and anger. 'I can't believe that Sanjay has cheated me like this,' she said to herself. 'I've lived with complete belief and trust in him ever since we got married. How am I going to live with him for the rest of my life? I don't know what to do.'

Soon, Sanjay came back from Malaysia. It was late at night when he reached home. He felt at once that something was amiss because Mridula did not get up to talk to him when he lay down next to her. Sishir was also absent since he was in Delhi with his friends. Early next morning, their driver, Nanja, told Sanjay that Mridula had not been to school for the last two days. Something was definitely wrong.

Sanjay thought, 'Mridula is talkative and doesn't stop talking even in adverse situations. A few friendly words to her will make her herself again. I'll go talk to her now. In spite of the servants at home, she makes coffee and breakfast for me every morning. My mother and Lakshmi would never do that for their husbands. Shankar really doesn't know how to get respect from his wife.'

When he went to their bedroom, Mridula was staring at the ceiling and had tears in her eyes. As soon as she saw Sanjay, she went to the guest bedroom and locked the door. He did not get a chance to say a word.

When Sanjay went to the dining table for breakfast, there was nothing to eat. The cook, Sakamma, came and he told her to make him a cup of coffee. She asked him, 'Sir, what do you want for breakfast?'

'Why're you asking me? Ask Madam.'

'No, sir, she hasn't eaten anything for the last two days. I'm really worried. I think she's unwell. I'm relieved that you are back.'

Now, Sanjay got really concerned. This was the first time that something like this had happened. He got up and knocked on Mridula's door, but she did not open it. He did not want to create a scene in front of the servants. So he quietly left for the nursing home and met Rosemary there. She said, 'Sir, what's wrong with Madam? I've been calling your house but I keep getting the answering machine. She had come for some documents a few days ago and I gave her the key to your cupboard. After that, she just went away without locking it or telling me.'

She handed over the keys to him. Understanding finally dawned on Sanjay. Mridula had seen the files and learnt about Lakshmi's assets. But he was not too worried. He thought, 'What's wrong with what I did? Lakshmi is my sister and when I didn't have anything, I stayed in her house for two years. She has a useless husband who can't afford to buy her a house. Anil is also not a good son. Besides, I have only given her black money. Mridula will complain that I didn't tell her. But why should I tell her everything? She'll say that everybody should earn his or her own money. But that's her theory, not mine. I am Dr Sanjay, Bangalore's most successful doctor and I've made the money on my own. I don't have to explain it to anyone. I'm not responsible for Mridula being upset. She's not short of money either. I have the right to decide what to do with my money.'

At the end of the day, when Sanjay was going back home in his car, he mentally prepared answers to Mridula's potential questions. But by the time he reached the house, Mridula had shifted bag and baggage to the guest bedroom and locked it again. There were no questions and no accusations—just a strange silence.

Over the next few days, Mridula stayed locked in the guest bedroom whenever Sanjay was at home. She did not feel like getting up from the bed or combing her hair or going to school. She felt like crying all the time and did not want to meet anyone. She stopped feeling hungry as well. She wanted to talk—but there was nobody to talk to. Her father was old and she could not trouble him with this. She could only confide in Anita who herself was facing personal issues. Still, Mridula decided to visit her.

When she reached Anita's house, there was an uneasy quietness everywhere. Anita hugged her and affectionately put her hand on Mridula's shoulder. Then she said, 'There must be something going on that you've come to see me. You look disturbed. What is it?'

Feeling Anita's genuine concern, Mridula could contain herself no longer and wept loudly. Sobbing, she told her the entire sequence of events. Anita smiled and gently said, 'Mridula, don't cry. What exists must perish. Sanjay has deceived you. But I believe that this wrong money won't help Lakshmi in the long run.'

'Anita, it is not about money. Money can be earned and lost. It is about faith that a wife has in her husband. That's more valuable than money and gold. Faith sustains a marriage and brings joy to the family. Without it, we have nothing. How can Sanjay destroy the faith and trust I had in him?'

'Mridula, you don't own Sanjay. He has emotional attachments to other people too. He has to keep everyone happy.'

'Anita, I know that. That's why I have maintained a relationship with his family, even when they are cold and when they ignore me. He should have told me about his intentions. He knows that I always give in at the end. Why did he cheat me like this?'

'Money, women and land are the three things that can ruin a family's happiness. We have both been cheated in different ways. Only faith in God can restore your peace.'

'But how? I don't know what to do. I don't feel like staying in my house. I don't want to talk to Sanjay either. Where should I go? And what will Sishir think of all this? Sometimes, I feel like dying but I know that that is not the solution.'

'Listen to me. Turn to God. Pray to Him to show you the right path.'

Mridula realized that there was no point in talking to Anita further and she left.

Her agony had not reduced. She knew that she must talk to someone older who loved her like a daughter. She wanted to cry and tell that person how she had been deceived and how much she was hurt. She decided to talk to Kantamma.

A few days later, Mridula went to see Kantamma who welcomed her. 'Come, come, Mridula. I'm seeing you after a long time!'

Mridula went inside and sat on the couch. Kantamma smiled and said, 'How is Sishir?'

'Fine.'

'Mridula, you look pale. Is there a problem, dear?'

Mridula started crying the moment she heard these kind words. She wanted to share everything but something held her back. Kantamma asked, 'Mridula, why are you crying? Did you fight with your husband? Your husband's such a nice man. He couldn't have said anything to you. He hardly talks. Did Sishir say something? Oh, children at his age definitely talk a lot and don't realize what they say. Forgive him.'

But Mridula did not say a word. Kantamma waited for her to speak. When she did not, Kantamma made coffee for her and continued to talk. 'Ups and downs are a part of life. But women must have more patience. Only then there is peace at home. Look at Sita. She suffered a lot but she persisted. Look at Draupadi. When goddesses themselves suffer so much, what are we? You know how my husband is. He was a principal for a long time and was strict at home too. My children never cared. But I had to obey him no matter what.'

Mridula was disappointed with Kantamma's value system. She knew now that she would only be told to adjust. Kantamma would not understand her grief. But Mridula could not stop crying. Kantamma quietly and firmly said, 'Crying is not the solution. Be courageous. God has been kind to you and the doctor respects you. Your mother-in-law also doesn't stay with you. Look at other people. Most people are worse off than you. Be happy with what you have.'

Mridula wanted to change the topic and asked, 'Where is Muniyappa sir?'

'He's gone to Kolar. We had a hundred sheep and his brother used to look after them. Just the other day, when we asked for the accounts, his brother said that the sheep are all dead. We don't know whether he sold them or not. My husband's gone to check. I told your sir to forget about the sheep and not get into any problems, but he doesn't listen to me. I pray to God to take care. He's been kind to us.'

Somehow, Mridula could not stay there any longer. When she got up to leave, Kantamma gave her flowers, a blouse piece and kumkum. Mridula hesitated to take them. Kantamma affectionately said, 'Today is Friday and you're like Mahalakshmi. When you came to Bangalore, your husband had nothing. You've brought good luck to him. Giving you this kumkum is a good omen. Please don't say no.'

Kantamma's love brought tears to Mridula's eyes again; she accepted the gift.

With the same broken heart, she returned home. The moment she entered, the phone rang. It was Sarla. Her aged parents had come from Hubli and wanted to see Mridula. Sarla insisted that she must visit them and said that she was sending Satish to bring her. Mridula did not feel like going anywhere but Sarla would not take no for an answer.

A few hours later, Satish came to pick Mridula up. When the doorbell rang, she was crying. She quickly washed her face and opened the door. Satish was observant enough to notice that she had been crying but did not ask her why. He could not. There was a distance between them now. He thought, 'When Mridula was a young girl, we shared everything except the fact that I loved her. But today, she is somebody's wife.'

Satish said, 'Mridula, you must come for lunch today.'

Mridula was in no mood to go. She said, 'Satish, how are the preparations for Tirupati going on?'

'Good. Prasanna has outsourced all tasks including the god's darshan. So there's not much for us to do.'

'What time are you reaching Tirupati?'

'Early morning, but Shyla and I are going to walk up the steps.'

'Why?'

Hesitantly, Satish said, 'Last year, Shyla was unwell and I prayed and promised that I'll climb the steps to Tirupati once she recovers.'

'Then you must do that, but why is Shyla climbing the steps?'

Satish blushed and said, 'Come on, Mridula. She's my wife and my better half. How can I go alone? She knows that I get bored without her.'

Mridula thought, 'There is charm in their marriage even after more than twenty years.' For the first time, Mridula was envious. She wanted to know how they lived. She asked, 'Do you do all the work together?'

'Yes. Shyla works too. So we divide the chores between us.'

'How do you manage your expenses?'

Satish was surprised by this question. Quietly, he said, 'We aren't rich like you, Mridula. We live on our monthly salary.

We calculate our expenses together, save some money and spend the rest. We have two daughters. They must also learn household work. It's important to learn to be independent. Each of my daughters is assigned chores and they are paid for doing them.'

Mridula fell silent. Such schemes would not work in her house because Sanjay could afford everything. Satish continued, 'Every morning, we go for a forty-five-minute walk during which we discuss our home matters. Then we do yoga at home together. In the evening after dinner, we spend fifteen minutes telling each other what we've done during the day. Shyla's been my best friend through the years.'

'Really?'

'It's true. My parents are old and are in their own world. My daughters will also go away in time. I'm a friend to Shyla and she's a friend to me. That's the absolute truth. Do you remember reading the Yaksha Prashna together when we were children?'

Mridula did but she said no. She wanted to hear more from Satish. Satish continued, 'There is a question in it: "Who is the best friend to a man and a woman?" The answer is: "A wife to her husband and a husband to his wife." Now, I agree. A husband and wife must share everything with each other and sit and sort out conflicts. Otherwise, how can a relationship develop? How can a family be happy?'

Mridula decided not to go for lunch to Sarla's house in her current state of mind. For the first time, she was thinking about another man. After Satish left, she wondered, 'Had I married Satish, I wouldn't have been as rich as I am today, but I would have had a contented life. If Satish had expressed his love before I met Sanjay, things may have been different. There's no relationship between money and happiness. The fact is that Satish shares and Sanjay doesn't—not even his emotions or sorrows. But Satish is content. That's why he's still a college professor. A content person distributes happiness. An unsatisfied person like Sanjay distributes restlessness.'

Mridula felt like a cuckoo in the Aladahalli trees. Even though mangoes grew around the cuckoo, she was unable to eat them. Maybe the cuckoo was truly unhappy.

Mridula silently sighed.

24

The Silent Cry

Mridula stopped getting up early to do her chores or look after the house. She continued to cry at the drop of a hat and felt depressed. She got out of bed after Sanjay left for work, had a bath, and sat in the veranda and gazed at the sky. She got angry at everybody and remembered how she used to run the house when they did not have money. At the time, Mridula knew everything about their finances. Now, she did not know what to think. To this day, Sanjay had never taken any money from the accounts that they had without her knowledge. She was under the illusion that she was managing all the financial transactions. But in reality, Sanjay was maintaining parallel financials elsewhere. He acted like an honest husband but he had stabbed her in the back. She felt trapped in her marriage.

Then she thought about Rosemary and got angry with her too. In the documents in the cupboard, she had seen Rosemary's signature on some of the bills. She thought, 'That means that Rosemary was aware of everything but didn't tell me. In spite of everything that I've done for her, she kept quiet and didn't give me a hint. But on the other hand, why should I blame someone else when my own husband's at fault? He didn't think of me at all! Sanjay has his walls around him. I feel all alone.'

At the same moment, in the nursing home, Rosemary's shift was over but she had not yet gone home. She did not want to. Her useless husband was busy betting on horse races or sitting in bars and her daughter Mary Shashikala was in Ooty in a boarding school. Before marriage, Rosemary used to dream about having a loving family, but that dream had remained just that—a dream.

When she was changing into her regular clothes, she thought about Mridula and felt helpless. 'Ever since Madam opened the cupboard, I've been feeling restless and sad. Did she find the files and documents in the cupboard? It isn't Madam's nature to walk out without talking to me. She always inquires about Joseph and Shashi. Madam and Dr Sanjay are poles apart. Madam is genuine and has an infectious smile. She understands and forgives people's mistakes. When Shashi used to fail in her class, Madam personally gave her free private tuitions at home. Then Shashi got good marks which helped her in getting admission to the boarding school. Madam also knew Joseph's drinking habits and convinced him to let Shashi stay in the hostel for her better future. She was right. Shashi is now happy and excels in studies. When my sister Saira was abandoned by her husband, it was Madam who bought her a sewing machine and helped her start a ladies' tailoring shop. Once Saira started doing well, her husband came back as the shop's manager. But now, both of them don't acknowledge Madam's help. Only Jesus knows the real truth.'

Rosemary got out of the changing room and went back to her desk. Her mind wandered to Sanjay. 'Dr Sanjay is the only person who can run a tight ship and keep control of his subordinates. It's difficult to please him. He gives good increments and salaries but doesn't help any employee personally. It's nice to have a boss like him but difficult to live with a husband like that. How does Madam stay with him? He doesn't forget anyone's mistake for years. He wants things done his way and in his time. Maybe all successful people are selfish. But why should I look at what's happening in other's people's lives? I should acknowledge what's happening in mine. Joseph is very stubborn. He was okay when we got married. As I started earning more, Joseph picked up bad habits—buying lottery tickets and drinking. So when Sanjay sir opened a new account with Lakshmi madam, I felt like telling him not to hide anything from his wife. Had he told her the truth, she would have respected him more. But I couldn't speak my mind. He keeps our relationship completely professional.'

Suddenly, Rosemary realized that a patient's relative was standing in front of her with a cheque. The cheque was for a new patient admission. The rule was that at least 50 per cent of the fees had to be given in advance by cash or DD. When Rosemary told the man to pay by cash or DD, he said, 'Why can't you take a cheque? Do you think we won't pay?'

'It isn't that. It's a rule.'

'We're close to the doctor. Can we talk to him?'

'Of course.'

Rosemary pushed the phone towards him. She knew what Sanjay would say. But the man muttered something, opened his wallet, pulled out a wad of notes and paid in cash. After taking the payment, Rosemary left the hospital.

A few days later, Sishir came back from his holidays and Mridula did not say anything to him. She did not argue with Sishir or Sanjay but cried in bed every night. Sishir got busy packing for London—his flight was in a few days. As a young man, he was enthusiastic about getting a chance to be independent. Sanjay advised him, 'Sishir, you must remember to behave differently with different people. The less emotional you are, the better your chances of success. You should not have a personal relationship with your subordinates. Only then can you fire them whenever you need to. You must also know your boss's weaknesses. Don't share everything with close friends. In a sentence: you must think only about yourself.'

Soon, it was time for Sishir to leave. It was the first time that Mridula and Sanjay were going to the airport to say goodbye to their son. Otherwise, going to airports for goodbyes had become a forgotten custom. Sishir had accompanied his father on international conferences several times. But this time, he would be alone in England until he completed his course. His parents would see him often, though, since he planned to come back during school breaks.

Mridula was unusually quiet as she saw Sishir go.

25

Connections

After Sishir cleared immigration, he learnt that his flight was delayed by two hours because of bad weather. He had a business-class ticket and went to the business lounge. It was full and there was no place to sit. He came out and saw Neha sitting in the economy lounge and reading a book. He was surprised to see her. He said, 'Hello, Neha.'

She put down the book and looked at him. There was no surprise on her face. Sishir asked, 'Where are you going?'

She smiled and said, 'England.'

'Me too. Where exactly in England?'

'Oxford. What about you? Are you on vacation?'

'No, I'm also going to Oxford.' Sishir sat down. 'Is it for another chess championship?' he joked.

'No, it's for my higher education.'

He smiled and reminisced.

A few years ago, two groups of college students had been selected for an all-India youth competition. The competition was in various fields such as dance, drama, oration and chess. There were two groups from Karnataka: one from Bangalore and a rural group from Chitradurga. The two groups consisting of five members each met in the office of the government Youth department in a colourless and lifeless building. Every student had excelled in at least one field; Sishir was a good orator and had been chosen from his medical college. When he saw the group from Chitradurga, he thought, 'Are they really up for a national competition? They would've been chosen because it must be mandatory for one group to be from a rural area.'

As was typical for a government employee, the department Secretary walked in late and started distributing forms. Without apologizing, he said, 'You have a five-day stay in Delhi. The government will take care of your stay and travel. You'll travel by train in second-class AC at a student concession and you'll get a daily allowance of five hundred rupees. Your food and accommodation will be taken care of in the government quarters. Since you're all adults, we are not responsible for any extracurricular activities. Remember that you represent Karnataka and you must bring glory to the state. Please sign the form if you accept these conditions.'

It was the most uninspiring and unmotivating speech that Sishir had ever heard. Everyone started signing their forms but Sishir said, 'The rules are okay with me but I won't travel by train. It'll take two days for us to reach Delhi from here. That's four days back and forth. I can't afford to waste that much time. I'll arrange for my own accommodation and transport. Is there a problem with that?'

The Secretary knew who he was and looked at him with disdain. He thought to himself, 'This boy is so arrogant.'

But to Sishir he said, 'As you wish. By the way, are you Sanjay Rao's son?'

'Yes, how do you know?'

'I saw it on your application and address form.'

Sishir did not waste any time and walked out of the room but before he did, he noticed that there were only two girls among the ten participants. One was from Mount Carmel College in Bangalore. He knew her since they often met at various competitions. The other one was an ordinary-looking and simply dressed girl in a salwar kameez. Her hair was in two plaits. He had seen her smile when the department Secretary and he were talking.

While going back home in the car, he browsed through the participant list. He learnt that the simply dressed girl was called Neha. He wondered, 'Why does the government select such girls who've probably never seen a city like Bangalore before? How can they hold their own in national-level competitions? She doesn't look like she came to the competition through connections.'

Then he became engrossed in his own thoughts about a party with his friends that night. There was a big farewell for him.

Sanjay and Mridula attended the event with him. Everybody cheered as if he had already brought the trophy to the college. Mridula said, 'Why are your friends celebrating so much without even going to the event? Enhancing the pressure will only affect the performance of the participants. Do you know that in the olden days in Greece, the Olympic Games took place and the winners got only olive-branch crowns. That made sportsmanship healthy and natural. There were no endorsements, no gold medals and no television. There was no doping either.'

'Amma, stop it. This isn't a history class,' Sishir replied.

'Mridula, please stop. You don't know how to encourage the youngsters today and give them confidence. I don't know what you teach in your school,' Sanjay said.

'I teach my students to have equilibrium in both victory and defeat.'

'Amma and Dad, stop giving me lessons. Both of you are wrong. I don't know whether I'll win the medal or not. I just want to enjoy the glory before I go. That's my perspective.'

Everyone laughed.

That's how he had met Neha for the first time. They had gone to Delhi for their respective competitions. Delhi was not a new place for Sishir. The first time that Mridula brought him there was when he was still a child. She wanted to show him the monuments and museums—just like a teacher. Though he did not like Delhi much, he enjoyed the kulfi, the roadside shopping and the air-conditioned Palika Bazaar.

During the competition, Sishir realized that the group from Chitradurga outperformed theirs by a large margin. Their music was rustic and folk but the tunes were undiluted, original and mesmerizing. Their dancers wore matching and colourful outfits. Sishir was surprised and felt a little ashamed of his prejudgement. Neha did not participate in either the dance or music competitions. Sishir learnt later that she was in the chess competition. This time, he thought that he should not underestimate her. Sishir did his level best in the oratory competition but he knew that he could not defeat the Delhi youths. They were excellent. It was a tough competition and he was happy with a consolation prize. Neha came third in the chess competition and he was duly impressed.

Out of the five days that they were in Delhi, all of them got a day off and they went to visit fashion studios, bars and Chandni Chowk. Everybody knew that Chandni Chowk had a paratha shop from Shah Jahan's time and wanted to see and taste the food. But Neha did not participate in the group outings. Sishir was curious to know where she had gone. When he saw her later, he asked, 'I didn't see you in the bars or in the fashion studios. Where were you?'

'I went to the national museum.'

'What's so great about museums? Have you come to Delhi only to see them?'

'No, I came for the competition, but I want to see all the museums while I'm here.'

Neha did not say any more. Sishir smiled and said, 'You're like my mother. She loves museums too.'

'Does she? What does she do?'

'She's a teacher in a school; but my dad, Dr Sanjay Rao, is a leading gynaecologist in Bangalore. Do you know about the infertility clinic called Samadhan? My dad started it.'

'Oh, I haven't heard of it. Sorry, I have to go now.' Her sharp words were like a needle that pricked the balloon of his enthusiasm.

After that, Sishir had met Neha for the second time in Bangalore. One evening, Mridula was getting ready to go out when the phone rang. Sishir picked it up—it was their driver. He was calling to inform Mridula that he was ill and could not come to work. Sishir was about to go out with his friends but when he realized that his mother was taking out the scooter from the garage, he called out to her and said, 'Amma, it's about to rain. Don't worry, I'll drive you to wherever you are going.'

Mridula happily agreed. When they were in the car, she said, 'Sishir, how will I come back?'

'Amma, if you don't spend too much time at your friend's house, I'll come back and pick you up in half an hour. By the way, where do you want to go?'

'To my colleague Chandrika's house in Thyagarajanagar. She has Varalakshmi Puja today.'

When they reached Thyagarajanagar, Sishir realized that the lanes were narrow. He had never been to this part of Bangalore before. Though Mridula was giving him directions, he found it difficult to manoeuvre his car. He felt uncomfortable when Mridula said, 'Most of my colleagues live here. It's near the school and affordable on a teacher's salary.'

They reached Chandrika's house; it was at a dead end. Sishir got irritated: 'Amma, how will I reverse the car here? There's no space in these small lanes. Will you tell someone to open the gate of the house? That'll help.'

Mridula got down, went inside and told the first person she met to open the gate. To Sishir's astonishment, Neha came out. She opened the gate and Sishir drove in and reversed the car. He smiled and said, 'Hello, Neha. What brings you here?'

'This is my cousin's house. I've come for the puja.'

Still sitting in the car, Sishir asked, 'All the way from Chitradurga just for a puja?'

'My sister Neerja stays in Bangalore too. So I thought I'll meet her. Why don't you come in?'

'No, I have to meet a friend.'

Neha found it strange that he did not want to come in and take prasad. So she said, 'At least come in and take blessings.'

He could have refused but by now, other people had come out of the house and were looking at his big car. He felt awkward and got out. When he went in, he saw that it was a simple lower-middle-class house with cramped rooms. There were too many people there. But Mridula was happy to see that Sishir had come inside and introduced him to her friends.

Neha came with a plate full of mithai and namkeen. Sishir said, 'No, I don't want to eat anything. I had a late lunch. Please excuse me.'

Even though he wanted to talk to Neha a little more, he did not get a chance and both mother and son left the house soon.

On the way back, Mridula asked, 'Sishir, how do you know Neha? She is Chandrika's niece. I really liked meeting her. Both her parents are working in LIC and they have two daughters. The older one is married to a software engineer.'

'Mom, I don't want to know about her family. I know her because she was one of the participants during our competition in Delhi.'

Sishir was rudely brought back to the present when there was a loud announcement from British Airways. He realized that this was his third meeting with Neha. She was packing her handbag and getting ready to board the plane. Sishir said, 'Well, see you in Oxford. Give me your email ID.'

She nodded her head and they exchanged email IDs.

A few minutes later, he boarded and settled down in his comfortable business-class seat. He wondered, 'How does Neha feel when she's going to a different country, especially with her background? Unlike me, it isn't easy for Neha to go from Chitradurga to Oxford. My life is like sailing on a boat under clear skies. I'm intelligent with good connections and great guidance. I appreciate Neha's hard work. She must have got a scholarship and taken a partial loan, at the very least.'

Sishir felt quite happy about the turn of events. Thirteen hours later, the plane reached London. Neha and Sishir met each other again at the baggage claim. Sishir's bags had priority tags on them, so they arrived almost immediately, but he decided to wait with her. Unfortunately, Neha's bags did not come and she looked worried. Sishir went to the airline counter and registered a complaint. He was asked to wait for another half hour. When Neha heard this, she said, 'Thank you for your help, but I don't want to hold you up.'

Sishir smiled and did not reply. Instead, he asked her, 'Is this your first trip to London?'

'Yes, in fact, it was my first plane ride.'

'How do you spend your vacations? Where do you go?'

'I go wherever my parents are. Both of them are in transferable jobs. They try to stay near Chitradurga—sometimes they are successful and sometimes they aren't. Depending on the circumstances, I make a trip to visit them. Otherwise, I stay alone in Chitradurga.'

'Isn't it difficult to stay in a small village by yourself? It's different from staying alone in a big city like Bangalore.'

Sishir had the independence to live alone but it was the first time that he comprehended that he liked staying with his parents. He might not always like their advice or suggestions but he knew that they loved him unconditionally and he loved the attention he got from them too.

Neha interrupted his thoughts saying, 'Sishir, it is not difficult. I have extended family there and my dad has also built a house. It may be small but it's our home. I like living there. I enjoy the company of my relatives and I participate in festivals with them.'

'What are you going to do in Oxford?'

'I'm pursuing my studies in sociology and human behaviour. I have received a fellowship for two years.'

'Are you going to continue to play chess?'

'Of course! It's my hobby.'

'Do you have any friends or relatives in the UK?'

'No. Almost all my contacts are in Chitradurga and I have a few cousins in Bangalore.'

'You must be away from your family for the first time for this long.'

'Yes.'

Sishir felt sorry for Neha—a girl who had never gone out of her country was going to stay on her own in a place like England without any relatives and with limited income. He suddenly remembered his mother. She had told him, 'Sishir, when I came to Bangalore, I cried for months. My Kannada and background were so different from the norm in Bangalore. It was as good as going to a foreign land. Many times, I wanted to go back home but I realized that your dad had a better future in Bangalore. So I started making new friends, learning their habits and the culture. But my heart lies in the village. For me, home will always be Aladahalli.'

Sishir thought, 'Neha must be feeling the same way Amma did all those years ago.'

He said, 'I'm going to be in John Radcliffe Hospital near Oxford. Please let me know whenever you need any help.'

Neha's bags finally arrived. As they walked out of the airport, Sishir asked, 'How are you going to Oxford?'

'The college website said that I should get down at Heathrow Airport, take the tube into town and then a bus to Oxford. I'll follow their instructions.'

'Why do you want to do that? I'm taking a taxi. I'll give you a ride.'

'No, I don't think so. I have troubled you enough. I can manage on my own.'

Sishir was a little annoyed and said firmly, 'Neha, try to understand. This is a new country. It is not even remotely like going to Delhi. I'm an Indian student like you who's going to stay here for four years. There's grace in accepting favours sometimes. Let me help you.'

Neha was silent for a minute and then said, 'Okay.'

They went out of Heathrow Airport and got into a taxi. Sishir knew the ins and outs of London.

As the taxi got going, Sishir noticed that Neha was looking on either side of the road, like a child looking at a beautiful toy for the first time. Her face was usually calm but he could see that she was excited now. He liked seeing her enjoy London. When her destination arrived, Neha got down with her bags and said, 'Thank you for the ride. I'll go to my room now.'

Sishir laughed. 'Do you have the keys?'

'Oh, I'm sure there's a chowkidar who will show me the room and give me the keys.'

Sishir was amused. 'This isn't India, Neha. There's a different system here. You need a special kind of key to get into your apartment.'

Sishir got down, talked to the apartment office and got the keys; Neha followed him quietly. Finally, he dropped her to her room. As they were saying goodbye, Neha felt alone; Sishir could see it in her moist eyes.

A week passed by and Neha sent Sishir an email giving the details of her apartment and her phone number. She said that she had started her classes. Though she was intelligent, she found it a little difficult to follow the British accent. Adjustment for Sishir was much easier. He had two seniors working in the same hospital but their shift timings were different. Apart from that, in one year, his seniors had also found girlfriends for themselves.

Sishir called Neha that evening and politely asked if they could meet on Saturday. He wanted her to have someone to talk to. Within a month, Neha had become a fish in water. She had adjusted well and made new friends. But she always felt the most comfortable with Sishir and liked meeting him. Sishir felt the same way. He had grown up an only child and had never had anybody to share with, to fight and reconcile with, to help hide his secrets, or compete with. Though he was friendly with both boys and girls, he preferred to keep to himself. For the first time, he felt a strong connection to someone whom he really respected.

26

Learning to Survive

A team of teachers came from Mridula's school to visit her. She had never taken such a long vacation and now, she had applied for medical leave. When they came to see her, everybody gave her different advice. Some said, 'Madam, since you are unwell, you should go to a hill station and rest. The change might be good for you.' Others said, 'You should go on a world tour since you don't have to worry about money.' But Leela said, 'I attended a swamiji's discourse in Jayanagar. He teaches relaxation techniques and I found it useful. Maybe you can try it.'

'Do you think my mind will be at rest after that?'

'I think so. I'll give you his address if you want.'

Mridula decided to enrol for the course and went there the next day. There were people from different age groups and everyone had a problem. Finally, the swamiji entered. He was young, lean and clean-shaven. He had a calm face and was wearing a white robe. He said, 'The main reason for unhappiness is disappointment. Disappointment disappears with detachment. Detachment comes through knowledge and knowledge is gained by dhyana. So you should learn the technique of dhyana.'

Mridula did not understand a word. She just wanted to be happy again. A devotee asked, 'Swamiji, I get upset quickly. How do I control my temper?'

'With your mind. I can't tell you a specific method because every individual is different and you have to find out what works best for you.'

Mridula thought, 'If I knew how to control my mind, then I wouldn't be here. I want to be the way I was and enjoy life and its beauty. But now, I dread the thought of living another day.'

Disappointed, Mridula came back home. The next morning at 10 a.m., the doorbell rang. She heard the sound but continued sitting on the sofa. The cook, Sakamma, opened the door. It was Vani, a former student of Mridula's. She was looking happy and holding a bunch of wedding cards in her hand. When she saw Mridula though, she stopped smiling. She knew that something was wrong. She said, 'Madam, what is it? What's the matter?'

Shocked, she sat down right next to Mridula.

Vani had been a student in Mridula's school. Her family was not well off: her father was a rickshaw driver and she did not have a mother. She was brillant in studies and always got good marks when she was younger. When she became Mridula's student, Mridula had called her father and told him, 'Don't stop her education. She has a bright future. She can become a doctor.'

'That may be true but I can't afford it.'

Mridula had thought about it for a day. Then she had called Vani's father and said, 'I'll sponsor your daughter till MBBS, only if you give me the assurance that you won't marry her off before she completes her degree.'

Vani's father had agreed happily.

Now, Vani had become a doctor and considered Mridula a mother figure and a mentor. Still, Mridula was unable to tell Vani anything. How could she tell her that the most famous and respected surgeon in Bangalore was cheating her?

Vani asked again, 'Madam, what's wrong?'

'Nothing.'

'Your eyes tell me that you're upset and sad.'

'It's nothing, Vani.'

Vani placed her hand on Mridula's lap and said gently, 'Madam, my mother is long gone. I look at you as a mother. If you think of me as your daughter, then you must tell me the truth.'

On hearing such kind words, Mridula started weeping. Vani held Mridula's hands and questioned her again: 'Madam, why are you crying?'

'I'm really tired.'

'Okay, then think of me as a doctor and tell me everything.'

'My palms sweat. And my fingers tremble. It happens often.'

'What else?'

'I feel like crying round the clock and don't feel like doing anything.'

'And?'

'My heart beats very fast. I have no enthusiasm for anything. I get scared and can't sleep at night.'

'Is there anything else?'

'I don't feel like getting ready or meeting people. But I don't want to be alone either. I get negative thoughts all the time.'

'Madam, I'm not an expert. But I think you need to talk to a psychiatrist.'

Since last year, Vani had been working at a psychiatric hospital. Mridula was concerned, 'Does that mean that something's wrong with my brain?'

'Oh, madam. If you meet a psychiatrist, it doesn't mean that you are mad or something's wrong with your brain. You are an educated lady. If you talk like that, what can we expect of others?'

Mridula did not answer.

'It may be difficult for you to share your personal problems with me. So you should see a professional. You know that there is a relationship between the mind and the body. It'll probably be a simple course of treatment.'

Mridula was worried. What if Sanjay and Sishir learnt about her psychiatric treatment? Vani read her mind. 'Madam, you don't have to tell anyone. Just go meet the doctor. You may need help immediately if you are in depression. I'm sure that you'll be fine quite quickly.'

Mridula was quiet. Vani changed the subject. 'Madam, my wedding date has been set. If you hadn't helped me, I wouldn't be here today.' She had tears of gratitude in her eyes.

Mridula wiped her own tears and said, 'That's really good. What do you plan to do after you get married?'

'I have to do my post-graduation. My professor has just retired and started a private practice. I'll give you all his details later. He's kind and experienced. You must meet him.'

'What does your husband do?'

'He was my senior in college and is now a doctor too. After a few years, we'll start our own hospital. You must come for our marriage and bless us.'

'I will.'

After Vani left, Mridula prayed for her. 'Every girl dreams of a wonderful marriage but for most, that dream never becomes real. Life after marriage is a battle. Only a few are truly lucky. Please let Vani be happy.'

The next day, Mridula took an autorickshaw and went to Dr Rao's clinic in Basavanagudi. She was glad that there were only a few people in the waiting room. Thankfully, nobody recognized her. After ten minutes, she was called inside the doctor's office.

Dr Rao was a stocky sixty-year-old man with grey hair and calm eyes. He smiled at Mridula as if he had known her for ever. At first, she was uncomfortable but the doctor's demeanour made her feel at home. Gently, he asked her name.

'Doctor, my name is Mridula. But first, I have a request—please don't tell anyone about my visits.'

'Don't worry. I won't.'

'Doctor, I'm suffering from depression. Will I be cured completely?'

'How do you know that it is depression?'

'Sorry, Doctor, I came up with it on my own. I searched the Internet for my symptoms.'

'That's okay. And yes, you'll be cured.'

'Do you mind if I ask you a few questions?'

'Not at all. The more you talk, the better it is. It shows that you're interested in getting better.'

'Doctor, I'm tired of everything.'

'Mridula, don't hold yourself back. You can cry if you want. It'll release the tension. Please know that you may need some time to come back to your normal self.'

'How much time, Doctor?'

'It depends. Depression is just the tip of the iceberg. On an average, it takes nine months to be cured. You must meet me every other day.'

'Okay, that's fine.' Mridula was disappointed because she was hoping to get well in a week.

'Is there a history of depression in your family?'

'As far as I know, no. Is it hereditary?'

'To some extent. Apart from that, external factors greatly influence it. Sometimes, medicines are needed and sometimes they aren't. You don't need them.'

Mridula started seeing Dr Rao thrice a week.

Sanjay went about his business and did not realize that Mridula was seeing a doctor on a regular basis. His routine remained the same and he did not make any effort to talk to her.

During one of their meetings, Dr Rao wanted Mridula to talk about her childhood and family. She said, 'Doctor, I'm the patient. Why do you need details about my family?'

'Mridula, I want to find the root cause of your depression. Then the treatment will be easier and quicker. Tell me, how do you feel when you see homeless people on the streets?'

'I feel that everyone is content except me.'

'And whom do you pity?'

'Beggars. They don't have anything.' Mridula started crying.

'Mridula, can you bring your husband with you next time?'

Mridula did not say anything. She had not told Dr Rao who her husband was.

Dr Rao insisted. 'Mridula, I want to talk to your husband. He plays an important role in your life. He needn't come every time but I want at least three or four sessions with him.'

Mridula agreed to talk to Sanjay. When she came home, Sanjay was watching CNBC news.

Mridula said, 'I am unwell.'

Without even lowering the volume of the TV, Sanjay replied, 'Well, what is it?'

'I have depression.' There was a pause. Mridula continued, 'I'm seeing Dr Rao on a regular basis.'

'Since when?'

'For three weeks now. He wants to meet you.'

Sanjay knew Dr Rao. He thought, 'What a disgrace! Despite all that I've given her, she has become a mental patient. Is she making me responsible for her problems? Well, she's wrong. What have I done to her? I just gave my sister money without asking her. If she's become a mental patient because of that, then that just shows how weak she is. I'm not going to Dr Rao. People will recognize me in the waiting room and then the news will spread. What will my patients think? What will happen to the nursing home and my reputation?'

Mridula repeated, 'Dr Rao wants to meet you.'

Sanjay did not respond.

Mridula knew that he did not want to go. But she said, 'I'll wait for you there at 4 p.m. tomorrow.'

The next day, Sanjay did not show up for the doctor's appointment. Mridula felt embarrassed. However, she told Dr Rao, 'Sanjay must have had an emergency.'

Dr Rao smiled and said, 'That's okay. Tell him to come for our next appointment.'

When Mridula got home, she saw Sanjay having dinner. She asked him, 'Why didn't you come to the doctor's office? I had to tell him that you had an emergency.'

Sanjay took his cue from Mridula and said, 'Yes, I did.'

'Then come next time.'

'Okay.'

But Sanjay never went for any of the sessions and gave Mridula a different excuse each time. In the end, Dr Rao said, 'Mridula, your husband doesn't have to come for our sessions. We'll work without him.'

As time passed, Mridula started feeling better. Dr Rao was no longer just a doctor to her. He had become a good friend. He did not give her any injections or pills. One day, she told him, 'Doctor, my husband wasn't like this when we got married. I was the decision-maker then. He never cared about finances or money.'

'The situation was different then. He was concentrating on studying and working hard. His motive wasn't making money and your decisions were important. He may have gone through difficult situations where he was humiliated because he wasn't powerful. Maybe that's why he believes that power is money.'

'Doctor, does a man not need gratitude and love?'

'Of course. But in highly competitive fields like politics and business, these are considered weak and unwanted emotions. There is only one place at the top and you have to climb over others to reach it.'

'But won't that affect one's family life?'

'Yes, it will and it does. But the rules for family are different from the rules for business. One shouldn't measure these two with the same yardstick. Softness is essential for a happy family. But a competitive attitude destroys a family. Statistics show that men are successful in business in the long term only if they have their family's support.'

Mridula said, 'Yes, I have always tried to support him. My husband never understands what I want—but he knows exactly what his sister wants.'

'Mridula, what do you want?'

Mridula was taken aback. She was unable to pinpoint what she wanted. Even though she had everything, she felt inadequate.

Dr Rao continued, 'In most marriages, women don't know what they want and men don't try to understand. The reverse is also true. Hence, spouses start blaming each other. I want to tell you a story.

'A long time ago, there was a handsome prince. He was defeated in a war and an emperor took away his land. The emperor wanted to kill the young prince but when he looked at his youth and intelligence, he changed his mind. The emperor said, "I'll give you a year to answer one question. If you answer it properly, I'll give you your freedom and your kingdom. Otherwise, you'll be executed."

'The prince asked, "What's the question?"

'"What does a woman want from a man?"

'The prince travelled to different kingdoms and asked many people but could not find the answer. Eventually, he learnt that there was an old witch who might be able to help him. When he approached her, she said, "I'll give you the answer, but my fee is high."

'"Please tell me."

'"You must marry me."

'The prince had no option and he agreed. The witch then said, "Every woman wants to change her life but no man understands how. He showers his wife with gifts that he likes but not with what she wants."

'When the emperor heard the answer, he was happy and the prince got his kingdom back. But now, he had to marry the old and ugly witch. On their wedding night, he was scared to sit next to her, but to his surprise, there was a beautiful maiden waiting for him. She smiled and said, "My prince, I appreciate your patience and word of honour. I have great power and I can remain beautiful either through the night or during the day. Which would you prefer?"

'The prince was lost in thought. If she looked beautiful during the day, everyone would appreciate her, but at night, she would become a witch and it would be difficult for him to handle. And if she looked beautiful at night, it would be awkward to have an ugly queen during the day.

'But by now, the prince knew what a woman wanted. So he said, "You can choose whichever you want."

'And the witch decided to stay beautiful all the time.'

After sharing this story, Dr Rao said, 'Mridula, in a male-dominated society like ours, all the important decisions are made by a man, including choices about what his wife wants. Every woman values her freedom to choose—much more than her husband's money or position. When I look at your life, you've been brought up in a progressive family but then you got married into a family with a different culture and economic status. That's also one of the reasons for your problems.'

Incidents flashed before Mridula's eyes.

Once, Sanjay had told her, 'Mridula, I ordered a new car for you because I really like it.'

'My car is only three years old and I like it just fine. I don't want to change it right now.'

'No, you don't understand. The car is old now and doesn't suit our status.'

Mridula had not known what to say.

Another day, Sanjay had said, 'I saw an advertisement for the new Siemens phone and told Rosemary to order one for our house.'

'Why? We don't need it. We barely make any calls. Sishir isn't here to use it either.'

'No, I want the latest technology in our house.'

At that time, Mridula had lost her patience and snapped, 'Is our house a laboratory that you want to keep getting new things and experimenting with them?'

'You can think whatever you want. This is my home and my decision is final.'

Mridula sighed and looked at Dr Rao. Though Mridula had not disclosed her husband's identity, Dr Rao was aware of who he was. But he kept this to himself.

During another session, Mridula told Dr Rao, 'Doctor, I respect my brother's wife, Vatsala, but she's not friendly. My sister-in-law, Lakshmi, also doesn't respect me. What's wrong with me?'

'There's nothing wrong with you, Mridula. In India, when you marry a person, you also marry his family. By default, people expect you to adjust to the husband's family. When a girl becomes a daughter-in-law, she's subjected to unnecessary criticism, irrespective of her good qualities. But look on the positive side. Your mother-in-law doesn't trouble you. Your husband isn't having an extramarital affair and your son doesn't have any bad habits. You should be grateful for that. Yes, your husband has cheated you financially. But there are men who cheat in ways that are much more hurtful. If you were a little practical and street-smart, things wouldn't have been so bad.'

'Do you think that Lakshmi could have been easily cheated like me?'

'I don't know Lakshmi and I can't answer that. Usually, people who are sensitive need more time to understand the real world. People who've been brought up in a tough atmosphere adjust fast.'

'But Sanjay never helped Lakshmi without my knowledge before.'

'Because Lakshmi was doing better than both of you financially.'

'Doctor, is money so important in life?'

Dr Rao replied, 'Yes, money is important. It's a change-triggering catalyst. Money brings power, status and confidence.'

'Why do people change with money?'

'Mridula, only philosophers can answer that question. But what I can tell you is that money brings out the best and the worst in people. It's a magnifying glass. When a person becomes rich, his inner desires are free to come to the forefront. If a selfish man becomes rich, he spends money on himself, but if a generous person becomes wealthy, he shares it with others. It's difficult to find people who aren't touched by money.'

'Doctor, what should I do when I get depressed?'

'Don't sit idle at home. Do whatever you like. Exercise is essential. But the most important thing to do is to share your anxiety with others. And remember that depression is curable. It just takes time.'

'With everything that's happened, I don't know how to behave with Sanjay. What should I do?'

'Mridula, your husband's a nice man. But he has a big ego because of his success. Money makes him feel powerful. He has an inferiority complex and an old value system where men are supposed to be the dominating partner. Unlike you, he's a complicated person. That's why he's never established good communication with you.'

Tears rolled down Mridula's cheeks. She thought, 'How did I live with Sanjay for such a long time? Today, he's given me money and position in society but he doesn't share my sorrows. I've held his hand and walked next to him on the thorny path to success. When a girl gets married, the extent of her happiness depends upon the husband's commitment and communication with her. A few kind words, a little appreciation and small gifts like flowers can make a girl feel special. But Sanjay just wanted to show that he was the boss.'

Mridula asked, 'Doctor, what should I do now?'

'That's up to you. Your husband thinks about money and his practice all the time. You can't change him. He's the one who has to be ready to make a change. Mridula, how do you feel when you look at beggars now?'

'I feel sad but not so much. Why?'

'Because beggars are synonymous with people who have nothing. When you came here, you felt empty inside. That's why you related to beggars. Over these past few months, you've regained your confidence and you're completely fine now. Please don't expect anything from your husband. The will to change has to come from him.'

'Thank you, Doctor.'

As Mridula left Dr Rao's office, she felt light and happy. When she looked at the people around her on the streets, she finally comprehended that everybody had their own problems.

27

Things Fall Apart

A few days later, Mridula wanted to try and talk to Sanjay about her treatment once more. Sanjay did not have time in the mornings so Mridula decided to talk to him the same night before she changed her mind. The phone rang, disturbing her thoughts. She picked up the extension and before she could say anything, she heard Alex say, 'Sanjay, I'm glad you picked up the phone. Did Mridula give her approval?'

Sanjay was already on the call. Mridula was about to hang up but she was curious when she heard her name and kept listening. Sanjay replied, 'No, I don't want to ask her. I've known her for almost twenty-five years. She won't cooperate with us. In fact, she'll create problems because she's an idealist. Instead of her, I want Lakshmi to be the silent director. She doesn't understand all this anyway. We can just ask her to sign papers whenever we want and, in return, we can give her some money. How are things at your end?'

'Anita doesn't want to get involved and my sister, Barbara, is shrewd. So I'll get Julie on board.'

'Good. So how should we price the product?'

Mridula kept the phone down. After hearing Sanjay and Alex, she did not want to talk to her husband any more. She did not care about their strategies or about why Lakshmi was being brought on board. If Sanjay kept hiding things from her, how could she continue living in the same house with him?

Had she been like Anita, she would have dedicated her life to serving God.

Had she been like Lakshmi, she would be happy with the money.

Had she been like Rosemary, she would have worked for her financial freedom.

But the truth was that she was like none of them.

She thought, 'If I continue staying here and in the same atmosphere, then I have a high chance of getting depressed again. I have to live life on my terms if I want to be happy. And that's not possible with Sanjay around. He ridicules and dominates me and it affects my confidence terribly. I can't take it any more. I have to do something. But what?'

Finally, it came to her. She knew what she had to do.

A month later, it was Sanjay and Mridula's wedding anniversary—they had been together for twenty-five years. Sishir called them from England in the morning to wish them.

A grand party was planned at The Leela Palace in the evening. Lakshmi, Rosemary, Shankar and Anil were busy with the arrangements for the event. There were cocktails at 7 p.m. followed by dinner and Mridula and Sanjay were to exchange garlands somewhere in between. Lakshmi wanted every guest to be presented with an expensive return gift. So she purchased silver items from an expensive jeweller's shop.

Sanjay had made a list of invitees and called senior officers, pharmaceutical directors and other important celebrities and businessmen of Bangalore. When Mridula's family received the invitation by mail, Bheemanna sent his best wishes through a telegram. Mridula recollected that once Sanjay had become successful, she had tried to return the three lakh rupees that she had taken from her father. Though Krishna and Vatsala wanted to take the money, Bheemanna had got upset and said, 'You can dump that money in the village lake or tie it to Hanuman's tail. It's left to you. I'm not doing any moneylending with my daughter. I can't accept it.'

So Mridula had used the money to repair the old school building of the village, where she had studied.

Among the people Mridula had invited, Sarla was coming to the party but Anita was not. She called Mridula and said, 'When we look towards God, he gives us a gift. Whatever he does, he does it to make us better. Accept it with happiness. That's all I wish for you.'

Mridula appreciated her words.

Ratnamma was busy with her chairman duties at the bank and sent her best wishes through her manager. However, Lakshmi was enthusiastic about the party and could not stop talking about it. She was still under the impression that Mridula was unaware of her financial transactions with Sanjay. She told Mridula, 'I'll buy you a white Kanjeevaram sari with a red border and a raw-silk kurta and pyjama for Sanjay. Diamond accessories will go well with the sari but I don't have that much money to gift it to you. I'll tell Sanjay to buy it for you.'

Mridula may have believed her a year ago but today, she was indifferent and did not say anything.

Sanjay was also excited about the party. He thought that Mridula was fine now and had come out of her problem. He asked her, 'Mridula, what do you want? Tell me. Do you want to go on a trip to Europe or do you want jewellery?'

He did not know that he could not give her back the faith she had lost in him.

It was evening and everybody was at The Leela Palace waiting for the couple to arrive. Twenty-five years ago, the simple and shy Mridula had been married to Sanjay in a simple ceremony at her house at Aladahalli. Ironically, her silver wedding anniversary was to be celebrated with more glamour than the original wedding.

At home, Sanjay was wearing his new Armani suit, specially purchased for the evening. He was ready and waiting for Mridula in the hallway. Mridula was inside her room busy doing something. Sanjay got upset because it was getting late. He called out to her loudly: 'Mridula, what are you doing in there? We're getting late. Everyone is waiting for us.'

Mridula came out in a white cotton sari with a glow of peace on her face. She said, 'I was packing my things. I've been transferred.'

'To where?'

'Aladahalli.'

Sanjay was surprised, but said at once, 'I know the Education minister. I'll get it cancelled.'

'Please don't. I asked for it.'

'But you never told me!'

'It wasn't important to you.'

'When will you be back?'

'Probably never.'

'Where will you stay there and what will you do?'

'I have bought Champakka's house. I should thank your mother who persuaded me to save some of my salary every month. I bought the house with my money.'

'Aren't you staying with your father?'

There was neither anger nor disappointment in Mridula's voice. She said, 'No, I've spent twenty-five of my most important years with you, and yet, I never felt like I belonged to you or your family. I'm still an outsider. My father's house now belongs to Vatsala and I don't want to be a burden on my brother and her. Sishir is independent and you can take care of him better than I can. My duty towards both of you is over. I've fulfilled all my duties as a wife, mother and daughter-in-law. Now, I want to live for myself. I have my job, my school and my village. You don't have to worry about me any longer. You and Sishir can visit me whenever you want.'

The clock on the wall struck six-thirty, the auspicious time. Mridula did not wait for Sanjay's response. She walked out of the house, found an autorickshaw, kept her small bag inside the auto and, without even looking back once, she left.

Sanjay was left standing in the veranda staring after her. He could not imagine in his wildest dreams that Mridula could leave him and go. He had taken Mridula for granted. Had she been like Sarla or Lakshmi, he would have been more careful in dealing with her. But Mridula had taken a tough decision and left without blaming anyone.

He did not know what to do.

He walked back into the house and sat down on the sofa. The phone was ringing. He ignored it. For the first time, he felt like he had lost something valuable. He believed that he could buy anything and anyone with money. But today, even with all his riches, he felt like a beggar.

Finally, the phone stopped ringing. After some time, he heard a car pull into the driveway. He did not get up to see who it was. The house was dark. Lakshmi came in and switched on the lights. Then she saw her brother sitting on a sofa—looking dazed and confused. In the bright lights, she could see Sanjay's pale face.

'Why are you sitting like this, Sanjay? I called you several times but there was no reply. Are you all right? Where's Mridula?'

Sanjay buried his face in his hands and said, 'Oh, Mridula, Mridula.'

Lakshmi walked around the house searching for her sister-in-law. Finally, she came back and stood in front of her brother and asked, 'What's going on? Where's Mridula?'

'She's gone.'

'What do you mean? Where and when did she go?'

Sanjay did not reply.

'What time will she be back?'

'I don't know.'

'Are you unwell or are you pulling my leg?'

Suddenly, Sanjay remembered the party. He collected himself and said, 'Lakshmi, go back to the party and tell everyone that Mridula has had a fracture. Wait, I'll come with you and let them know. Tell them to have their dinner and leave.'

'But why did she leave? And when?'

Sanjay did not answer despite Lakshmi's repeated questions.

Sanjay and Lakshmi drove to The Leela Palace. It was filled with people. Sanjay forced himself to smile and apologized to everyone: 'Thank you for your patience. I'm extremely sorry for having made you wait. Mridula has had a fracture and I had to rush to attend to her. Please have dinner and enjoy yourselves.' Sanjay instructed Rosemary and Shankar to manage everything and left the party.

When he came back home, he felt really upset with Mridula. He was mad at the way she had embarrassed him in public. He decided that he would not call her back. He thought, 'I haven't harmed her in any way. There's no reason for her to leave. She's the wife of a famous gynaecologist in Bangalore. How dare she disobey me? Let her realize who I am. Then she herself will come back to me. It's not easy for an Indian woman to live alone. Meanwhile, Sakamma, Chikki and Nanja are capable enough to look after the house.'

He changed his clothes and went off to sleep.

Suddenly he got up and looked at the clock. It was 2 a.m. Sanjay was not a light sleeper. But today, he could not sleep properly. His mind kept flashing back to the day he had met Mridula, how he had courted her and how life had been with her then.

When he woke up in the morning, Sakamma, Chikki and Nanja were waiting for his orders.

Sakamma asked, 'What should I cook today?'

Nanja said, 'I need money for petrol.'

Chikki added, 'The water tank is leaking.'

For a minute, Sanjay was at a loss. Then he said to Nanja and Chikki, 'Talk to Rosemary and take the money from her.'

He turned to Sakamma and said, 'Make whatever you feel like.'

'When will Madam be back?'

'Maybe in a month.'

Sanjay left for the nursing home. He thought that once he got there, he would get busy and life would go back to normal. But he felt like an orphan. He was worried that if he took a vacation or cancelled any operations, it would affect the reputation of his nursing home.

When he came out of his room in the evening, he saw Rosemary's husband standing at her desk with a bunch of red roses. He was neatly dressed and clean-shaven and waiting for Rosemary. Sanjay looked down upon Joseph and hardly ever spoke to him; but today he asked, 'Is it a special occasion, Joseph? You've come with a bouquet.'

'Today is Rosemary's birthday.'

A minute later, Rosemary came back to her desk and asked Sanjay if she could leave for the day. Sanjay nodded and went back inside his room. From his window, he could see them holding hands and crossing the road. He was surprised that a simple bouquet of flowers had made Rosemary so happy. He had never made Mridula this happy.

Then he checked the cash register. The collection was around six lakh, but he did not feel elated. His phone rang. It was Anita. She asked him, 'Sanjay, what happened yesterday?'

'Nothing.'

'I know that Mridula left you and went back to her village.'

'Who told you that?'

'I called up your house, took Mridula's father's number in Aladahalli and managed to speak to her.'

Sanjay did not know what to say. Anita continued, 'I don't want to tell Mridula to come back. She won't get any happiness from you. Sanjay, you were lucky to get married to her. You should have been grateful to God. Now that you've lost her, all the money you earn from your nursing home is of no use. You may not like what I'm saying, but a true friend should tell the truth even if it hurts. Yes, you have friends in high positions. They'll be nice to you and smile but they'll laugh at you behind your back. I've known Mridula well for the last twenty-three years. She's shared all your difficulties. Your mother or sister or son can't take her place. Sishir will marry and have his own family. After that, a father is just a guest. Regarding your mother, the less said the better. Your sister just looks for a chance to make money off of you. Nobody can match Mridula in terms of simplicity, innocence and affection. I'm sorry that I have taken the liberty to speak so much about your personal issues. But I have to listen to my conscience.'

Before he could reply, she disconnected the phone. Sanjay knew that Anita was straightforward. He kept standing next to the phone like a statue.

After a few minutes, he heard Lakshmi's voice outside. Finally, she peeped in. She had dyed her hair and was wearing matching jewellery. She looked much younger than him. He signalled her to come in and both Shankar and Lakshmi walked in and sat down. Lakshmi said, 'Sanjay, you want me to become a director in your new company. So when is the inauguration? Will there be a press release? I've already told the women in my ladies' club. By the way, there weren't many gifts yesterday evening. Most of them were bouquets . . .'

Lakshmi did not talk about Mridula or about what had happened last evening. She just wanted to talk business. Sanjay realized that Lakshmi was interested more in her new post than in her brother's personal life. He said, 'I don't know much about it. Alex is working on it. Ask him.'

'Do you know any good girls for Anil? I want to get him married after I become director.'

Sanjay got a call on his cell phone and walked out of the room, leaving the couple inside. When he finished the call and came back in, he found Shankar scolding his wife, 'You don't have any common sense. Why did you tell him to find a girl for Anil? He married that villager and so he'll probably suggest a village girl for Anil too. Mridula is totally useless. Even though she's good-looking, she's dumb. Anybody can look beautiful with make-up. If a girl is ordinary looking, that's fine with me but she should be the only child of rich parents.'

When Shankar saw Sanjay, he stopped short. Sanjay felt bad about the way they spoke about Mridula. He knew that it was his fault. He used to take her for granted and talk rudely to her in front of them. That was why they also behaved the same way with her.

He went home. The house seemed empty. He worried that every evening would be like this from now on. At first, he had been upset at the way Anita had talked to him. But now at home, he pondered over her words. Even though he talked to Mridula only for a few minutes every night and even though she fought with him, she was still an integral part of his life. He looked around and saw the old clock in the room that had been bought with Mridula's first salary. She had bought him the old scooter in the garage too.

Though Sakamma served him hot food on his silver plate, he was unable to eat. He saw his wedding picture on the wall. Mridula and he were both smiling in it. He thought about their failed marriage and remembered that she had married him despite his handicap and loved him without expecting much.

There was so much emptiness without her.

28
Growing Pains

Time rushed by for Sishir and Neha who continued to meet regularly. Sishir, who never showed any interest in history and the humanities, was impressed with the way Neha explained these to him.

Neha and Sishir both joined the Indian Youth Club and found that there were three more people there from Bangalore— Ramesh, Usha and Raghu. All of them spoke Kannada too. Among the five, only Sishir owned a car. Everyone except Neha became dependent on him. Circumstances made Sishir a leader and he loved it. He was the one who took decisions about where to go, where to dine and what to do. At times, the others did not like his choice but it was easy and comfortable for them to be with him. They only had to pay for their share of the food; Sishir took care of the rest.

Neha did not like this. So she did not join the group sometimes. But Sishir would insist: 'Come on, Neha. It's good for you.'

Neha knew that this was not true but did not want to be impolite because he had helped her so much. One day, Sishir decided that they should go punting in the river, which was a usual practice for most students.

While the five were punting, they started talking about their future. Ramesh was studying law and said, 'I want to marry a lawyer. Then we can set up a good law firm.'

Usha said, 'I want to marry a rich man so that I don't have to work. I can read, travel and enjoy life.'

Raghu said, 'I want my wife to be beautiful like a model, and modern in her outlook.'

When Sishir's turn came, he said, 'I want a girl who won't argue with me and who'll adjust to any situation. A woman defines the culture and environment at home. But she should be modern outside the house. She must be intelligent and understand how I think and act accordingly.'

Everyone laughed at him. They said, 'Then you need to marry four girls.'

'Why? Is it that difficult to find a girl like that? I'm sure that there are plenty of girls who would love to live that way. Finding a good husband is also an achievement.'

Everyone laughed again. Now, it was Neha's turn. She said, 'I want a man who respects me as a woman. We must give each other the freedom to grow together and individually, as people. Money doesn't matter to me. His job doesn't matter either.'

'Oh, Neha, you're thinking of an imaginary man who doesn't exist,' said Usha.

A few months went by and Neha continued to keep her distance from Sishir. She maintained their friendship, however. Though Sishir was used to girls falling for him and hanging on to his every word, Neha stood out because of her coolness. That attracted Sishir more and he really liked her. He wanted to ask Neha out on a date. They moved in a group most of the time and he had never invited her to dinner alone. He phoned Neha and said, 'Will you join me for a movie tonight followed by dinner? It'll be a date.'

There was no response. He said, 'Neha, I'm waiting for you to say something.'

After a pause, Neha replied, 'Sorry, I can't come.'

'Why? Do you have a prior commitment? Are you meeting someone else?'

'No, I don't have other plans. I just don't want to come.'

'Come on, Neha. It'll be a good change for you. I'll see you at the theatre at 6 p.m.'

Sishir disconnected the phone. At home, when he insisted a little bit, his mother eventually agreed. He was sure that Neha would also give in.

He went to the theatre but she did not turn up in time. He waited for half an hour and felt bad that she had not come. He called her. Neha picked up and said, 'I'm not coming. That means that I'm really not coming.'

Sishir was livid. He decided to go back to the theatre and see the movie by himself. Though the movie was playing on the screen, his mind was not at rest. 'How can anyone say no to me?' he thought. 'I'm handsome, rich, intelligent and have achieved a lot. My father's a big man. He owns a nursing home. We have great prestige in society. What else does a girl want?' He could not believe his ears. He had never heard the word 'no' in his life. He had got everything he wanted through his hard work, intelligence and money and, at times, through his aggressiveness. Had he called Dolly, she would have sailed the seven seas to be here with him.

'An ordinary girl from Chitradurga, a nobody who is anonymous in any crowd, will never get a boy better than me. If she says "no", she's either impractical or foolish. Maybe she's not destined for a good life,' he thought.

Sishir thought of Neeta and the other girls in his college who were much better than Neha in terms of looks and position in society. They would have begged him to ask them for a date. His anger knew no bounds. His palpitations rose. His palms started sweating. He forced himself to calm down and thought, 'Why do I care about this girl from Chitradurga? She's not equal to me in any way. Why am I attracted to her? I didn't propose marriage to her. I only invited her for a date.'

Sishir came out of the theatre midway through the movie, cancelled his dinner reservation and went back to his room.

The next day, he still wanted to know the reason behind Neha's refusal. He went to Neha's college and waited for lunchtime. Soon, he located her having lunch and sat down with his own lunch at her table. In an angry voice, he asked, 'May I know why you didn't come yesterday?'

'Sishir, you don't need to know why. You can't insist in such matters.'

'That means you have someone else in mind? If so, why didn't you tell me earlier?' He became jealous.

'No, there's no one else. You're a good friend and a good person. However, I thought about it and took the decision. I'm aware of the consequences. I may not get someone as rich, famous and handsome as you but that's fine by me. That's not my ambition. I don't want to date you.'

'Still, I want to know the reason,' Sishir insisted. 'At least I'll be happy knowing the truth.'

'Sishir, telling the truth is not a big deal but it depends on how people take it. Some people react badly, some people accept it easily and correct themselves, while others take it emotionally and break down. If you have the capacity to digest it without bitterness, then I'll tell you.'

'I'll digest it. But I want the truth.'

'The truth is that we're different. Your upbringing is different. More than that, your attitude towards life is different. Despite modern education, your mindset has not changed. You expect a woman to remain a subordinate. She should adjust under every circumstance. Her compromising nature is considered a virtue. I don't want to live like that. I don't want to be a doormat. Marriage is not the final destination for me. There are other ways that a woman can live her life.'

'What do you mean my attitude to life is different?'

'The attitude that money can buy everything may be appropriate in today's society. But the fact is that money can't really buy everything. Life is more than money. It's about having concern for one another. That gives a person more satisfaction and happiness. There are three types of men in this world. The majority of them belong to the first category where a man leads and thinks he's superior and makes his wife follow him. He's happy to look after her as long as she remains subordinate to him. He assumes that she's not as exposed to life as he is or as intelligent as he is. He makes decisions on her behalf. Most women accept this as a way of life and people who don't accept it or rebel against it have to suffer in society.

'The second category is of men who allow women to excel. They adjust their life according to the woman in their life and respect her as an individual rather than a wife. But there are very few people in this category.

'The third category is of men who treat their women as true and equal partners in life and walk side by side with them. I don't want the first category of men at all . . .'

Sishir interrupted her, 'Are you saying that I ill-treat women and call them inferior? How dare you talk to me like that?'

'Sishir, take it easy. I didn't say anything like that. But your attitude shows that the woman has to make all the adjustments. It worries me. It's better to know each other before a relationship than regret it later. Because of that, my family has suffered a lot already.'

'What do you mean?'

'I haven't shared my personal life with you. My sister Neerja got married to her classmate whom she had known for a long time. We all felt that though he was a good-looking young boy, he and his family were very dominating. My parents gave her a warning but Neerja just ignored it. She said at the time that he was only an acquaintance. Acquaintance led to love and love led to marriage. Ultimately, she suffered a lot. Her husband was nice to everyone outside the home but he dominated every aspect of her life—choosing a job, buying a house, having a baby. She could never be herself. She was suffocating every day and couldn't take it any more. Then they separated and divorced. She advised me, "Love is blind and that's why I never understood his true nature. Had I kept my mind cool and looked at him objectively, I would've made a better decision." Going through a divorce is hell, particularly for a girl in our society. He got remarried within a year but Neerja still doesn't look at other boys. She's so scared. Once bitten, twice shy. If two people feel incompatible in the beginning of a relationship, neither friendship nor marriage will change that. It's better to be unmarried than to go through this process. That's why I said that I want an equal partnership the day we went punting. Ask your conscience. Do you really respect women in the true sense? Do you consider them equal partners? Your own leadership dictates that others should follow. True leadership is when you take everybody's opinion and needs into account and then make a judgement that is best for all. A true leader leads with affection and not power. Your conscience is your best judge.'

Neha left the table quietly without waiting for Sishir's answer.

Sishir was very upset about the whole episode. It took a while for him to calm down. He continued sitting at the table. He thought, 'The most interaction I've had with a woman is with my mother. But how much have I shared with her? I idolize my father and the way he treats his wife is an indication that I'll also treat a woman like that. Amma says that role models don't exist outside the family. It's the parents who become role models. She's right.'

He knew that unlike other girls, Neha was not trying to hook him. For that matter, she was not even aware of who he was when she had met him for the first time. She was an honest and transparent girl—just like his mother. He wondered, 'What authority does my mother have in any household decisions except in the kitchen? She doesn't have freedom anywhere. Everywhere, my father makes the decisions and my mother has to follow them. If she doesn't do so, the decision is still made and it brings her pain. But no one ever tells my father about my mother's sufferings or his mistakes. Though she has sacrificed so much, today she's still a nonentity.'

Suddenly, he understood what Neha was talking about. It jolted him. That meant that his mother must have gone through tremendous pain in an effort to stay with his father. Neha being a modern girl realized that good men did exist but Mridula was not even aware of it. Sishir did not want to lose Neha. She was honest, caring and bold. She would make a perfectly balanced partner for him—but only if he changed for the better and for his own sake. Change may not be easy but it was not impossible. If he did not change, he would lose the benefit he may have got from a happy married life.

His mind kept oscillating between Neha and Mridula. His mother used to say, 'Sishir, things are different today. Girls are independent now. Their expectations from a partner are high. Boys have to change to adjust with girls now. Traditionally, only the woman was expected to adjust and change. But the modern world demands that boys change too. You can't treat your wife the way you treat me. No modern girl will be happy only with money. Care, partnership and responsibility are the key ingredients of a modern marriage.'

He thought, 'My mother has undergone so much silently—she has a right to be happy.' He suddenly felt homesick—like a small child. He wanted to hug his mother and his eyes filled with tears, thinking of her difficulties. For the first time, Sishir saw his mother from an altered perspective. He took out his cell phone and called home. He wanted to speak to her.

The phone rang. Sanjay picked it up. Sishir said, 'Hi, Dad. I want to talk to Amma. How were your anniversary celebrations?'

Sanjay said softly and tearfully, 'The party didn't happen.'

'But why?'

'Because your mother left and went to Aladahalli.'

'Oh, when she will be back?'

'I don't know.'

'Come on, Dad! Amma can't be angry for ever. It isn't her nature. She'll be back soon. Don't get upset.'

'Sishir, she's taken a transfer there.'

'Then it must be serious. You always neglect her and take her for granted. At least, try and get her back. If you really try, you'll succeed.'

'So, Sishir, how's work?'

'Work's okay, but I miss home and Amma. When I was there, I never realized how important she is. When I see women here, I realize Amma's selfless sacrifice. She's great like you too, but in a different way. Dad, without her help, you would've never built such a big empire. She has been and is your strength. When I was there, I laughed at her advice, but today, I follow everything she used to say, including going to bed early and getting up early. Dad, home is not just made of four walls and luxury items. Home is home because of a father and a mother. Cheer up, Dad. Amma must be finding it hard to live without you too. Don't wait for her to call you. You should make the first move. But I'll try and talk to her too.'

Sanjay was surprised. Their son, who had always hero-worshipped him, had changed after being away from home. He was seeing life in a different light.

The next day, Sanjay kept waiting for Mridula's call. He picked up all his phone calls eagerly but none of them were from her. She did not call. His ego did not allow him to phone her either.

Days went by. Sanjay was slowly losing interest in everything he did. Within a few weeks, he had lost interest in his nursing home too.

Sishir called him every day to check up on him.

29

Hope

Two months passed by.

Mridula was sitting on the swing under the big banyan tree opposite the Hanuman temple. It was Ugadi time, in the month of February or March. Summer had just arrived. The mango trees sported soft reddish-green leaves and the cuckoos were making lovely coo-coo sounds. Everyone in the village was busy preparing for the festival. Yet, there was a pin-drop silence near the temple.

But for Mridula, nothing mattered. She was swinging without any bondage and with a free mind. From the swing, she could see her house. She was happy.

Mridula was not like everybody, she was different. She had enormous enthusiasm for life and unlimited energy. She wanted to spend every minute of the day fruitfully. It seemed that the sun rose for her and the rainbow colours were meant only for her. Every day was to be lived to its fullest and every beautiful minute to be enjoyed.

Suddenly, Mridula felt that someone was trying to stop the swing. Surprised, she turned to look.

Sanjay was holding the swing, with his one good arm.